VIATICUM

VIATICUM

PATRICK
MORGAN

Phase Publishing, LLC
Seattle

Text copyright © 2021 by Patrick Morgan
Cover art copyright © 2021 by Patrick Morgan

Cover art by Tugboat Design
http://www.tugboatdesign.net

Phase Publishing, LLC first paperback edition
July 2021

ISBN 978-1-952103-27-8
Library of Congress Control Number 2021912380
Cataloging-in-Publication Data on file.

More from Phase Publishing

CHAPTER ONE

I'm about ninety-nine percent sure I'm about to get fired from my own company, and I have no idea why.

All that I've been told so far is that Chad wants to meet with me. Chad himself wasn't even the one who told me. This despite the fact that he's had my cell phone number now for over twelve years, *and* despite the fact he's never once shown a shred of reluctance about using that number as often as it pleases him.

No, it was Margo Maloney, our unfortunately-named human resources manager, who finally managed to get ahold of me last night in the midst of what had otherwise been a perfectly lovely dinner with Allie at our favorite restaurant in town. All Margo had cryptically been able to reveal was that my presence was requested in the conference room tomorrow morning at nine o'clock sharp.

So here I am now at nine o'clock sharp, sitting in this plush, black rolling chair that I probably bought once upon a time with my own personal credit card, trying my best to look 'normal'—whatever that looks like—while I await my fate in a pretty, glass zoo cage that I helped design.

I keep seeing coworkers hurry past the sleek, see-through conference room that we so sparingly use for actual conferences. Every single one of them seems to be taking great pains to avoid making any kind of accidental eye contact with me.

It's as if I wasn't an actual groomsman in Mark's wedding party a little more than a year ago.

As if I didn't personally recommend my wife's old hair stylist, Jillian, to fill our vacant bookkeeper position when she suddenly decided she wanted a career change and then practically begged Allie to talk to me on her behalf.

As if I didn't once escort a sobbing Hector into my office to assure him that he could take as much time off as he needed when his marriage of two decades unexpectedly imploded last year.

Frankly, the utter *ingratitude* of these people astounds me.

They all scurry past with their gaze pointed any direction but in here, looking for all the world like a bunch of poorly trained film extras on a movie set, each trying desperately to outdo the others at *acting* like they're busy working rather than actually *being* busy working.

I can't bear to look at them anymore. My focus shifts instead to the various trappings of this conference room, and I wonder at just how much of it I'm personally responsible for.

A little more than four years ago, this room was basically a cavernous storage closet for janitorial supplies and holiday decorations. The only illumination was a hanging lightbulb with a pull-string switch. There wasn't even a knob or a lock on the door, just a crudely cut circular hole in the wood to let mice in and out.

And now look at this place. Four shining glass walls

that stretch from tastefully carpeted floor clear up to industrial-chic ceiling. One of those walls has a door cut right into it that comes complete with a sleek, brushed chrome handle. High up above, the ceiling is speckled with inlaid LED sconces that are both dimmable and fully controllable by an app on your phone. Not to mention, we have heating and air conditioning in this room now.

Then there's the furniture. Twelve ergonomic rolling chairs with adjustable headrests, armrests, and footrests, each with a back that boasts a full ninety-degree tilt range. An abstractly shaped oblong table that is both easy on the eyes in terms of its unique shape and modern aesthetic as well as highly functional and practical, since it has built-in power outlets, USB ports, Bluetooth speakers, and even cupholders.

Most everything in here was my brainchild once upon a time. And while a good amount of it was purchased with the company expense account, I just know that I personally footed the bill for a lot of it too. The chairs, for sure. And now it's all getting ripped out from under me.

My knuckles tighten possessively on the genuine leather armrests that are both keeping me contained and keeping me together. How could they do this to me? How could *he* do this to me?

Chad and I were freshman-year dormmates at Michigan. Neither one of us arrived in college expecting to become business majors. He wanted to be poli-sci, and I had every intention of graduating with a degree in either visual arts, architecture, or both. But despite those best-laid plans, we each left Ann Arbor with a boatload of debt and a diploma from Ross.

We had been out of school for about four years when he called me out of the blue one evening. What started as simple reminiscing about the good old days somehow transitioned into a serious heart to heart, one in which we both somewhat sheepishly admitted that we'd somehow lost our way post-grad.

At the time, Chad held two jobs in Chicago: he was an office manager for a construction company by day, and a bartender on weekends.

When he called, I was working as a gallery manager for a struggling arthouse in downtown Los Angeles. Most of my day-to-day consisted of posting inane updates on our company's Twitter feed, Facebook wall, and Instagram page about the mediocre talents we were 'proud' to call our featured clients... and trying my best not to blow my brains out from sheer boredom.

Needless to say, neither one of us was very happy.

Maybe that was what made VitaLyfe so intoxicatingly appealing. Chad had already mapped out all the logistics for starting a real fruit-infused bottled water company when he called. He'd also somehow already raised seventy-five percent of the necessary funding, mainly through networking connections, loans, and sheer charismatic willpower.

What he said he needed was someone who could think outside the box, someone who had good taste in both design and people, and someone who could talk him off a ledge and be the voice of reason when he needed it most. He also wanted a friend he could trust, and as far as he could tell, I fit that bill better than anyone else in his life.

It wasn't until he flew out to L.A. and we met face to face that he revealed the other major reason he wanted me in with him as a partner in the company. After nearly three hours of lubing me up with stiff cocktails and verbal foreplay, he finally let it slip that he'd noticed on social media that I was engaged to Allison Kagan, the daughter of Bill Kagan—a businessman who owned a modest but successful chain of convenience stores in Southern California.

And there it was: the real reason he had wanted to talk to me about this venture.

Yes, I was still 'the perfect person for the job', but it certainly didn't hurt that my soon-to-be father-in-law was both loaded and well connected in the very industry that Chad hoped to infiltrate.

But who was I to argue? Here he was, promising me the thrill of adventure and the opportunity to build something that was unequivocally ours. He knew I was unhappy, and he knew that I was bored. With VitaLyfe, I could quit my dead-end job, come work with my best friend from college, and we'd be our own bosses. The only people we'd have to answer to would be each other, the six investors Chad had assembled for the bulk of his initial funding, and—assuming he'd put up the remaining twenty-five percent we needed—my future father-in-law.

It was any and every entrepreneur's wet dream, and it was there for the taking. So, I took it.

And for the past four years, it's been pretty good; at least, in terms of the business. Things started off very hard, but we were mostly prepared for that. We purposefully gave ourselves the wiggle room and requisite buffer we needed to survive the early setbacks and surprises that always seem to accompany a startup in its infancy.

For the most part, our investors have been patient with us. Not surprisingly, my father-in-law, Bill Kagan, has repeatedly proven himself to be both a godsend and a goddamn asshole. Without him bringing VitaLyfe into all his stores, there's no way we would have made it past our second year. Unfortunately, no one knows this better than Bill himself.

Some of the emotional and mental struggles that came from those early days were less expected, but we managed to overcome all that, too.

Or at least, *I* thought we did. And yet, here I am, sitting and sweating in the very heart of the company I gave birth to, wondering what in the hell is going on right now.

It took Margo Maloney from H.R. three tries to finally get ahold of me last night. Allie and I had just finished our appetizers at Gwen's on Sunset. We have a ritual of eating out on Sunday nights. It's one of the relics from our pre-nuptial days that we've surprisingly somehow managed to maintain despite all that life has thrown at us. Whether we go somewhere we've been before or we try someplace new, we always commit to putting our phones on vibrate and ignoring them for the full duration of the meal.

Truth be told, it's probably an easier assignment for her than it is for me. With all due respect to my wife's job as a daytime social worker at a senior center in Pasadena, her phone's not exactly ringing off the hook most evenings or weekends.

Mine, on the other hand, just would not stop last night. Finally, I did what I normally do in those types of situations, and I excused myself to go to the bathroom so I could sneak a peek at just what was so urgent in the sheltered privacy of a stall.

There were three missed calls from Margo… and a *text*. Sure, the text was only three words—*Call me back*—but in four years at VitaLyfe, I'd never once received a text message from the middle-aged divorcee, let alone a phone call.

When I called her back, she wouldn't reveal anything other than the fact that Chad wanted to talk to me one on one about something extremely important. She wouldn't say whether she knew what it was about, and she refused to speculate as to why Chad couldn't just contact me himself. All she would do is give me the message, which she did, and then she hung up.

Perhaps understandably, Allie and I did not end up staying for dessert. My wife's misgivings about me violating the religious sanctimony of our Sunday night tradition to take a phone call in the bathroom quickly transformed into something bordering on genuine panic when I told her just what that call was about.

Chad could have saved us from a long night filled with too much fruitless speculation and too little sleep, but he proved to be better at completely ignoring his phone yesterday than I was.

Speaking of Chad, he finally arrives, followed close behind by the same woman he had do his dirty work for him a dozen hours ago. Chad holds the glass door ajar as Margo enters with a pleasant smile on her face, and I'm less taken aback by the fact that she's in here with us than I am by her sustained eye contact. I don't know her half as well as any of the other people out there in our office, but you'd never know that based off the warmth of her present greeting.

Chad's demeanor is similarly friendly. At least on the

surface, he's gone to great lengths to either make me or make himself feel comfortable. Rather than taking the empty seat next to Margo at the opposite end of the table, he decides to change course and pull back a rolling chair that's two down from me.

It's a simple gesture, though I can't help but read it as him trying to somehow disassociate himself from her by choosing to sit on 'my side' of the table. He mumbles my name and gives me some kind of smirk, like we're sharing an inside joke together even though we're not.

Chad has nothing with him, but Margo came prepared. She opens a large manila folder filled with documents that I can't read from this far away, but most of them look like they've been typed out on letterhead. Margo lays a yellow notepad and a pen down on top of it, then speaks as she lowers her briefcase to the floor beside her.

"Just about ready here."

"Ready for what?"

It's the first time I've spoken aloud in probably twenty minutes at least. Though I was told to be here "at nine o'clock sharp," I know from a quick glance at the gold watch on my wrist that it's almost nine thirty now.

Chad just smirks at me again but says nothing. I can hear Margo's fingers scratching around in the recesses of her leather bag before they pull up what they've been fishing for: a silver electronic device. She presses a button on the side of it, sets it down matter-of-factly on the table in front of her, and angles it in my general direction. I realize we're being recorded.

"Big-time company, and we're still out here using old-fashioned tape recorders, huh?"

I guess Chad can speak after all. He chuckles and

rolls his eyes before giving Margo a smarmy wink. I feel like maybe I'd normally find this sort of thing from my old college buddy charming, but right now, he just comes across as greasy and a bit juvenile.

For her part though, Margo doesn't seem to mind.

"You know, I say that myself all the time. It'd be so much easier just to use my cell phone, but every job I ever worked at before here, it was always customary and expected to use the recorder. I think people like having a hard copy sometimes? Anywho, I got in the habit of using one, and now it's a hard habit to break, so I–"

"I'm sorry, but what the fuck is going on here?"

I'm about as surprised by the volume of my own voice as they are. It's not quite an outburst, but the words still come tumbling out before I've fully formed them. The room is suddenly ninety degrees, at minimum, and I'm wondering what happened to the high-powered air conditioning that I once hired a contractor to install in here four years ago.

Chad looks increasingly nervous. I can tell now that whatever facade of routine comfortability he'd hoped to preserve just vaporized in the wake of my exclamation. His left leg bounces up and down on the ball of his foot under the table like he's had too much coffee this morning; which he probably has, knowing him.

"Ethan, my man, this is not what I wanted to be doing with my morning, believe you me."

He actually has the *gall* to chuckle.

"But I guess it falls on me to be 'the guy' in these types of situations, even if it goes against my own best interests, so to speak. Or even if it's a conflict of interest. You know what I'm getting at."

"I honestly don't."

And it's the truth. There's no malice there, just naked sincerity.

Chad gives a quick glance in Margo's direction before returning his attention to me. He places one hand on his bouncing knee to suppress the movement, and, with the air of a captain resigning himself to go down with the ship, slaps his other hand flat on the table, stares at me, and clears his throat.

"You and I go back a long ways, obviously. We went to school together; we kind of came of age together. It's why I approached you to help me run this whole song-and-dance routine four years ago. We've already gotten farther than where we ever thought we'd be at this point, and that's fantastic. We're a full year ahead of schedule and then some, as you know. So, I think it's time—*we* think it's time—that we started acting like the player that we are in our industry sector, rather than the player that we were four years ago."

I give him a moment to continue on with his little soliloquy, but once it's clear he's not going to, I cut in.

"So… you're firing me… because of what?"

Chad smiles self-consciously, and his eyes dart around the conference room like moths.

"I wouldn't go so far as to say anyone is 'firing' anybody. What's more accurate, what's a better representation of where we're at right now as a company, is that we're *right there*, right on the precipice of an exciting new chapter in the story of VitaLyfe, and…"

He seems to run out of gas midway through his own bullshit. Chad runs a hand through his gelled hair and slaps it back down on the table. The sensation both buys him a bit of time and seems to give him an extra jolt of energy, because all of a sudden, he plunges full force into more verbal vomit.

"Fucking *Christ*, Ethan. You know your schedule better than anyone. You're never here when you're supposed to be in the mornings; you come in casually mid-afternoon like it's no big deal. Yeah, you did a great job in helping us get set up in the very beginning, but we're so far beyond that now. And you know it! You know we're at that sweet spot, that make-or-break juncture that separates the flash-in-a-pan upstarts from the companies that actually stand the test of time."

Chad has finally found his voice. He folds his hands together and slides the bonded nucleus across the table in my direction like it's some kind of weird, fleshy peace offering.

"It's not just punctuality, of course. Like, I could live with the haphazard hours from my COO if you, you know, *did more*. But all the leaps and bounds we've made as a company these past fourteen months, they're not because of you. Truthfully, they're *in spite* of you. You can't possibly be surprised that we're sitting here right now, can you?"

If I'm being totally and perfectly honest, on some level, I'm not. Sure, there have been times over the past few years where I felt like more of a figurehead than a pioneer. I'm in the same boat as the vast majority of the American workforce when I say that I've done a good job, if not a great job, in fulfilling all the basic expectations associated with my chosen vocation.

But there's a reason for that, of course. And he and I both know what it is.

"So, what are you telling me?"

He blinks a couple of times, plays with his hands,

looks at Margo, then looks back at me.

"What… you want me to spell it out for you?"

"Yeah, why don't you, actually."

"If that's what you really want from me, then fuck it, I'll tell you the truth."

Chad straightens as he sits bolt-upright in the chair.

"When I first came to you about VitaLyfe and it was just you and me, we had practically nothing. Now, we have over twenty-five hundred stores across ten different states and counting, and yet the way you approach this company hasn't changed one iota. You're still acting like it's a given you even have a job in the first place based off your relationship with me. I gave you the COO position despite the fact that you had no practical or relevant experience in this industry, and that you've never run a company before–"

"The same exact thing could be said of you, Chad. I mean, you were a fucking *bartender* in Chicago before this. Don't pretend like you're some Tim Cook-type who paid your dues and came in well prepared for this."

There's no way that Margo or anyone else in this office knows about those meager years Chad spent slinging drinks in Boystown. He has meticulously and intentionally veiled the interim era of his life between graduating college and founding VitaLyfe, and now his complexion reddens immediately, as I know he's both embarrassed and angry that I've breached his trust and poked a hole in his carefully constructed company persona.

"There are many, many differences between you and I, Ethan. As it pertains to this current discussion and the matter at hand—which, just so we're clear, is your immediate termination of employment from this company—the only real difference that matters is that our shareholders have complete and utter confidence in my continuing performance as CEO. Unfortunately, they don't have that same level of confidence in you."

Chad pushes his chair back from the table and gets to his feet. For a second, I think he's actually about to hit me, but he turns and walks over toward Margo instead and holds out his hand expectantly.

"I'm ready for the papers now, Margo."

She nods and hands him the manila folder on the table. Absurdly, she still has that perfectly peaceful, sunny disposition about her, as if she couldn't care less that two grown men are trading highly personal barbs right out in the open in front of her… or that one of them is about to have his entire life ripped to shreds.

But then again, why should she? She's not the one getting axed for absolutely no reason whatsoever.

"You can read and sign these here if you want, or you can take them home with you and show them to a lawyer; it doesn't matter to me. It might make Margo's life a little easier if you do it now, but I'm sure she'll understand if you need a little more time… to process everything."

He takes a couple steps and slides the folder down the table at me, then places a hand casually on the door handle, signaling he might be as finished with this conversation as he is with me.

"There's all the usual stuff in there—info about your NDA, non-compete, severance, benefits transferal, yada yada yada—plus what your options are as far as stocks are concerned. Not to rush you, but there's a limited time window in which the other shareholders are willing to give you a more-than-generous compensation package for the percentages you own. If you decide to hold onto them past that point, the number drops precipitously. So, again, no rush, but maybe think things over quickly. Everyone really wants you and Allie to land on your feet after this."

I spring up to those feet and the room is absolutely spinning now.

"Don't you ever say her fucking name again, you hear me?!"

Chad and Margo both appear stunned. I'm vaguely aware of people watching me from outside the glass, but it doesn't matter anymore. All I can see through a haze of red and black and gold spots is Chad standing right there at the door, just barely out of reach, and I'm having an impossible time keeping the thoughts and mental images away right now.

"Ever. Do you hear me?!"

Chad's eyes dart nervously toward Margo and then come back to rest on me. He's wondering if I'm about to talk about it. So am I.

"When was it?"

Chad blinks at me.

"When was what?"

"The vote. When did you guys do it? And where?"

Chad actually looks relieved by this particular line of questioning, and it makes me instantly reconsider whether I *do* want to rehash a private conversation he and I had three years ago… a conversation that, until today, I had every intention of keeping buried and otherwise forgotten in the darkest, most distant corner of my mind.

"When and where doesn't really matter now, does it?"

"It matters. Of course it matters. It should matter a

great deal to me, don't you think?"

Chad's knuckles whiten on the door handle.

"Be that as it may, Ethan, I'm neither legally required nor personally interested in revealing any of that information. And I'm well within my rights to say that."

"Oh, *come on*, Chad. You can give me that much, at least, after everything else you're taking from me. I'm asking as your former best friend and business partner to at least give me the common courtesy of letting me know when, where, how, and by whom I came to be fucked out of my own company."

Chad bristles.

"It was never *your* company. It *was* our company, but now it's *my* company. As soon as the vote happened, your position here and on the board was nullified. I could have just had Margo meet with you one on one, but I thought you deserved better than that."

"Well, thanks for being so considerate and deigning to make an appearance here yourself. It's an honor you decided to fuck me in person rather than sending another minion to do it for you. I'm actually surprised you didn't just have her tell me everything last night. That would've been more your style, you chickenshit prick."

Chad lifts his index finger at me in warning. It's an absurd gesture, and I can see even through the fabric of his perfectly tailored blazer that his arm is trembling.

"I've said all I'm going to say to you. You can act like an adult now, gather your things from your office, and leave with dignity… or we can do this the theatrical way. I told Margo that we wouldn't need Rich for this, and I hope that I was right."

Rich is the amiable, elderly security guard who mans the front desk of our office building. Not only am I the guy who hired Rich; I'm also the guy who stops and actually talks with Rich every single morning. It's hard to imagine Rich coming in here at Chad's behest to escort me out, and it's even harder to imagine a scenario where he'd be able to physically overpower me if I didn't want to go quietly. But I'd never do that Rich, so I guess it doesn't really matter anyway.

Chad taps his foot impatiently on the carpet.

"Are you going to be all right if I leave now, Margo? I've got a few other things I need to take care of before I have another meeting."

He's acting like he's about to leave her alone with a caged animal. Hell, maybe he's right.

But Margo is apparently old hat at this sort of thing. If she's fazed in the slightest by anything I've said or done up to this point, she sure doesn't look it.

"We'll be just fine, thank you, Chad."

Palpable relief washes over the face of my one-time college roommate, best friend, and business partner. He sets his jaw and lets out a weary sigh, all 'heavy lies the crown'.

"I honestly thought this would go better. Maybe I'm naïve, but I thought we'd at least be able to shake hands at the end."

Now, it's my turn to audibly chuckle.

"Chad, you're not naïve. You're an idiot."

He stares back at me for a second, his expression inscrutable. Then he turns to the door, pushes it open, and walks off down the hallway, probably to go prepare himself for the staff meeting where he'll break the news of what's just happened and spin it however he sees fit.

Once he's completely gone, I turn my attention back to Margo, who is waiting patiently for me.

"Well, now. I'm sorry about all this, Mr. Birch."

I can't remember if she has always called me Mr. Birch or if she's only doing it now out of professional courtesy, and I have half a mind to correct her and ask to be called 'Ethan'. But then I remember that it doesn't matter anymore, since this is going to be our final interaction anyway.

"It's fine."

Of course, it's really not fine. But what else am I supposed to say?

"Do you want to go through that folder now together, or do you think you'll need some time?"

Her demeanor is rehearsed but gentle. I have the ridiculous thought that she's actually quite good at her job, and I try to remember if I'm the one who hired her. I'd like to think that I am.

"Honestly, I don't think I'm in the right state of mind right now. Is that all right?"

Margo's quick to put me at ease.

"Of course! I know you have my information already, but my card is stapled in there to the top sheet in case you have any questions or concerns down the line. You have several options as far as returning all the completed paperwork is concerned: you can mail it back to me, you can scan and email it back to me, or you can drop it off in person. I'd just ask that if you do decide to drop it off, you leave it up front with Rich rather than bringing it inside yourself."

That sounds less like Margo's ask and more like Chad's, but I nod my understanding all the same.

"Now, then. Would you like to go to your office

together?"

She phrases it like it's a question, but I know it's actually a direction. Margo stops her little tape recorder and puts it away as she gets to her feet, then moves to the door and holds it open for me in the same way Chad did earlier for her.

Once we're in the hallway, she allows me to lead her to the room that used to be my office. Neither one of us says anything—what is there really to say?—and the silence seems to suit both of us just fine.

Mercifully, we don't run into any other living souls on the short walk there. In the time I spent waiting alone in the conference room for Chad, it felt like every single employee in the company walked by at some point to try and steal a glance without getting caught. Now, though, they're all conspicuously absent from the hallways and common areas. Maybe Chad locked them in a room together so I couldn't say anything to anyone on my way out.

Someone has done me the great courtesy of assembling a couple large, empty boxes and leaving them on the floor next to my desk. How thoughtful.

I move quickly and a bit carelessly. Truthfully, there's not much even here, since most of my things are at home in a room I've about halfway converted into a home office.

It's impossible not to start psychoanalyzing the last four years of my life as I finish stripping my office of any evidence I've ever been here. Somewhere, some long time ago, I must have known this day would come. There's only so much healing and reconstructing a human being can do. Beyond that, perhaps all that's really left is to break away and start anew all over again.

Still, I want to know how the vote went. Chad obviously voted against me, but who else? It's one thing if the other votes that went against me came from his early investors. But if one of those votes came from my father-in-law? That's something I would need to know.

"Do you need any help with that?"

Margo's voice breaks into my train of thought. She's stood quietly patient as I packed everything up. It's only now after I've precariously stacked one large and heavy box on top of the other and slid my fingers beneath the combined load hanging off my desk that she looks a bit concerned.

"It's all right. I've got it. Can you just get the door?"

"Of course."

She flattens her body up against the wall after pulling the door as wide as it will go, and I shuffle past her, trying to make sure I can see where I'm going around the box tower that I've barely got a hold of in front of me.

Quickly, clumsily, I stumble down the hallway. The boxes are good for two reasons: they'll make anyone think twice about getting in my way right now, and they'll hide the emotion in my face from any curious onlookers.

Up ahead, I see that Rich already has the front door open and waiting for me. That's nice. His face is upturned, and he seems to be enjoying standing outside in the fresh air and warm Southern California sunlight for a change, using just the toe of his boot to keep the door from closing.

"Thanks, Rich."

I grunt the words from a distance, partly to show my honest appreciation and partly just to get his attention so he knows I'm coming through.

The guard looks a little surprised at my sudden appearance, but he doesn't flinch or lose his foothold on the door.

"Not a problem, Mr. Birch."

There it is again. Only this time, I know for a fact that it's intentional. Rich called me Mr. Birch for the first couple weeks after I hired him until I finally broke him of the habit, and he's called me Ethan ever since. Until now.

"Wow. It's already back to Mr. Birch, huh? Just like that?"

Rich blushes, and I immediately regret saying it.

"I'm sorry about that. Ethan."

He seems genuinely mortified and miserable as he lopes after me into the parking lot.

"I just don't know what I'm supposed to say or how I'm supposed to act in this type of situation."

"That makes two of us, Rich."

I drop the boxes on the asphalt as soon as I reach the trunk of my car… and maybe a bit too hastily. The resulting crash is a surefire sign that something—maybe several things—have just broken inside.

Rich winces and looks down at the boxes.

"That didn't sound too good."

I fish my keys out from my pocket, pop the trunk, and smile sadly at him.

"No, Rich. No, it did not."

He helps me lift both of the boxes and arrange them side by side in the empty trunk space. It's a particularly kind gesture, especially since I know he has a bad back and wears a brace beneath his shirt.

When we're done, I pull the trunk closed and look

at him. Margo is still standing out here in the parking lot with us too, though it's clear she hung back a bit to give us some space, I guess. I put out my hand and Rich shakes it.

"Thanks for the help with the boxes, Rich. I appreciate it. I'll miss our morning talks."

His mouth twitches, but it looks like he still doesn't know what to say... and it's getting weird now. I give his hand a pat with my free one and disengage, then take a small step toward Margo and give her a wave. She waves back.

"Don't forget to reach out if you need anything at all now, you hear? You have all my information."

Of course I have all her information. She called me three times and sent me a text message last night.

"I will."

Despite all the professionalism, it's still an awkward goodbye. There's just no getting around how unnatural and uncomfortable this situation is for all parties involved. I need to get out of here.

Wordlessly, I turn away from these people whose very livelihoods I've spent years providing for so I can step inside the merciful solitude of my car. Of all the individuals I know and have worked with at VitaLyfe, it's strange that these two people are the last ones I might ever see or talk to. I never in a million years would have imagined that's how it would be.

The Jaguar roars to life as I back it slowly out of my parking space. It takes everything in my power not to look up at the white sign in front of me that I know reads 'RESERVED FOR MR. BIRCH.' Thankfully, neither Rich nor Margo wave at me in my rearview mirror as I steal one last look past them at the building I helped select as our headquarters once upon a time.

And then all it takes is a slight turn out onto the road, and everything behind me fully disappears from view.

Chapter Two

For a while, I just drive mindlessly forward. My hands are at ten and two on the smooth, leather steering wheel, my foot alternates back and forth between the brake and the gas pedal, and my eyes stare straight ahead at the cars in front of me without really seeing any of them.

People come, people go, some grow young, some grow cold...

Tom Petty's "You Don't Know How It Feels" is about midway through on the radio before I even realize I have the radio on to begin with. I punch the dial to turn it off, drive in torturous silence for about ten seconds, change my mind, and punch the dial to bring it back.

Let's head on down the road, there's somewhere I gotta goooooo...

I sing the chorus and the rest of the song with Tom as best I can with what lyrics I think I know.

When it ends and the radio DJ comes on to talk, I decide maybe it's time for me to formulate some kind of plan. Nothing too grandiose or significant, of course. Not like what I'm going to tell Allie, what I'm going to do with my life now, how I'm going to afford to keep a roof over our head. None of that, obviously. No, something much simpler is what I need right now.

A glance at the small digital clock on the car's console tells me it's just past 10:30. What can a person do at 10:30 a.m. on a Monday? It's too early for lunch, and I've already had breakfast. I kind of have to pee. And for whatever reason, the idea of going home right now without a finite plan in place just scares me shitless.

My options are scarce. I can either drive around aimlessly until I come up with said plan, or I can go to a physical location, park, and either do something inside that location or do nothing outside it in my car.

Of these possibilities, the most appealing is to go somewhere and go inside.

Good. I'm making progress. Now, where would I like to go? I'd *like* to go to work and still have a job. But that's impossible.

Seeing as I'm not hungry but I have to pee, it seems like my only options are to go to a coffee shop, go to a bar, go to some sort of retail location like a store or a mall, or go to a public place like a library, a park, or the beach. I'm also not about to surrender what little dignity I have left by stopping at a gas station in my own home city just so I can take a leak.

Bar, it is, then…

I justify the notion of visiting a bar before noon on a weekday as being sort of cinematic. Especially in a city like Los Angeles, you learn to appreciate the moments in your life that feel like they could have been scripted for film or television.

Just got fired? Better get a drink.

Just got fired from your own company? Better get two.

As soon as I see a promising spot, I pull off into the

parking lot. True to the way my day is already going, I can't see the hours from the outside and the door is shut. I have to park, get out, walk up to the door, and try the handle before I conclude that it's definitely not open.

I pull out my phone and do a quick search for nearby alcoholic establishments that are for sure already open. On a whim, I end up selecting a little hole-in-the-wall tiki bar on Sunset that's not too far from our house in Silver Lake.

Best-case scenario, I have a Mai Tai or two and work up the courage to make what looks like a five-minute drive home. Worst-case scenario, I leave my car behind on my own side of town and get a cheap Uber ride there when I'm ready.

There are no other cars in the parking lot outside of Shangri-La when I arrive, which isn't a good sign. I double-check the information on my phone to make sure it's actually supposed to be open, and it is; at least online. I'm half-expecting this door to be locked just like the last one was when I grab the handle and pull, but mercifully, it swings wide open and allows me to step inside.

You'd never know it from the outside, but this place is *huge*. From the street, or even from the parking lot, it looks like it could pass for a mom-and-pop taco stand or a tiny little pawn shop. The exterior of the building is a boring beige, and it's as boxy as they come, almost like God Himself just dropped an unwrapped package on the side of the road and somebody decided to open up a bar inside of it.

The interior is something altogether different, though. Hanging paper lanterns provide most of the illumination from above, and in their soft, multicolor glow, I see that the faux straw and bamboo patchwork steeple ceiling goes back a good fifty feet or so.

All manner of baubles, trinkets, tchotchkes, and knickknacks line the ceiling, the floor, the walls, and the shelves behind the bar. Nothing really looks like it serves much purpose other than to take up space. It's as if somewhere along the line, the bar's owners decided that if they covered every square inch with décor, patrons would have no choice but to surrender themselves over to this ridiculous theme and accept the illusion they'd just stepped inside a tropical hut somewhere in the Pacific.

Even without a drink in my system, I can appreciate the level of effort that went into this place. I'm still too sober to forget the fact that I'm in Southern California—and that I just got fired—but it's disarming and even a tad bit enchanting just seeing so much *stuff* everywhere you look.

This place is perfect, because it's chock full of distractions. If the drinks are at least passable, there's a decent chance I can lose myself here for a couple hours or more.

The one thing Shangri-La doesn't have right now is people; which, frankly, suits my purposes just fine. Although there's a momentary jumbled flash of guilt and self-loathing when I realize there aren't a ton of other souls having a cocktail on a Monday morning with me, I'm also a bit relieved at the peace and relative quiet of the place. Other than some soft 'island music' playing in the background, a few whirring, wall-mounted, oscillating fans, and an old man in a bright orange Hawaiian shirt topping off bottles behind the bar, there's not a whole lot of action here.

Maybe I'll move to one of the many empty wooden pub tables after I get my drink, just to be sure no one sits beside me at the bar. But for the time being, I take a load off by clambering up onto the nearest metallic spinning barstool by the door.

If the bartender knows I'm here, he doesn't give a damn. This place is pretty dark, so I have to imagine he noticed the sudden spear of sunlight cutting in from outside when I opened the door, even if he didn't hear me come in.

Either way, he keeps at what he's doing: tilting bottles of nearly empty dark rum into nearly full bottles and then tossing away the empty ones when he's finished. I notice a few of the bottles he's pouring out from are different brands than the ones he's pouring into, but I'm not about to rat him out.

When he's finally done, he takes a step back and admires his handiwork, then turns and walks over in my direction. Without so much as a word of apology or even a friendly hello, he pinches up a brown cocktail napkin from a stack on the counter, flips it in front of me, crosses his arms, and speaks.

"What'll it be?"

If it wasn't for the garish Hawaiian shirt, I'd think this guy stepped straight out of an old-timey Western flick. He's got all the appearance and swagger of a saloon barkeep, with scores of crusty wrinkles around his eyes, matted facial hair, a permanent frown, and just the faintest odor about him that reminds me of campfire.

Briefly, I'm taken aback by the bluntness of his question, but then I remember that it's not even 11:00 a.m. yet on a Monday. He knows I don't want to see a menu or a drink list.

"I'm assuming you make a good Mai Tai."

He nods.

"I'll have one of those, thanks."

He sets off making me one, and I decide it's high time that I relieve my bladder.

It's a straight shot to the back of the bar, and even with my eyes still adjusting to the darkness of this place, I can make out a pair of wooden doors bathed in yellow light. One bears the image of a half-naked hula girl and the other sports a half-naked fisherman. I almost walk through the hula girl door just because I can right now, but years of social conditioning steer me automatically to and through the fisherman door instead.

Pissing when you really have to go is one of life's most underrated pleasures. People talk endlessly about things like sex, chocolate, wine, sleeping… but nobody talks about the simple joy of urinary release. I shiver just a bit and lift a heel, finish, flush, and wash my hands.

My eyes are finishing up their adjustments to these dim surroundings as I make the walk back to my stool. Hawaiian-tourist Sam Elliott looks like he's doing inventory now as he checks various bottle quantities and scribbles on a worn legal pad.

Waiting for me on the countertop is a beautiful orange and red cocktail in a tall, whimsical glass with a turquoise toothpick umbrella and a pineapple wedge on the rim. Next to it is a small shot glass that is filled to the brim with brown liquid. What a kind gesture.

"Hey, thanks for this."

I'd lift the shot glass up to salute him, but I'm afraid I'd spill it if I tried. Better to wait until he's not looking and take it then.

Tiki cowboy glances back in my direction from the

other end of the bar.

"It's not from me. It's from them."

He tilts his head to the right over his shoulder, and for the first time, I realize we're not alone. Maybe they've been here this whole time, and I just didn't see them in the dark—though I don't know how I could have missed them sitting in the corner booth not too far from the bathroom.

True, the booth is fairly well obscured by the bar itself and by all the junk hanging everywhere. I can see it now from my vantage point, but it'd be easy to overlook unless you knew it was there to begin with. The more reasonable explanation is that they arrived while I was in the bathroom.

But even that seems a bit farfetched. The music in here is barely audible, so I probably would've heard them come in from the other side of the door. And even if I didn't, why would they buy a random stranger they hadn't even seen yet a drink?

They must have already been here, because they each have a drink in front of them, and one looks about empty. That settles it, then. Somehow, I must have walked right past them twice without noticing. Shit happens when you're dealing with emotional trauma, after all.

The booth seems to be the only one of its kind in here, tucked in the corner between the end of the bar counter and a small, wooden ledge with a few random wicker stools adjacent to the bathrooms. There are no paper lanterns above the booth, but there's a small, red votive candle burning low that's flanked between two glass drinks in the center of the table.

It's two of them, two guys, one older and one

younger, who are sitting together at the table this Monday morning.

The younger man is the one with the half-empty glass. He looks to be about my age, somewhere between his late twenties to his mid-thirties. I can see from here that he's either got blonde or red hair, cut close to his scalp in a buzz cut. Judging by the way his pale skin glows in the dusky candlelight, he's probably a redhead. If he has eyebrows or eyelashes at all, I can't see them from here.

The older man more than makes up for what his companion otherwise lacks in hair. He's probably somewhere in his sixties or seventies, and yet he still has a full head of hair that might be pulled back in a ponytail. The hair lines a long, narrow face until it becomes a pointed beard and a curving moustache. His eyebrows are thick and wooly, and they look darker than the hair on his head. He has a giant, sloping nose that I can distinguish even from here in these inky conditions.

The younger man leans forward and sips on what's left of his drink through a straw he holds in place with his mouth. His hands are too busy clutching a smartphone atop the table that he types furiously upon with his thumbs.

The older man has one elbow resting on top of the table and is slowly, sensuously stroking the tip of his beard between his thumb and forefinger. He's also just staring at me, unless there's something incredible happening right behind me right now.

But he did just buy me a shot... for whatever reason. Honestly, I don't know if anyone's ever bought me a drink before. I'm not sure how I'm supposed to react. I don't think I bought that many women drinks before I met Allie either, if any at all, so this whole concept is unfamiliar territory to me.

What exactly is expected on my part now? In the movies, it's always a guy who buys a girl a drink with the hope or expectation I guess that the gesture might earn him an opportunity to talk to her. There's also obviously a decent amount of romantic or sexual subtext there, and that's not something I'm looking to cultivate or encourage. For all I know, this place is a gay bar. Maybe these guys are some kind of odd couple looking for fun with a third wheel.

Or maybe this is all just my imagination running wild. I am suffering from emotional trauma, after all. Best to just thank them from afar so as to acknowledge the gift and leave it at that. Even if the right thing to do would be to go over there, I really don't want to. Nor should I have to, given the way my morning's gone.

I make up my mind to lift the shot glass high in a salute to the peculiar strangers at the other end of the room, knowing full well just how much of it is going to spill out around the edges onto my hand as I do so. I guess I'll definitely smell like rum when I see Allie later tonight, which is just peachy, of course.

"Thank you, guys! I actually really needed this."

My voice is embarrassingly loud in the quiet cavern of the empty bar, but I want to make sure I'm loud enough that they can hear me without having to actually get up and go over there.

Younger guy glances up from his phone. The bartender turns around as well, looking a bit startled and probably annoyed at my sudden outburst.

I give it a couple seconds in case somebody wants to say something... the young guy, the old guy, the bartender, the invisible voiceover narrator in the movie of my sad, pathetic excuse for a life right now. When nobody speaks up, I bring the shot glass to my lips and do my best to throw it back.

Easier said than done. I've never been that big of a drinker—despite the present appearance to the contrary. Whatever rum doesn't get on my hand, my chin, or my lap manages to find its way down my throat in a couple quick gulps rather than one smooth swallow.

Feeling the urge to gag and without any water nearby, I reach for the Mai Tai and take a long pull through the straw to chase down the pure liquor. My eyes might be watering a bit, but no one can tell from this far away—not in this dusky fake twilight, anyway. I didn't hurl, either, so at least there's that.

When I blink away the hot tears, the bartender's back to his inventory and the redhead's back to his cell phone. Only the bearded guy continues to look in my direction… and it still doesn't feel like a look so much as a lingering gaze.

What more does he want from me? I'm not going over there. If I wanted the company of strange men right now, I would have gone straight to Santa Monica Boulevard in West Hollywood. I came here to be left alone and to have a quick diversion and a dose of liquid courage before coming to grips with my grim new reality.

"Thanks again."

I'm a little less loud and abrasive this time as I lift the empty shot glass high in the air in some kind of dumb, victorious symbol of my masculinity or courage or gratitude; I'm not exactly sure which. All I know is that I intend it to be a signing-off of sorts when it comes to whatever this interaction is or might be.

I turn my attention back to the cocktail in front of me and to the wall of bottles and random tropical detritus, pretending like I'm not still watching the booth from the corner of my eye and mentally steeling myself for the worst.

In one fluid movement, the older man leans toward his younger companion. It looks like he might be saying something to him now, as the young guy immediately sets his phone down and turns his head to listen. From my periphery, I can't tell if the old man is actually talking or not, nor can I tell if he's still staring in my direction.

What I do see is him stand up suddenly and maneuver his way gracefully around the table and out of the booth. My heart stops as I realize this might be it. He's likely about to stride right over here and initiate something. And sure enough, he takes a few long, confident steps in my general direction.

But then he slides a hand under the end of the bar countertop, lifts up a metal gate, mumbles something unintelligible to the bartender, and walks right on in behind the bar. The bartender chuckles without stopping his work as the old man pauses and soaks in one last prolonged look at me. Then, he presses a large hand up against a row of bottles behind the bar and walks right through the wall in a sudden burst of white light.

It's at least fifteen seconds or so before I understand that I didn't just witness some real-life Harry Potter shit right before my eyes. The white light lingers a bit after the old man disappears, and then it slowly fades as the wall of bottles swings back into view.

With an air of complete and utter nonchalance, the

bartender reaches for a specific bottle on the moving wall and pulls it toward him. Suddenly, it's clear that this section of the bar wall isn't real; it's a secret door, more Scooby-Doo than Harry Potter. The bottles on those shelves aren't for serving or drinking; they actually are for décor alone, like most everything else in here.

This sort of thing isn't exactly uncommon nowadays, especially not in major cities where speakeasies and novelty bars are all the rage. Still, it's a strange and disconcerting thing to see if you're not really expecting it.

Stranger still is the idea that a bar patron would be allowed back behind the bar to use such a door. Maybe the old man wasn't a patron at all though; maybe he's the manager, or maybe even the owner of the place. That would make a lot more sense.

I'm still putting all this together in my head when I realize with a start that the younger guy with the phone and the buzzed head is standing pretty much right next to me. I can't help but jump in my seat on the barstool, and he cautiously puts out a hand as if to stop or catch me from falling, though he doesn't actually make physical contact.

"Woah, there. Steady now. Steady, bud. You okay?"

From up close, he's definitely a redhead. His pale, white skin is dotted with freckles along his nose, under his eyes, and everywhere on his forehead. Trace acne scars here and there wage war with the freckles for territory in the endless barren tundra of his complexion. I was right; he has no real eyebrows or eyelashes to speak of. They're there, but just barely.

What's very much there, however, are two bright, white eyes surrounding small ponds of pale blue with beady black pupils set in the center. He's wearing a dark navy Henley shirt that looks like it's one size too small; but it also looks like that might be intentional. The fabric is tight around his chest and his biceps, accentuating what is certainly a sculpted and imposing figure.

Even his smile is a bit imposing right now. I'm not sure if he means for it to be friendly or intimidating or both, but it honestly comes across as much challenging smirk as it does wolfish grin of hello.

"You good, bud?" The smirk spreads. "You look like you just saw a ghost or something."

He talks funny, like he's imitating a tough guy from the Bronx or Philadelphia, some thug or mafioso from a seedy, low-class neighborhood somewhere on the East Coast. Maybe he's actually from one of those places. Hell, maybe he's actually one of those types of people, too.

"Yeah, I'm good. You just—I didn't see you there, that's all."

He lifts both hands and wiggles his fingers in my face.

"*Wooooooooo…* spooky."

I guess I don't give him the reaction he's after, because his skull pivots on a swivel to track down the bartender.

"*Ay, Ron!* One more for me, plus another Bacardi 151 for my friend over here."

He smacks his mouth loudly. I *think* he's chewing gum. With a quick sideways glance and another smirk in my direction, he calls back out to the bartender.

"*Ehh,* fuck it! I'll do one with him."

Ron the bartender nods and grabs a bottle from a high shelf nearby, as well as two shot glasses, and starts to pour.

I turn to face this guy.

"No, no, no, no, no… I appreciate it, but I actually shouldn't be drinking anything else. The shot you already got me was more than enough. More than generous and—and kind, I mean."

He just chews his gum and smirks at me, so I soldier on.

"Thanks again. If you didn't hear me before."

Ron sets the two shot glasses down on the bar top before us, filled to the brim once again. Somehow, he doesn't manage to spill any of the rum when he does it, but I guess that comes with the territory of being a grizzled bartender with presumably years of experience.

My new companion gives me an exaggerated comical shrug.

"Too late."

He picks up both shot glasses and makes to hand me one as Ron shuffles off to make him another cocktail.

This is the moment. Either I put my foot down and tell this guy 'thanks, but no thanks', or I see how far down the rabbit hole goes. My hand is starting to move toward the shot glass when I see Allie's face in my mind. She's not even giving me a 'look', but her on-cue materialization is enough to make up my mind for me.

"Hey, I can't. I'm sorry, though. Thank you. And I appreciate it."

He purses his lips and studies me, holding the shot glasses in mid-air all the while.

"You sure you can't?"

It could be a challenge, or it could be a come-on; I honestly have no idea which. So, I slide my Mai Tai away from me toward the inner bar rail as further proof that I've made up my mind. It's nowhere near finished, but I could swear I'm already starting to feel the effects of the drink, especially combined with the shot of straight liquor.

"I may be down and out, but I'm not desperate."

It's not necessarily meant to be a personal rebuke, but I'm also not entirely upset if that's how it lands. I still have zero clue what this dude's intentions are, and I'll be damned if I'm going to let a complete stranger peer-pressure me right now.

Buzz Cut snickers to himself.

"Suit yourself, bud."

He takes something out of his pocket. It's a compact but gorgeous wooden box, maybe about the size of a cell phone, outlined in shining gold and ornamented all over with strange markings or runes of some sort. He lifts open the top of this box and digs out something that looks like a cross between a chalky pill capsule and a thin Eucharist wafer. Without a second's hesitation, he tosses the unidentified substance into the back of his throat, chases it with one of the shots, swallows, then gulps down the other shot glass in rapid succession.

There's no denying it's an impressive feat. I'm no heavy drinker, and I certainly don't know my rums, but I know that if the two shots he just inhaled came from the same stuff they gave me, this guy's definitely going to be feeling it... and *fast*. Especially if he just took some kind of drug first. Unless, of course, this is all just standard operating behavior for this person on an early Monday afternoon.

If he does feel any of it at all, he doesn't show it— at least, not in front of me. Buzz doesn't blink, his eyes don't water, and his face remains blanch white. He just lets out a guttural sigh that maybe indicates satisfaction as he flips the two empty shot glasses and sets them back upside-down on the bar top, then closes his mysterious box and buries it back inside his pocket.

"I gotta scram. But before I go, I'm supposed to give you this."

He produces what might be a black metal credit card from the same pocket and sets it on the counter in front of me.

"I'm not sure what your current work situation is, and I don't wanna come across like a total dick or anything, but my boss thought maybe you looked like you could use a job."

A quick downward glance reveals it's not a credit card at all, but a business card. There's some thin, metallic gold script along the lower edge of the card that looks like an address and maybe a phone number. But it's too small of print, and it's way too dark in here to really make anything out for sure. What's easily legible though is the lone word in big, embossed, shiny, all-capital gold lettering in the center of the card with a thin, gold rectangle outlining it: *OLYMPUS*.

I slide it back in his direction.

"I appreciate that, but I actually have a job. Thank you, though."

He just stands there and smirks at me. What's with this guy?

Finally, he decides to check the time on his phone, whistles, looks back up at me, and pats me on the shoulder.

"Maybe you want a better one, then."

Before I can really process how much of an asshole

comment that is to make to someone you don't even know, he's moving away from me and down to the other end of the counter. Like his boss did earlier, he lifts the metal divider and steps right behind the bar like he owns the place.

"Catch ya later, Ron."

He slaps the bartender on the shoulder, strides past him through the false wall door, and then disappears out of sight.

I can't really see Ron's reaction, but he looks a little stiff and annoyed. Perhaps he's not as familiar or as cordial with the young guy as he was the older guy. Or perhaps he's annoyed that he's holding a fresh cocktail that he just finished making, and now the person who ordered it is gone. Or maybe he's just like everyone else on Earth and he doesn't like getting his back aggressively smacked without warning.

Now that both men from the booth are gone, I take a minute to pick up the business card and really study it. My assumptions are correct. Beneath the word Olympus is a brief address and a phone number, both of which indicate an office in the Beverly Hills area. Nowhere on the card does it say what this company is or what it does; because that would just be too easy, of course. The back of it is blank. There's no name or title anywhere on it that would belong to an individual person.

For a second, I consider tossing it into the large trash can I see in front of me on the other side of this corner of the bar. It's halfway out of my hand when I sigh and decide to at least do a quick Google search on my smartphone for Olympus.

There's a Japanese optics corporation that sells cameras, a Wikipedia page about Greek mythology, and not a whole lot else. I click through a few pages of results to see if there's anything buried in the search engine that could relate. Maybe something local to the area or at least headquartered here in California. But as best as I can tell, nothing exists.

I type in the address and pull it up on Google Maps, then click on the street view option. The image that pulls up is one of a black, nondescript office building with several stories, located right in the part of the Hills that starts to blend in with Century City amongst a thousand other businesses and offices. There are other companies with the same address but different suites, and yet none of them are labelled Olympus.

Feeling bold but also drunk, I dial the phone number on the card. It doesn't even ring—it just goes straight into a pre-recorded message saying the number I've dialed has a full voicemail box and that I won't be able to leave a message.

This has to be a scam. It has scam written all over it. Either that, or it's something nefarious like a porno company or some kind of illegal drug operation. That would explain why the two of those guys would be here in a bar on a Monday and why I can't find any more information about their company anywhere online.

I'm feeling a bit sad all of a sudden, like it's finally settled in that the wind is no longer in my sails. I don't know if it's the booze that's fully kicking in or if it's the full severity of my situation. It could even be the frustration I feel over the fact that I couldn't find anything in my search for Olympus, or that I wasted my time searching for something that bogus in the first place. Whatever the reason, though, I decide that it's time to go home.

"Hey, Ron? Can I settle up over here?"

Ron the bartender appears miffed that I now know his first name. He doesn't make any immediate move to head in my direction, but he does give me the courtesy of at least turning his head to show he's heard me this time.

"It's all settled for you, thanks to the gentlemen that just left."

I'm flattered and surprised... but I'm also uneasy. What if they're waiting outside to pounce on me, scoop me up, throw me in the back of a van, and gang-rape me or force me into some kind of manual labor factory? The degree of interest they've exhibited in me is wholly unexpected, inappropriate, and overwhelming.

"Everything? They took care of everything?"

Ron sighs and gives me a pained expression. Here is a man who has clearly mastered the fine arts of hospitality and customer service.

"Yep. Everything. They took care of the one drink you ordered. You're all set if you want to go."

Normally, I'd be put off by his passive-aggressive and then downright aggressive-aggressive tone, but my head is starting to swim. Plus, I no longer have a good reason to be here unless I'm going to keep drinking, which I'm not. I get up off the barstool... a little more unsteadily than I'd like to admit.

Ashamed as I am that I'm such a lightweight today after one shot and less than half of a Mai Tai, I'm even more ashamed when I slip the card from the bar top into my pocket instead of letting it fall from my hand into the trash can.

CHAPTER THREE

The streets of Beverly Hills are strangely empty today. Maybe it's the rain; which is unusual for this city no matter what time of year it is, but especially now. Perhaps everyone just decided not to deal with it today, and they all either stayed home or took cabs or rideshares to work, because there are barely any cars out here on the city streets.

I'm currently parked outside the very building that, exactly one month ago today, I swore to Allie I would never enter.

Funny how life goes sometimes, isn't it?

She'd been understandably confused, surprised, concerned, and a whole swath of other emotions when she came home from work on Monday and discovered that the worst of our fears from Sunday night had been realized. Any ideas I may have had about lying to her went out the window real quick. Soon, I was spilling my guts in a blubbering hysterical mess that must have been truly embarrassing to behold.

My emotions had come as a bit of a shock even to me. I had found myself absurdly on the verge of tears for the first time that I could remember since our wedding. I'd held it together the best I could for most of the morning, but seeing her face and then trying to explain how everything would be all right for us even without my high-paying job was enough to finally break me down into a million little pieces.

True to form, she handled the adversity much better than I did. While she made no efforts to conceal her obvious alarm and disappointment in the situation—and perhaps in me—she was also the first to start thinking about what comes next. She immediately called her father and put him on speakerphone; something he may have been expecting, but nevertheless didn't appreciate.

Bill Kagan was vague and evasive in his responses to her questions, spouting off some random misdirection here and rattling off some jumbled legalese there. He was also significantly more pointed and abrasive any time I dared speak up to ask a question, making it abundantly clear that he thought I had no one to blame but myself, even if he didn't say it out loud in those exact same words.

At the end of an excruciating hour that mainly consisted of Allie berating Bill and Bill deftly re-routing that abuse onto me, my wife abruptly hung up on her father and announced that she needed to take a walk. Before I could offer her my company, she was already out the door and had it slammed shut behind her.

Mostly, I just sat in silence with my head in my hands on the sofa while she was gone. If she'd noticed the rum on my breath, she hadn't said anything. I guess it didn't matter that much in the grand scheme of things with everything else that was going on.

After what felt like centuries, she finally returned with a plan, just as I knew she would. We'd sit down together and brainstorm my next move on paper, listing all of my interests, our mutual connections and friends, and pretty much any leads whatsoever that could potentially amount to something that might stave off the utter collapse of our financial future.

And over the course of the past month, I'd exhausted all of our options and come up empty-handed each and every time. Most places weren't hiring at all, and if they were, the positions they had open quite simply wouldn't pay enough to support us or our lifestyle.

Asking Bill for money was also out of the question, given everything that had happened and his role in it. Though he'd refused to go into details about the vote, the more I thought about it, the more I was convinced he'd voted against me. There was no way I'd be going back to that wellspring ever again.

It was also out of the question to ask Allie to consider leaving her job for a more lucrative one. Not only did she love her work at the senior center, but she also was responsible for the trust fund that had primarily supported us during the first year or so of our marriage. And that was on top of all the money her father had put into my company, and not to mention all the lavish wedding and honeymoon expenses the Kagan family had also covered for us in full.

So, yeah… this one was solely on me to figure out.

Everything might have eventually been fine if she hadn't found the Olympus card over that first weekend of unemployment. I'd forgotten it was still in my pants pocket, and it was all too easy for her to come across the thick piece of metal while doing laundry. Naturally, she asked me about it, and I told her about my bizarre encounter at the tiki bar.

As it turned out, Allie wasn't mad about me going to a bar that day at all. Instead, she spun the whole incident as fate, and she insisted that it was meant to be that I ended up there when I did and came across those two strange men.

I attempted to explain the lack of information I had on the company and the strong possibility that the whole thing was either a scam or something we wouldn't want to be a part of. But the more time that passed without me finding work elsewhere—and the more our bank accounts slowly but surely bled out each day without replenishment—the more I began to lose what little leverage I'd had with that argument to begin with. Once I'd finally struck out on all our other leads, Allie wisely pointed out that I had nothing left to lose by at least going in for an interview and seeing what it was all about.

So here I am today, parked outside the address on the card and staring up at the imposing façade of the large, black office building that supposedly houses this supposed company called Olympus.

I tried to call ahead of time on Friday to set up an appointment, but again, my phone went straight to the pre-recorded message saying the voicemail box was full. There was no email address or website with a contact form. My only option was just to show up at the physical location and hope to talk to somebody in person.

With one last adjustment of my necktie—which I absolutely *despise* wearing, by the way—I take a deep breath and step out of my car into the misting rain. I don't have an umbrella with me, so I quickly throw the door shut and traipse up the slick steps leading to the covered front entryway. There's no callbox or anything, and the doors are unlocked, so I step right through two sets of tinted glass swinging doors and wipe my feet on a mat once I'm safely inside and out of the rain.

I'm surprised to find myself standing in the middle of a relatively ordinary-looking commercial lobby. I guess I was expecting it to be either totally gorgeous or totally run-down, but I definitely didn't think it'd be totally plain. There's no seating anywhere, just a few odd indoor houseplants placed here and there, all surrounding a kiosk in the middle of the room.

At the kiosk are two security guards dressed smartly in matching black-and-white shirts, ties, and blazers. They look up in unison as I approach their set-up, and I can't help but think of Rich and how he's probably the furthest thing from a true security guard. He was always friendly and welcoming, but he'd never be able to stop someone from getting past him if he ever really needed to. These guys, on the other hand, look like they could have been former NFL players.

The guard on the left smiles and speaks first.

"Good morning, sir. How can we help you today?"

Suddenly, this whole gambit feels a bit foolish and ill-conceived. I have no appointment to speak of, plus I don't even know the name of the guy who gave me this card. Why the hell would anyone let me through?

"Hi, yeah, good morning. Um… I'm here to speak to someone about a job. At Olympus?"

"Do you have an appointment?"

That would be nice, wouldn't it?

"I do not. Actually, I tried to call a few times now, but every time, I just kept getting a message saying the voicemail inbox is full."

The guard folds his hands together in front of him.

"Unfortunately, there's not a whole lot I can do for

you, sir, without an appointment."

He's not unfriendly at all in the way he says it, but that still doesn't stop me from feeling the sharp pang of rejection. Briefly, I contemplate turning around and going home, but the idea of telling Allie I gave up so easily stops me in my tracks.

"I don't know if this helps at all, but I was actually *invited* to come here. About a month ago or so, by someone who works here, I believe. This isn't like a cold-call or anything."

The guard on the right is the one who speaks up now.

"Do you know who it was that invited you, sir?"

I dig around in my suit pants, find the black business card, and offer it to the guy, who takes it from me and examines it.

"I don't know his name. And I know that sounds weird, but he never gave it to me. We met at a bar, and he gave me that card and asked if I wanted a job. Red-headed guy with a buzz cut; maybe in his thirties? He was with another guy who was older and who had a beard and a ponytail, I think? I don't know if any of this information helps at all…"

The guards exchange a quick glance as they pass the card between them. The one on the left studies it briefly before handing it back to me and picking up a phone.

"Do you mind waiting just a minute while I call up?"

Relief floods over my body like a tidal wave.

"Not at all."

I step to the side to give them a bit of space and privacy, and I judge myself for feeling such profound elation at the simple prospect of being allowed to pass through. This is what happens when you live in L.A. for too long. You get stupidly excited and irrationally proud just at the idea of getting past bouncers and red velvet ropes into someplace exclusive.

After a brief, hushed conversation, the guard who made the phone call hangs up, stands, and places a computer tablet and a stylus on the kiosk counter.

"All right, you're good to go, sir. Just need you to sign in here with your name and then you can head on up."

I scribble my full name and the current time on the top row of an otherwise blank page on the screen. Looks like it hasn't been a very busy day here so far, in terms of guests.

When I'm done, the same guard retrieves the tablet and replaces it on his side of the kiosk, then comes around and escorts me toward a solitary elevator at the other end of the lobby that up until now, I hadn't even noticed.

"Right this way, sir, if you don't mind."

He presses the button, the doors open a few seconds later, and he gestures for me to step inside.

"What floor am I going to?"

That question turns out to be unnecessary, since it looks like he's going up with me. I wiggle toward one of the walls to allow his hulking frame enough space alongside the other, and he selects the top-most button, marked with a 9.

As the elevator starts to glide smoothly upward, I decide to attempt a bit of small talk.

"So, how many offices are there in this building?"

The guard turns his head to face me.

"Right now, just one, sir. It was before my time, but I believe there used to be multiple offices here—a couple talent agencies, an orthodontist, a shared workspace. But Dr. Charon bought them all out last year, and the building was empty by January."

Questions bubble up inside my head. Who's Dr. Charon? What's so special about this particular office building that he had to buy everyone else out to set up here? What does Olympus even do in the first place?

The question that I say out loud isn't any of those, though.

"So, is he planning on renting out all the other floors, or what?"

The guard smiles and turns back to face the doors as we hear a soft *ding,* and they open.

"You'll have to ask him yourself, sir. That's above my pay grade."

This lobby is absolutely nothing like the one down below.

High up above, the ceiling is maybe twice as far away from the floor as it was on the ground level, and everywhere along it, there are contoured ridges illuminated from within by unseen light sources. The effect is like gazing through the caverns of a sunlit desert canyon shaped millennia ago by rivers that have long since dried up. Shades of sand, beige, orange, cream, and terracotta blend together to make a color palette taken straight from high-definition space pictures of the planet Jupiter.

At random spots along the sloping ceiling ridges, soft, white tubes of light poke out at varying lengths and angles. It's as if some Olympic athlete was asked to stand on the ceiling and unload an entire arsenal of electric javelins in every possible direction.

The ceiling is connected to the floor... *by water.*

Every visible vertical wall surface around me is *moving*. The walls themselves might be some kind of tan slate or marble; it's honestly impossible to tell exactly what they are, since every square inch of their surface has water cascading down it.

Somehow, none of this makes any noise whatsoever. There's no splashing or trickling, and if there are motors above or below in the walls, floors, or ceiling that maintain this whole mesmerizing effect, I can't see or hear them.

Even the floor is spectacular. Polished onyx tiles are speckled with little metallic flecks of gold and silver. The baseline black of the floor hints at mirroring the colorful patterns and shapes of the ceiling, while the tiny flakes catch the light off the glowing lances and reflect it back upward. Altogether, this floor could easily be mistaken for a glossy night sky littered with twinkling pinprick stars.

At the other end of the lobby is a closed pair of large, white doors that stretch from the floor all the way up to the ceiling. I'm not sure if I've ever seen doors this *large* before. The doors are tall and skinny, though they seem to get wider as they go up, like something out of Alice in Wonderland. They're also outlined in the same soft, white glow of the spike lights that are everywhere on the ceiling.

In between me and those doors is a whole lot of empty space, broken up in just four places by what I assume are couches, even though they don't look like any kind of couches I've ever seen before. There are two on both sides, spread evenly apart from each other so that all four corners of this lobby boast a piece of furniture. It looks like they're maybe ten feet long and built extremely close to the ground with a low back. Each is a different shape and a different color: midnight blue, eggplant purple, wine-red burgundy, and jet black.

"Sir, you can have a seat wherever you'd like. Someone should be out shortly to come and get you."

I've completely forgotten about the guard, who's still waiting patiently beside me with one arm wrapped backward around the retracted elevator door.

"Oh, okay. Thank you."

As soon as I step out of the elevator and into the lobby, he pulls his arm back, the doors shut, and I'm left alone up here. If it was eerily quiet before, it's freakishly silent now that the guard and his steady, heavy breathing are gone.

I still can't even hear the water from where I am, so I walk over to one of the walls to get a closer look and listen. Somehow, it's impossibly silent even when I'm standing right next to it. After a furtive look down across the great room at those glowing, strange white doors, I'm bold enough to reach out my index finger and touch the liquid wall in front of me. The water is cool but not cold, and my finger splits the cascade and makes a gentle curtain.

I tilt my head back to scan all the way up the waterfall and search for the source. The only thing I see now that I didn't see before is way high up above where the water magically appears out of thin air near the ceiling. It's not a motor, a faucet, or a hole—it's a small, glass disc that's practically invisible. But from within it, I can just make out a camouflaged black apparatus and a tiny bead of blood-red light. It has to be a camera.

I walk the length of the wall I'm standing by, dragging my finger through the water along the smooth surface on the other side, keeping my chin upturned the whole time as I count the hidden camera discs up above. When I'm finished, I cross the wide, cavernous space—eyeing the double white doors curiously as I pass—and then I do the same thing on the other side of the room until I've essentially walked the massive perimeter of the lobby.

All in all, I count twelve cameras that I can see. It seems a bit excessive, even for a space this large, when you consider just how empty and sparse of a room it is. Besides, there are only two ways in or out: the elevator and the double white doors at opposite ends of the lobby.

It occurs to me that perhaps I'm being watched. I'm fairly certain I didn't see any monitors or computer screens down at the guard kiosk on the first floor. While I guess it's possible there's another room somewhere in the building with more guards whose sole purpose is to watch the surveillance footage, it seems unlikely; especially now that I know most of this building is empty.

Maybe the system's not set up yet. That's what I tell myself, anyway, as I move toward the closest couch/chaise lounge/moon pod thing. It's an easier explanation to accept than the alternative: that these camera feeds are being watched by someone who might be about to interview me. Creepy.

Time passes.

There are far worse places to sit alone with your thoughts than in here, but I'm still getting a little anxious. I have no idea who I'm interviewing with or what I'm interviewing for. I'm not too sure I even know where I am anymore; I'd sooner believe I'd just stepped inside a planetarium or some kind of modern art exhibit than a waiting room in a Beverly Hills office building.

At least this sofa thing is extraordinarily comfortable.

Finally, the big, white doors split down the seam and swing out into the room like sails from wooden booms moving in the wind on a ship. Two massive, coal-black dogs come racing out from beyond the gap and thunder across the tile in my direction.

My reactions spiral rapidly from surprise to shock to terror. I try to stand up quickly, but I've been sitting so long that my feet have fallen asleep. Worse, the couch I've been sitting on has also sort of molded itself around me, and getting up and off it now feels like trying to crawl out of a waterbed. The dogs are maybe six feet away from me, tops, and I'm only halfway standing when I hear a woman's voice bellow out from across the chamber.

"*HEEL!*"

Eight paws come skidding to a stop so suddenly it takes my breath away. Every muscle in their bodies is still straining against the smooth iridescent sheen of their fur, but the two Great Danes instantly obey the command and become rigidly locked in place. Only their mouths still move as they pant for air, tongues lolling out comically in goofy-looking grins; all four eyes are still trained, unblinking, on me.

"They'll let you pet them if you'd like."

My attention shifts away from the dogs to the woman speaking to me now.

It's Laura Dern.

Or... at least, it looks *exactly* like Laura Dern.

No, it has to be her. She has all the same features as

the Hollywood star. This woman is very tall and thin, and she has wavy blonde hair that falls just above her chest, high cheekbones, and kind blue eyes. There's an austerity to her visage that counterbalances the warmth in her voice and the friendliness of her expression— something I'm familiar with from seeing so many of her performances in film and television over the years.

It sounds like she might have a British accent though, which doesn't quite make sense. I'm almost positive Laura Dern is American. So, unless she's doing a character right now, that's a discrepancy I can't quite wrap my mind around.

She's wearing a white silk blouse tucked neatly into black chinos. Around her waist is a thick black velvet belt with an overlarge silver buckle, and she's sporting a sheer scarf or ascot type of thing around her neck that looks like it could be modeled after a Monet print.

I notice as she takes several long strides to close the distance between us that she's also barefoot, which is odd. Her feet are pale like the rest of the skin she shows, but her toenails are painted a bright fire-engine red.

She walks right in between the dogs—who could be statues now if it weren't for their steady panting—and extends her hand as she finally reaches me.

"Isla Charon. Pleasure to make your acquaintance."

Her handshake is surprisingly strong, and the British accent doesn't falter. Unless she's method acting or psychotic, I guess this isn't Laura Dern after all.

Isla looks like she's waiting for me to say something. I remember what it is.

"Hi… hi, Dr. Charon. I'm Ethan Birch. I really appreciate you meeting with me today."

She laughs, waves her hand in the air, and takes a

seat on the sofa pod.

"Just Isla is fine. I'm Mrs. Dr. Charon, too, for the record. Not the doctor myself."

She pats the space on the cushion next to her.

"Perhaps not the Charon you were expecting? Please do sit."

I take a seat at the other end of the couch.

Isla immediately pouts and pats the space right next to her again, this time a bit more forcefully.

"Oh, come now, darling, that's much too far away. I promise you, I won't bite… and neither will they."

She crosses her legs, looks up at the dogs, gives a loud snap of her fingers, and then points at the floor in front of her foot. Right on cue, the two dogs trot over and lie down side by side, flat on their bellies facing her, each one with their muzzle angled toward her foot and about six inches away from it.

I scooch across the couch a couple feet closer, but not as close as she seemingly wants me to be. Even if she's perfectly comfortable with zero personal space, I'm definitely not. Besides, those Great Danes are humongous… and now they're even closer to me.

Maybe Isla sees the look on my face because she laughs again and gives a sweeping gesture with her fingers in the air.

"Suit yourself."

There's something girlish and whimsical about her demeanor that seems to belie her true age. Up close, I can see she's quite a bit older than I initially thought. Wrinkles and lines around her forehead, under her eyes, at the corners of her lips, and stretching across her long neck are now much more visible. If she's wearing any makeup at all, I can't tell.

"So, Ethan Birch. What brings you to Olympus today? "

It's a simple question, and one I wish I had a simple answer for, but I don't. I'm not exactly sure how much I intend to tell her yet about VitaLyfe, but I *am* sure I don't want to discuss why I'm no longer there unless I'm directly asked about it. First, though, it seems much more prudent to ask her about what the hell Olympus is and does before we get into any of that.

"Well, this is a bit embarrassing, but I'm just going to be completely honest with you."

Isla's eyes sparkle as she shifts her weight and draws her legs up onto the couch, tucking her feet behind her.

"*Ooh*, yes, please. Absolute and naked honesty. Always."

I pull the black metal business card from my pocket and offer it to her as I speak, but she makes no immediate move to take it, instead keeping her focus on my face.

"About a month ago, I stopped by a little tiki bar on Sunset called Shangri-La to have a drink. Two men were in there, and they bought me a shot while I was in the bathroom and then covered my bar bill in full. Neither one told me his name, but one of them gave me this card and told me I should keep it if I needed a job."

Isla still hasn't shown any interest in taking the card from me, so I slide it back into my pocket self-consciously.

"Anyway, this all happened a month ago, like I said. I tried to call the number on the card several times to see if I could make an appointment, but I couldn't get through to anyone. Finally, I just decided to come in person myself. I hope that's all right?"

An impish grin spreads across Isla's face as she raises an eyebrow.

"Nolan told us the gentleman from the bar said he already had a job."

It takes me a couple seconds to understand. Nolan must be the name of the buzz cut guy with the sneer who gave me the card. And that would make me the gentleman from the bar.

"Well... yes. I did say that."

Do I lie to Isla now or admit that I lied to Nolan then? Either way, it exposes me as a liar. And in the midst of a potential job interview, no less.

"Honestly, it was a unique situation. Two complete strangers in a bar buy you drinks. Neither one says who they are or what they do, but one of them offers you a job at a place you've never heard of. You can understand why I'd keep my cards a little close to the chest."

Isla does the graceful air-sweeping gesture with her hand again.

"One hundred percent, darling, of course. But you still haven't answered the question now, have you? Do you have a job... or do you not?"

She leans forward to reach across the space between us and places her fingers lightly on my shoulder.

"I don't mean to pry or press you. I'm just trying to ascertain the exact nature of your visit, you understand."

That makes two of us. I think about it for a second and then make a spontaneous decision.

"I... do have a job... but I'm always open to exploring other ventures, of course. If an opportunity presents itself that's advantageous, for me and for my wife, then I think I owe it to myself—and to her—to at least explore and entertain it... of course."

Isla smiles.

"Of course."

Slowly, she lets her fingers fall away from my shoulder, folds her hands together in her lap, and leans back into the sofa.

"Tell me, Mr. Birch. Are you familiar with a dating program called Signals?"

My heart skips a beat, because I'm extremely familiar with Signals. Besides being one of the most popular dating apps since Tinder and Bumble, Allie and I first met on Signals.

This woman doesn't need to know that, though.

"I am, yes."

Her eyes light up again.

"*Oh, grand!* I was hoping you'd say that. Well, that's us."

She flicks both of her hands through the air this time and gives a quick glance in each direction at our surrounding environment before leveling a warm smile on me once again.

"That's what's responsible for everything you see here today."

Isla tilts her head to the side and nods to the dogs.

"Well, everything except for them, that is. Castor and Pollux predate even Signals, don't you, lads?"

Neither makes a sound, but they're both still very much awake, eyes glued to their master.

Isla drifts her gaze back up to me, and her smile morphs into something mischievous again.

"Now, then, you must be wondering what Olympus is, right?"

Truthfully, I'm not. I've kind of forgotten all about Olympus, the black card, and what I'm doing here in the first place. That's how much I'm still reeling and trying to process the idea that the person I'm sitting next to right now is somehow responsible for not only one of the most successful apps of all time, but also for my marriage.

I need to clear my throat and blink a bit before I talk again.

"I take it that's your name? Or, the name of your company, I mean? The developer?"

"Not quite."

Her blue eyes glint as her grin widens. Isla seems to be milking this moment and reveling in the suspense she's created.

"Olympus, darling… *is what comes next.*"

She lets the mood linger, drinking in the delicious mystery she's conjured up for me, before finally punctuating her pause with a pixie wink.

"Behind those double white doors is the future, Ethan Birch. A small but profound team of visionaries, each with his or her own unique backstory, belief system, and motivations. Hand-picked—*hand-selected*, actually—for what they can bring to this project that no one else on the planet can. Together, we're building something that's never been seen before. Something so unique, so powerful, so *perfect…* it will change the world forever."

She certainly has a way with words, I'll give her that. The very air around us feels like it's suddenly crackling with magic. I almost don't want to say anything for fear of breaking her spell.

"So… it's an app?"

For one infinitesimally small fraction of a second, her mouth tightens, her eyes flash, and she looks like she might actually slap me hard across the face. But as quick as it arrives, it departs. And then her expression is lost as she throws her head back and explodes into a peal of laughter that rockets up to the high ceiling and echoes off the chamber walls around us. When she's finished, she wipes glistening tears from the wrinkles around her eyes and smiles at me, and she looks herself again.

"Yes, darling, I suppose you're right."

Isla glances down at the two dogs still lying flat and calm on the floor, then readjusts her weight on the couch until she's sitting cross-legged facing me.

"But enough about us. Tell me about you, Ethan Birch. What are your dreams, your desires, your expectations of life?"

The way she says it makes me feel like we're a couple of high school kids gossiping at a sleepover in someone's basement.

I give her the full rundown of my professional life, starting with my college degree and academic credentials, before going chronologically through the jobs I'm proud of while casually omitting the ones I'm not.

Obviously, I spend the majority of my time discussing VitaLyfe and bombarding her with numbers to show just how successful we became and how important my role in creating that success was.

Obviously, I say nothing about the fact that I'm no longer employed with VitaLyfe because I got fired four weeks ago.

It turns out that Isla is as familiar with our product as I am with hers—"the watermelon mint one is just exquisite, darling"—and she gently pokes and prods me for more information about our story from beginning to end. Playfully but firmly, she chides me any time I gloss over the details, and we end up discussing more intimate aspects and facets of the operation than I originally intend to.

More than once, I find myself saying something I probably shouldn't. But then I remind myself that technically I no longer work there anyway, I think of Chad, and then I boldly continue on with the conversation right where I left off without even an ounce of remorse about violating my NDA.

When she finally seems content with everything she's learned, Isla stops peppering me with questions, leans back into the couch, and shakes her head wondrously at me.

"What an *adventure* you've had, Ethan. What a *story*."

She pauses to study me, and the effect is a bit uncomfortable. I'm reminded of the twelve little cameras hung all around us, each a silent electronic sentinel, watching, listening, and recording. Let's just hope this feed never gets hacked, because I'm positive I said some things I shouldn't have.

Isla leans forward again and reaches out to touch my shoulder.

"Listen, darling. I don't want to pressure you into leaving something so precious. Especially since you built it yourself from the ground up. If anyone knows what that's like, it's me and my husband."

Her grip tightens ever so slightly.

"But I do want you to know what you could be a part of here. Someone with your background, expertise, artistry, and leadership skills could do very, *very* well for himself here. I don't believe anything happens by accident or by chance. Frankly, I believe it was fate that

Nolan and my husband crossed paths with you at the Shangri-La."

She lets that sink in before releasing my shoulder and bringing her hands back together in her lap. There's something serene and yogi-like about her expression and posture now.

"I know it's a lot to take in and that it's even more to trust from someone you've only just met. But hopefully, you know enough about what we've done to get here that you'll believe me when I say this: all of that was only the beginning. I say this now with complete love, respect, and pride: Signals was an *earthquake*, yes. But Olympus? Olympus is the *Earth*."

Isla waits a moment, then smiles, sighs, claps her hands, and gets to her feet—much more nimbly than I did earlier, too, I might add.

"Richard loves to give me a hard time for being so esoteric. He says I delight in speaking in riddles. I always love to ask him then where he thinks I learned it from."

She winks at me, reaches into her pants pocket, and produces a card that looks identical to the one Nolan gave me in the bar.

I stand up, too. As she passes it over to me, I notice this card has her full name on it—Isla Charon—in slightly smaller lettering than the word OLYMPUS. There's also a title in italics beneath her name: *'Director of Recruiting'*. The phone number and office address look to be the same—there's no cell phone or anything listed— but there is an extra line for an email address this time around that simply reads: 'isla@olympus.com.'

"In the interest of both plain speaking and plain dealing, then, why don't you email me how much you'd need to earn to make this transition work for you and

Allie? I can't guarantee we'll be able to match or beat your base annual salary as VitaLyfe COO right off the bat, but I'm confident we can get creative with stock options, bonuses, and other performance-based incentives to close the gap if necessary."

She puts out her hand, and as I go to shake it, she takes her other hand and clasps mine between both of hers firmly.

"Something else my husband likes to say is that 'a man has to make at least one bet a day, or else he could be walking around lucky and never know it.' As I mentioned earlier, I'm more of a believer in fate than luck. But either way, darling, you're sitting on a winning lottery ticket. All you have to do now is cash in."

Isla gives me one last wink and a hand squeeze, then releases me, turns on her heel, and pads across the center of the room toward the way she came in. About halfway there, she emits a high-pitched whistle without turning around or breaking stride. The two dogs spring up from the floor, spin around, and go galloping off after her across the tile. Each one takes a side as they draw level with Isla, flanking her as she opens the great big Alice in Wonderland double doors.

I try to peer past them from where I'm standing and steal a glimpse of what's on the other side. It seems much brighter in there, almost as if the architect of this building decided to put all the windows and natural light in that room rather than in this one. But before I really have a chance to make anything definitive out or to move any closer to get a better look, the giant white doors swing shut, taking with them Isla Charon and her twin canine companions.

I just stand there for a second or two, breathing in

63

everything I've seen, heard, and been offered.

Five weeks ago today, I was the COO of a fast-growing beverage company that my best friend and I created together.

Four weeks ago today, my best friend fired me from that same company.

And today, some British barefoot Laura Dern lookalike offered me a position without a title or a job description at the same company that's ultimately responsible for introducing me to my wife six years ago.

I have to get home to talk to her about all this. There's no way she'll ever believe me.

CHAPTER FOUR

This Barbie doll is proving extraordinarily difficult to giftwrap while sitting in the passenger seat of a moving vehicle. It's hard enough trying to get the wrapping paper folded, tucked, cut, and taped in all the right places while using my knees and thigh muscles to hold the doll box still in my lap. It's even harder trying to do all this while having a fight with my wife at the same time.

Allie's driving, like she normally does when we go anywhere together in the Jag. Sometimes I'll drive, and she'll ride shotgun, but I'd say most of the time it's the other way around. She loves her Volvo and swears she doesn't need a fancy car to make her happy, but then again, she *really* loves to drive my car whenever she gets a chance.

We're currently en route to Allie's sister's house in Oxnard for our niece's tenth birthday party. Since Allie's behind the wheel, it's my unlucky job to wrap the doll we just bought at Target fifteen minutes ago because we only decided this morning that we'd actually be going to this party in the first place.

"So, explain to me again what your hang-up is? Because I'm having a really hard time understanding what the problem here is."

It's at least the third or fourth time now she's asked me some variation of that same basic question. As mad as I am that she keeps asking it, I'm also mad at myself for being unable to give her a satisfactory answer.

I pull a flap of some glittery pink wrapping paper against the Barbie box and see that I'm short once again. You can still easily make out the buxom figurine in her plastic prison cell through the negative space I've failed to completely cover up. With a heavy sigh, I un-tape my work and start all over.

"The problem is that I have no idea what this job is. You're asking me to say yes to something that I have absolutely no clue about what I'm even supposed to be doing."

I can see the little vein throbbing at the corner of Allie's temple. It's a sight I'm quite familiar with after three-and-a-half years of marriage and after six years of knowing each other. She has them on both sides of her face—like we all do—but it's only this one on her right-hand side that bulges out like this when she really gets worked up about something.

Other than the pulsing vein, though, her face is actually pretty well controlled and neutral. She's certainly not smiling, but she's not exactly clenching her teeth either. Allie's knuckles aren't white on the steering wheel. Her face isn't flushed red with anger. I know she's self-conscious about sweating under her arms and having pit stains there sometimes, but as far as I can tell, she's dry right now.

The temple vein speaks volumes, though. As much as she might be trying to control her emotions and keep them in check for the sake of this conversation and this car ride, I can tell she's quickly losing patience with me.

"Let me ask you this, though. When you started with VitaLyfe, did you really know what you were doing back then? You went into that pretty blind, and you still figured it out, didn't you?"

I turn the air conditioner up another notch. She might not have pit stains yet, but I can feel the sweat starting to build and drip down my sides.

"Yeah, but it took us months of trial and error to get to that point. You were there, Al—you remember what it was like those first couple years. All the long hours and the unpredictability of it all. Is that really something you'd want to go through all over again?"

She gives a quick jerk of her head to shake the bangs from her eyes. It's a newer hairstyle she's experimenting with, and I know she's not entirely sold on it yet. Ever since Jillian left to become VitaLyfe's bookkeeper, Allie's been searching for a new style… and a new stylist.

"How unpredictable do you think this Olympus thing is actually going to be, though? I don't know anything about apps or tech, but it sure sounds like a sure thing to me. I mean… Signals? Dr. Richard Charon? That all sounds like the very *definition* of a sure thing to me."

She's not wrong. While I hadn't been able to find much of anything online about Olympus, there was of course all kinds of information to be mined on Signals.

The app first launched almost ten years ago now, but it took less than a year after its release to become a phenomenon in the dating scene. Within its first two years of existence, Signals overtook all its competitors in users and profitability. Within five years, several updated versions of the app allowed users more catered experiences finding romantic partners, sexual partners, friends, professional connections, and even special interest groups. Within seven years, Signals was a name-brand sponsor and featured logo on the uniforms of an NBA team.

The app's creator himself, Dr. Richard Charon, was a significantly more difficult subject to read up on and research. His Wikipedia page was surprisingly sparse on personal information, though there was no shortage of op-ed pieces out there on the web speculating about his nebulous background as well as his meteoric rise to fame and fortune.

He definitely wasn't a recluse, though. Far from it. A quick image search revealed hundreds of photos: some of him speaking on stage at tech conferences; some of him posing with his wife, Isla, at fancy red-carpet events and Hollywood soirees; and some of him strolling down the street in dark sunglasses and a thick woolen coat, walking a pair of Great Danes and looking for all the world like a celebrity trying to grab a cup of coffee or a quick bite to eat while evading the paparazzi.

Interviews with Charon were less prevalent, but they, too, existed. Everything I could find seemed to be with the same digital magazine, TrendBeat, and the same journalist—Elle Maguire. I read a few of the articles I came across but didn't really find anything of major interest. Mostly, they were just puff pieces hailing him as the next great genius savior messiah in tech. Certainly there was nothing he said in any of the articles that swayed my opinion on him one way or the other.

I wouldn't be surprised if Allie had read all of them, though. Pretty much from the moment I got home and started filling her in on everything, she seemed to make up her mind that this was it: the answer to all our problems.

I'd convinced her on Monday not to get her hopes up before I'd even emailed Isla and received a response about my salary.

But that argument flew out the window fast after I messaged Isla Monday night and received a detailed contract proposal in my inbox Tuesday morning— particularly after it became clear that if I hit all my incentives and the app met even the most modest of projections, I could feasibly make *more* money working as Olympus's director of development than I ever did as VitaLyfe's COO.

True to form, Isla hadn't given me a deadline date to accept or decline the contract via email. Instead, she'd included a simple directive at the bottom of her message to me:

P.S. No need to write me back. If it's right for you, we hope to see you Monday morning at nine. If it's not, we hope you and your company continue flourishing all the same. ☺

I was—and still am—pretty taken aback by such a cavalier approach. For a company with so much on the line, and for a position this well compensated, it makes no sense to be so devil-may-care or Zen or whatever you want to call it.

Unsurprisingly, Allie doesn't agree. She said she found the postscript "bold" and "refreshingly progressive." Allie even liked the little smiley face at the end.

So now, here we are, four days later and less than forty-eight hours out from when I need to either show up or not show up for my first day of work at Olympus.

And to make matters worse, we're on our way to see Allie's entire family for the first time since I got canned—and that includes her father.

"Charon isn't the problem, and neither is Signals, Allie. Look, don't you think it's a bit weird how all this happened? They met me at a *bar*. They offered me a job when they didn't know anything about me. I go in for one interview and they offer me director of development, just like that. I didn't have to send in a resume, and they sure as shit didn't check my references, because if they did, they'd know that I'm not working for VitaLyfe anymore. All of that, plus they're somehow totally fine with potentially paying me *more* than what I was already making? None of it makes any sense."

The vein has subdued just a bit in her temple, but I can see a sweat splotch beginning to form ever so slightly beneath her armpit as she drives. I angle one of the air conditioning vents more in her direction and she gives me a look as she registers what I'm doing.

"Maybe they were really impressed with you."

She glances at me again, and her face seems a bit kinder, if no less desperate and determined. I can feel how much she wants this for us from across our car seats.

"You're very charming, Ethan, and you underestimate how intelligent and passionate you come across when you talk. I'm sure they could pick up on all that."

I can't tell if she's being earnest or if this is some kind of new stratagem she's testing out. Allie's not one to flatter or fawn. She's always been a strong, independent woman, from the moment I met her on our first date. Even before I picked up on it in person, it was obvious in the little bio she wrote for herself and in her choices of famous quotations, books, movies, and TV shows on her Signals profile.

Unable to decipher what she's doing right now, I turn my attention back to wrapping the Barbie doll and realize that I've almost run out of paper. Down at my feet are at least half a dozen crumpled-up sparkly pink balls, each one a physical manifestation of my inability to complete even, such a simple task. There's also a sizeable smattering of glitter on the floor mat now, and when I look at my pants, shirt, and hands, I realize with dismay that it's pretty much everywhere on my body, too.

"Look, Al, I could be the most charming man alive—which I'm not—and they still wouldn't offer me this kind of job and salary on that alone."

We're only about fifteen minutes away now. I recognize we have just a few exits left before we have to get off the freeway and head into beach town suburbia. Time is running out for us to do the one thing that I really wanted us to do during this car ride, which is to game plan our interaction with Allie's father. That seems a whole lot more pressing and pertinent to me right now than a conversation we've been having on repeat ad nauseam since Tuesday.

"So, what are you saying? That this is a scam? Because the way you described it to me on Monday, they have a whole entire building bought out in Beverly Hills with a penthouse office that looks like something out of Tomorrowland. And when we looked at pictures online of the Charons, you told me that the woman is definitely who you met with on Monday, and that you think the man is the same guy you saw at the bar last month."

She flicks her bangs away from her forehead again and turns to look at me.

"So, what—they're lying to you? This very famous, very rich, very in-the-limelight-and-center-of-public-attention techie power couple are just... stringing you along? For what purpose? And why? Why would they do that? Any of that?"

Very early on in our relationship, I learned two things about Allie and me.

The first thing I learned was that she was almost always right. And not like almost always right in the 'women are always right' kind of way that boyfriends and husbands are conditioned to say about their female partners. Like, *actually*, Allie was almost always right... and about everything. It would be irritating if it wasn't so bizarre, so uncanny, and—ultimately—so often beneficial for us both as a couple.

The second thing I learned was to choose my battles on those rare occasions where I couldn't be convinced that she was right. Honestly, I'd stopped even putting up a fight about most issues by the time we got engaged, because it's not often that I can't be convinced by Allie in an argument. Especially since she's easily the smartest person I've ever met, and I know she only has both of our best interests in mind at all times.

But right now, I'm really having a hard time not choosing this particular battle as one I want to fight. And it's not that I like fighting. I actually hate it. What's the point when you're wrong so often anyway? For once though, I just can't shake the nagging thought that my argument might be on a level playing field with hers. She brings up plenty of good points, but I can't wrap my mind around this situation. It feels too good to be true.

So, maybe that's exactly what I need to tell her.

"Listen, Al. You're right. It's not a scam; it's a real company. And you're right—they're very successful at what they do. It *is* a sure thing, whatever this Olympus thing even is, just because of who's behind it. I get why it seems like I'd have to be a complete moron to turn this down, because the whole thing feels like it's a one-in-a-million opportunity. And maybe it is."

We merge into the far-right lane and prepare to take our exit. I can see the green sign coming up ahead, and I know I've got about ten minutes left at this point.

"I want it to be. For me, for you, for us. Of course I want it to be that. But what if it's not? This whole thing—the way it came about, the Tomorrowland office, the ridiculous salary—it all seems too good to be true. Multi-billion-dollar companies don't just hire guys off the street they find sitting alone in some bar off Sunset. If VitaLyfe taught me nothing else, it's that you have to fail a million times over and scratch and claw your way to success in this world. Nothing ever just gets handed to you for free."

We pull up to a stoplight after taking the exit. Once the car slows to a stop, Allie takes both hands off the wheel, removes her glasses, and polishes them on her shirt. I can see from here that they've fogged up a bit, which is crazy, since the air is on full blast and it's really not that hot in here at all. Outside, it's an uncharacteristically balmy eighty-five degrees, but with the windows up and the A/C cranked, I'm surprised to see her like this.

She carefully slides her glasses back into place, and as she does so, I notice the small dark spot beneath her arm has become much more pronounced. Internally, I make a note to say something to her before we show up at the party, just in case it's something she might not be aware of. Who knows if it's something she'd even care about right now, but I do know that normally she'd want me to say something if I noticed, and I have.

"That's not true."

Allie brings both hands back to the wheel as the light turns green and we slide back into motion, turning right on a street that will take us most of the remaining way there.

"What's not true?"

She tries to flick her bangs off her forehead, but a few strands of hair have become stuck there with sweat. I can see that she feels it and it irritates her before she uses her left hand to smooth the hair off her face and push it to the side.

"You said that nothing ever just gets handed to you for free. But that's not true. What would you call my situation? Me and my sister were born into wealth."

I can't tell if there's a tinge of pride, shame, both, or neither in her voice as she says it.

"Is that fair? I don't know… probably not. But I didn't choose it. It chose me. I can't control who my father is, who my mother is, who my family is. All I can control is who I am and what I choose to do with my life, and how I choose to play the hand that's been dealt to me—which, some would say, was a pretty great hand. Financially speaking, at least. You and I both know that my dad can be a royal pain in the ass and a real bastard when he wants to be. But he's also given us a lot."

Yeah, I really loved it when he gave me that pink slip last month.

She takes her right hand off the wheel and places it on my thigh before giving me a meaningful look and then returning her eyes to the road, leaving her hand there.

"Ethan, you've been dealt a great hand here. I understand what you're saying, that it sounds too good to be true. But really, that's all relative. My life, your life, our life together, our house, VitaLyfe, this opportunity with Olympus… it's all too good to be true in the eyes of so many people less fortunate than us. Why should we let that stop us?"

It's moments like this one that re-confirm why I believe Allie is always right and why I need to pick my battles even when I think she's wrong. I know she was never on the debate team in high school, but she should have been. She's so wickedly intelligent and effortlessly persuasive when she wants to be.

Still, despite everything, I just can't help myself.

"What if we wait just a little bit longer? My severance package should be kicking in any day now, and we still have some VitaLyfe stocks. If nothing else materializes—say, we give it one more month—and there's truly nothing else, then I'll go back, hat-in-hand, to Isla Charon or Richard Charon or Elon Musk or whoever I need to go to about a job."

I rest a hand on her hand atop my thigh.

"We don't *need* this one, Al. If the company really wants me that badly today, there's no reason they won't want me just as bad four weeks from now. And even if it's a different position with less money, you said it yourself: this is as sure of a sure thing as they come. We'd be set hopping aboard at any time in the future."

Suddenly, she jerks her hand out from under mine,

puts it back on the steering wheel, glances up in the rearview mirror for a split-second, and then pulls the wheel hard to the right. Tires squeal as the vehicle takes a sharp turn and we veer off onto a random residential side street. We're still several blocks away from her sister's house, and I know there's no reason for us to have turned onto this road.

Allie glides the car to a stop behind a parked car on the right side of the quiet street. As soon as we're there, she throws the gearshift into park, takes her foot off the gas pedal, pulls off her glasses, moves both of her hands up to cover her face, and takes a humongous breath in… and then out… and then in… and then out again.

We sit here like this for at least thirty seconds or so before I work up the courage to break the silence.

"Are you all right?"

From behind her hands there comes a grunt.

"No."

It almost sounds like a sob, or at least a stifled sob. Allie's the furthest thing from a crier, though, so this throws me quite a bit. Blood rushes to my cheeks. I'm frankly embarrassed by the unfolding situation and by my lack of knowledge to properly navigate it.

"What can I do?"

When I ask the question, I obviously mean it in reference to her pulling off onto this random road, guiding the car to a stop, breathing heavily, and experiencing whatever it is that she's experiencing right now. But I also know my wife well enough that I'm not surprised in the slightest by the muffled answer that comes out from behind her hands in between slow, drawn-out breaths.

"You can take the job."

Now it's my turn to sigh and bring a hand up to my face. I rub my forehead with my thumb and stare down at the half-wrapped Barbie doll in my lap. Bet they never had a fight like this, Barbie and Ken.

It's not even a legitimate fight, though. I know that Allie's right—that I'd be a fool not to take the director of development job and just see where it goes, if nothing else. After all, what do I have to lose? I'm already unemployed.

"So, you don't think we can wait? Or you don't trust me to get a job somewhere else? Or what?"

There's a long, slow breath in. This time, there's no immediate breath out that follows. Rather, Allie falls back into the car seat with her lungs still fully expanded, melting softly into the leather like a hot air balloon that's just bumped up against a skyscraper. She shudders and makes a guttural sound I'm not sure I've ever heard her make before from behind her hands.

"Ethan… I'm pregnant."

It's not as if I'm keeping track, but this time, at least a full minute goes by in complete silence, other than Allie's steady deep breaths in and out, before I manage to find something that vaguely resembles my voice again.

"What?"

The hands still completely obscure her face, the breath still comes in and out of her body like a bellows, the air conditioner still whirs on high inside the car, and the random little street around us still remains noticeably quiet and empty. My eyes are staring at nothing in particular outside the windshield. Her eyes are probably staring into the black nothingness of her own flesh pressed up against them in her palms.

"I said I'm pregnant, goddammit."

My complete shock is compounded a billion times over when I hear Allie stifle a short but altogether solid laugh in her hands.

"*Fuck…*"

I realize that I've never loved and hated a person as much as I do her right in this very moment. I also realize that whatever I say in this very moment needs to be very well thought out and very well articulated, as there's a great chance she'll remember my reaction exactly as it was long after I've forgotten it.

"Wow. That's… that's great."

So far, not so good. I can hear myself talk, and I don't sound very convincing.

"Do you know how it happened?"

Again, I'm taken aback when what sounds like a short laugh comes out from behind her hands.

"I'm sure it happened the same way it usually does, Ethan."

My internal scale tilts a bit more toward hate than love.

"Okay, yeah, but do you know… like… when it happened?"

She lowers her hands from her eyes and turns to face me head-on. If she's cried at all, I can't tell. Maybe her palms soaked up whatever renegade tears threatened to brim over.

"All I know is that I went and got a test after I was late and that the test came back positive. That was on Sunday. I took another test yesterday, and that one was positive too. So… now you know as much as I do."

I can't help feeling a bit hurt that Allie's been sitting on this for almost a week now, whether she believed the first test or not.

Allie's still staring at me.

"Is that it?"

"What?"

"Is that all you have to say?"

Get it together, Ethan. In the movie of your marriage, this is a pivotal, climactic scene. Don't blow it.

"Allie…"

I tentatively reach across the center divider that separates our car seats and take her hands in mind. She lets me, and her chestnut-brown eyes grow wide, beautiful, and suppliant.

"I couldn't be happier. Seriously. It's… it's absolutely incredible."

And it is. The timing of it all is absolutely incredible. For going on a year now, we've been trying to get pregnant. It's something we've both wanted from the very start; we honestly probably talked about our mutual desire to be parents on our second or third date.

Especially for Allie, becoming a mother has been a lifelong dream. We'd agreed to wait until our financial situation looked particularly solid with VitaLyfe, so it made perfect sense for us to start trying when we did. If she'd broken this news to me six months ago or even six weeks ago, I'm sure my reaction would have been one-hundred percent pure and utter bliss.

As things currently stand, though—and in light of recent unfortunate developments—I don't feel particularly guilty about the mixed emotions I'm currently experiencing. And I'm sure I'm not alone in feeling them either, given everything I've just seen from Allie over the last portion of this car ride.

She squeezes my hands gently.

"Ethan, now that you know, hopefully you can understand better where all this is coming from. I'm not trying to rush you into something you're not comfortable with. But, truthfully, we're kind of past that point now, whether we want to be or not."

She's right again. Allie's always right. I give her hands a little squeeze back and turn to look out the windshield.

Finally, there's a bit of movement on this quiet street. An attractive couple, perhaps only a few years younger than us, are walking down the sidewalk and pushing a baby stroller between them. How perfectly cinematic.

Allie puts her hand on my thigh again.

"I'll call my doctor and schedule an appointment for us to go in so we can find out just how far along I am. In the meantime, though, I really think you should go in on Monday with an open mind. This could be the start of something really special for us. All of it. The job… the baby… And if somewhere down the line, it turns out that Olympus isn't the right fit, at least we'll have saved up more money by then, and you'll have incredible experience on your resume for wherever or whoever you want to apply to then. Sound good?"

The happy couple walks past our car, oblivious to everything but each other and this new miniature being they've generated out of their love. I watch them walk past my window before turning to face Allie once again.

"Sounds good."

She looks like she needs more convincing. That makes two of us.

"Sounds like a plan. I'll go in on Monday… and we'll take it from there."

Allie smiles at me and holds my gaze another few seconds before putting her glasses back on and then shifting the car into drive. Slowly, she lurches us forward, loops the car around, and pulls us back out onto the main street. We drive in silence for a while, with the only sound the steady whirring of the air conditioner.

I wonder now just how much of my wife's perspiration was related to the heat, how much was related to our argument, and how much was undoubtedly related to the insane things that are happening on a physiological level right now in her body.

I wonder just how far along she is in this pregnancy.

I wonder if I'm ready to be a father.

It's funny how rapidly and randomly your worries and priorities can shift. In the span of a single car ride, my greatest concern in life has alternated between facing my father-in-law, to wrapping a Barbie doll, to arguing with my wife about a new job opportunity, to staring down the unforgiving barrel of the shotgun called parenthood.

"Are we telling your family?"

Allie gives me an incredulous look.

"Are you kidding me? I still don't know if I'm even going to speak to my dad after what they did to you. Definitely not."

I can't help but smile. This is why I married this woman.

The short remainder of the drive goes by quickly. Despite everything that's changed, the mood between us feels noticeably and significantly lighter now than it did before. Once again, we're on the same team, and our minds and hearts are aligned. Allie even takes pity on me

81

and wraps the Barbie doll herself with what little paper I've left her once we've parked a bit down the street from her sister's house.

I have the present under one arm, and my other arm is wrapped around her waist as we walk together up the sidewalk. Our nerves may be frayed, and the future may be uncertain and daunting. But it's also beginning to look a bit exciting to me, too. No matter what, at least we have each other. And there's a real comfort in that.

As we step up onto the stoop outside the front door of the massive Southern California home, I squeeze Allie even tighter by my side. Silently, I make a promise not to let anything that happens inside over the next couple hours ruin the honeymoon feeling of this newfound depth and strength we've stumbled upon in our relationship.

Bring on the noisy kids I can already hear running around inside. Bring on the inevitable nosy questions about what happened at VitaLyfe. Bring on Bill Kagan, even—*if* Allie decides we're going to acknowledge her father exists, that is.

Bring it all on, I think, as I press the glowing doorbell button. There's nothing we can't beat, now that we're a unified front once again.

CHAPTER FIVE

It's the same two guards in the lobby from last week. But this time, they seem to be expecting me. The one who had previously escorted me up the elevator stands and shakes my hand as I walk up to their kiosk in the center of the room.

"Mr. Birch. It's good to see you again."

I'm reminded immediately of Rich, my old security guard at VitaLyfe, and I briefly consider asking to be called Ethan from this point on. But I don't even know what this guy's name is yet, let alone what I'm actually doing here for a job. There will be time for all that personal stuff later on down the road.

"Before you head up, I just need you to fill out some new-hire paperwork for me, if you don't mind."

I'm a bit surprised. While filling out new-hire paperwork should be absolutely routine and expected on the first day of a brand-new job, I wouldn't have pegged Olympus as being the type of place where anything ever happens that's absolutely routine and expected.

The guard places a small tablet and stylus up on the counter between us. Of course, this is what they mean by 'paperwork'. Nice. I pick up the tablet and stylus before looking around the lobby for a place to sit down.

The guard must realize what I'm thinking because he's quick to chirp up.

"Oh, it's just one page and one signature. You should be able to knock it out real fast. All the usual suspects—W2, I9, employee handbook forms, etcetera—that'll all come via email later on today."

I nod.

"Do you need to make a copy of my passport?"

He shakes his head and smiles.

"You can send a digital copy later with everything else, if you have one. We don't have a copier here or anything like that."

I'm far from an expert on employment laws, but something still tells me this process isn't exactly by the book. That feeling gets magnified by a thousand when I realize the one-page document I'm looking at on the screen is some kind of photo release form.

It's pretty straightforward as far as what I'd expect a photo release form to look like. Living as long as I have in this city, I've seen plenty of them at restaurants, bars, and outside random buildings around town.

It's just peculiar that I'm signing one now to start work at a tech company. While it doesn't say anything about what the filming is for or how my likeness will be used, it does explain that by agreeing to work at Olympus, I consent to any and all video and audio recordings being made of me for as long as I'm employed here. It also states that those recordings are the property of the company and can be used in whatever manner they see fit.

"What is this?"

The guard looks up at me from the seat he's taken behind the desk.

"It's a release form."

He says it like it's the most ordinary thing in the world to give to someone on their first day of work anywhere.

"I know, but... I mean... why? What's it for?"

The guard shrugs and smiles, a bit sheepishly.

"Once again, Mr. Birch, I'm going to suggest you ask *them* that. That's another question that's above my pay grade, unfortunately."

His companion to my right, silent until now, speaks up.

"We all signed one our first day here, if that helps any."

It doesn't really. I read over the form again just to make sure there's nothing I've missed. I'm still not exactly sure why a photo release form is necessary, but I'm also not exactly in a position to refuse signing it. Even asking to speak to Isla or someone first seems like a bad idea since it wouldn't make for a great impression.

Whatever. I'll sign it and see if there's time later today to ask her about it. I'm sure there's a perfectly reasonable explanation that I'm just not seeing right now. After I scribble my signature on the tablet surface with the stylus, I hand it back to the guard.

"Thank you, Mr. Birch. Do you need me to show you the way up again?"

I glance at the elevator behind them.

"I think I can manage, unless it's changed since last Monday."

"Very good."

The guards go back to whatever it is they do while guarding.

I walk around their station and press the 'up' button

next to the metal doors, which open instantly. Once inside, I press the button with the 9, watch the doors shut, and ride up in silence to the top floor.

For some reason, I'm vaguely disappointed when the doors open and the chamber on the other side looks exactly the way I remember it from a week ago. It's still every bit as awe-inspiring, eye-catching, and futuristic as it was the first time around, but I guess I maybe expected it to be a completely different room altogether, as if by magic.

Just like last week, though, it appears I'm alone. The glowing white Alice in Wonderland double doors at the other end of the room are shut. I kind of expected Isla to be waiting here for me, barefoot and accompanied by her massive dogs once again, but the room is empty save for those weird colorful couch pods in the four corners.

What's next? Maybe the guard assumed I knew my way in through those white doors, too? They seemed to be unlocked when Isla came and went through them a week ago. Maybe I'm just supposed to go straight on in?

I cross the great room quietly, as if the sound of my footsteps on the polished black star-tiles might be enough to shake the electric white stalactites free from the ceiling if I'm not careful.

The double doors are even more bizarre up close than I remember them. Standing at the base looking up, I can see how they dramatically grow wider and wider as they climb skyward toward the ceiling. The effect is a little nauseating, like I'm drunk in a carnival funhouse.

Cautiously, I put a hand up flat against the door on the right and give it a slight push. Nothing happens. So, I try the other door. Same result; nothing happens. I try turning the handles on both doors, but neither gives an inch. It seems like everything's locked.

Feeling foolish, I move away from the doors and walk back into the center of the room. I can't tell if I'm more annoyed that no one's here to greet me or that I might have to ride the elevator all the way back down and ask the guards for help. Surely, they called up to Isla or whoever it is that's supposed to be receiving me to let them know I was here, right?

My watch says it's 9:05 am. A light sweat is starting to break out on my chest and under my arms beneath the button-up shirt and necktie I begrudgingly forced myself to wear this morning. I did my part in showing up ten minutes early. It's certainly not my fault that the doors are locked and nobody gave me any more information about what to do up here.

As my eyes rove around the moving waterfall walls and rippled ceiling, I spot some of those tiny black camera globes way up high, almost out of sight. Moving closer to one, I can just make out a faint red dot glowing from within the orb.

No one asked me to sign a release last week. They definitely must have videotaped my interview with Isla. The realization turns my stomach as I move my gaze away from the camera and head back toward the center of the room.

Then again, there are cameras just about everywhere nowadays. No one asks you to sign a release form every time you step inside a bank, a supermarket, a shopping mall. And yet, there are cameras in all those places recording your every move, too.

I'm about to take a seat on the wine-colored couch when the sound of doors opening makes me stop and turn around.

It's Nolan, the younger man with the red buzz cut and the freckles from the bar. Today, he's sporting a milk-colored Henley shirt, a fitted pair of khaki capris, and bright white canvas boat shoes with no socks. When combined with his pallid skin tone and the silvery wisps he calls eyebrows and eyelashes, he looks like the ghost of an Ivy League trust fund kid who drowned on a sailing trip.

"Mr. Mai Tai! Our paths cross again."

As he draws closer, I can't help but think again that this guy has no concept of what his actual clothing size should be. Especially now that he's wearing a brighter-colored shirt—and standing beneath a veritable galaxy of lights—I can practically see the freckles on his torso through the skin-tight shirt. I can definitely see his nipples, and it's an uncomfortable realization to have.

Also, this 'Mr. Mai Tai' moniker had better only be a one-time thing.

He greets me with an extremely firm handshake.

We get it, dude. You work out.

"You're Nolan, right?"

A thin, wide smile breaks out across his face.

"I see my reputation precedes me. Heard only good things, I hope?"

"Honestly, I haven't really heard much of anything. Isla mentioned your name during our interview last week, and I kind of put it together that you must have been the guy from the tiki bar."

The smile melts instantly from his face.

"You 'haven't really heard much of anything?' Well, fuck me, I guess. Nice to meet you, too."

Is he being serious right now? I want to believe he's joking. He has to be. Yet the look on his face is definitely hostile and shows no outward signs of cracking. What should I say? I don't know how to undo whatever unintended slight he seems to have suffered.

After a miserably uncomfortable moment of awkward tension, he suddenly lets out a high-pitched, wheezing laugh that rocks his body from head to toe. Mid-laugh, he reaches out a hand and grips my shoulder to steady himself, as if he's about to completely topple over.

"I'm just fucking with you, bud. Relax."

I force a wholly unnatural chuckle out for his benefit alone. Hopefully, this douche and I will end up working in two very separate, very distant departments. I'm not sure I can handle Nolan's energy on a day-to-day basis in the workplace; or anywhere else, for that matter.

I'm just about to step out from under his grip when he finally removes his hand from my shoulder, reaches into his pocket, and fishes out that pretty wooden container he had at the bar. This time, though, it's a stick of chewing gum he produces from inside, rather than those mysterious wafer-pill things.

"Want some?"

He offers me a piece, but I hold up my hand and politely decline. For all I know, he probably laces it with something.

"Suit yourself, bud."

Nolan unwraps a stick and tosses it into his mouth, then closes the box and puts it back in his pocket.

"So. You're Ethan Birch. *'Director of development'*, huh?"

This just isn't getting any easier. I have no idea who this guy is or what his professional relationship is to me, but the way he drew out the words of my title in between wet smacks and pops of his bubblegum chewing gives me an ominous feeling. At this point, I'm not sure which prospect is more repulsive: that Nolan and I might be working closely together as partners, or that I might have to answer to him directly as my supervisor.

"That's me. Do you have a first and last name and a job title, too?"

Nolan studies me for sarcasm. It's there, for sure, and I'm not convinced I did a good enough job hiding it. Then again, I'm also not convinced I really care.

"Why, yes. Yes, I do, Mr. Mai Tai."

Damn it.

"Nolan Best. Director of marketing. At your service."

Fuck. Every company is different, but there's probably no way I'm going to be able to avoid this guy if he's director of marketing and I'm director of development. Those departments go pretty much hand in hand; especially as we get closer to launch date, I'll bet. But at least he's not like a VP or something. That would have been worse.

"Well, now that we're besties, should we go in and meet everybody? Or at least all the important people?"

This guy is unreal.

"Sure, I'll follow your lead. I don't really know anything other than I was told to be here at nine."

Nolan jerks his head back toward the double white doors and starts walking in that direction.

"Sounds like you're crushing it so far."

Before I can marshal a proper reaction, he throws open both doors dramatically and we step into an absolutely breathtaking office space… if such a location can even be called an office space.

Most of the room is windows. Where the lounge area we've just come from is entirely surrounded by dark walls of falling water, this room is pure glass and light. Platinum-blue Los Angeles skies stretch out in every direction, and beneath them, a full nine stories down, I can gaze out over the urban sprawl of civilization in much the same way that God must look down upon us.

The ceiling is *alive*. Quite literally. Every inch of real estate up there is smothered in growing plant life. There are countless shades of colored moss mixed in with ferns, flowers, grass, and leaves of all shapes and sizes. The overwhelmingly predominant color is green, but every version and variation of the color green imaginable. Here and there is a burst of orange, pink, or yellow—usually in the form of some gorgeous tropical flowering masterpiece that looks like it better belongs in Barbados or in a master gardener's acid trip than in the ceiling of a Beverly Hills skyscraper.

And the ceiling isn't the only living surface in this space either. So is the floor. All around us on the ground, as far as the eye can see, is *grass*.

There are small pockets of space scattered about where the grass stops and is replaced by traditional concrete flooring, and in each of these pockets is a desk, a chair, and—sometimes—a person. Some of the desks are wooden, some are metal, and some are glass. They all seem different from one another and are all set at different heights or widths or depths. The chairs, too, seem to run the gamut as far as variety is concerned.

Evidently, all of this can be personalized to suit the individual's preference; a theory that is reinforced by the varying levels of décor and personalization I'm seeing at each specific station. Some desks are adorned with picture frames, books, bonsai trees, flower vases, glowing Himalayan salt lamps, color-changing LED light strips, stuffed animals, children's toys, action figures, protein powder tubs, mini-fridges, one laptop, one desktop, one laptop and one desktop, two desktops, two laptops… you name it. And then some are absolutely barren save for the desk itself and the chair beneath it.

The great unifier amongst these individual islands is the lush sea of perfectly manicured grass that surrounds and connects them all. Considering people's allergies— not to mention considering basic maintenance concerns—I have to believe it's all synthetic. There's no way they actually planted sod in the floor of the ninth story of an office building. How would that even be possible? And yet it all looks stunningly real.

"You can take your shoes and socks off here if you want."

Nolan's already doing it. He slips his white canvas shoes off and tosses them down amongst numerous other pairs of discarded footwear. It's like the warehouse of a shoe factory over here along this window wall next to the double white doors we just came through.

He must see the look on my face because Nolan immediately sneers.

"You don't *have to*, of course, if you're worried about your feet stinking or you haven't trimmed your toenails in a while."

Ignoring him, I do a quick scan around the interior expanse. It appears everyone else is indeed barefoot. Some have their shoes nearby at the base of their desk, but the vast majority of them presumably did as Nolan's doing now and left their shoes at the door.

"You'd take your shoes off before coming inside someone's home, wouldn't you? It's kind of like that."

Nolan smirks and puts his hand on my shoulder again.

"Besides, we want everyone to feel totally comfortable here. You know what I mean, bud?"

He accentuates the question by moving his hand to the knot of my tie and giving it a gentle shake before letting go. If it wasn't already abundantly clear that I'm overdressed, it sure is now.

Nolan's not the only one dressed casually. Most of the men and women I see are wearing street clothes. Some look a bit more put together than others, but I imagine that has less to do with position or rank and more to do with individual preference and fashion sense. I don't get the feeling that there's any kind of dress code here... other than maybe being barefoot.

Reluctantly, I bend over to untie and remove my dress shoes. I briefly contemplate taking my socks off too, but as much as I hate to admit it, I actually am worried about the state of my feet. It's a muggy September day in Southern California, and they've been wrapped in thick, black socks and tight Italian leather for hours. I can't vouch for how they'd smell right about now.

When I'm done setting my shoes aside, I straighten back up and look at Nolan. He stares down at my socks with disdain for a couple seconds before he finally shrugs, shakes his head, and starts striding forward again.

"Suit yourself, bud."

Why do you even care so much, 'bud?'

The grass feels plush, cool, comfortable, and

luxurious beneath my stockinged feet as we walk. It's almost enough to make me want to turn around and leave my socks back with my shoes after all. I can't remember the last time I was actually barefoot on grass, artificial or otherwise. It's the kind of sensation you associate with childhood, summertime, and play.

As we walk further into the room, I try to take in as many of the sights as I can around me. It's much easier said than done, though, because there's just *so much* to see.

Over here is a gigantic coffee and espresso bar stocked with the kind of high-tech machines that probably cost more than some automobiles. It's the exact sort of set-up I begged Chad for years to let us have at VitaLyfe, but he was always too cheap and too practical to go for anything other than an office Keurig.

Over there through an open doorway is what can only be described as a miniature movie theater of sorts, complete with a giant projection screen, several rows of recliner seats, a vintage popcorn machine, and drawn red velvet curtains hanging in the corners of what look like soundproofed walls.

To my left is the biggest kitchen I've ever seen in my life. It's stockpiled with fresh fruit and vegetable baskets, a row of gleaming silver refrigerators, another row of stainless-steel sinks, a compost bin, and a polished marble countertop lined with sparkling electric blenders. Apparently, this isn't even the main employee kitchen or cafeteria, because there's a sign by the entrance to the space that labels it as a juice and smoothie bar.

To my right is a velvety lounge area littered with all manner of liquor and wine bottles, more refrigerators, more sinks, a trash can, and another polished marble countertop. Only this counter is lined with glassware, shakers, strainers, and stirring spoons. It must be an actual *bar* bar.

Some of the people we pass are sitting at their desks quite normally, like I imagine ninety percent of the American office workforce does for forty hours a week. Others are at standing desks, their rolling chairs either pushed to the side or buried underneath the desk in front of them.

And still others are working in much stranger fashion altogether. I count at least three treadmill desks spread out around the room, one of which currently has a young woman powerwalking atop it, feverishly and violently stabbing away at a laptop on a pedestal stand in front of her. I note that she's not barefoot, but instead seems to be getting great use out of her running shoes at work.

Numerous individuals are splayed out on the ground around the office space. Some lie on their stomachs working; some lie on their backs working; some lie on their sides working. There are even some who are seated up against the floor-to-ceiling windows along the outer perimeter of the magnificent room, perhaps enjoying the feel of the warm sunlight streaming through on their backs.

I'm pretty sure at least two people I come across aren't working at all. They're just lying on their backs in the grass with their eyes closed and their hands behind their heads, apparently napping. I can't help myself from checking in with Nolan to see if he notices, but if he does, he doesn't seem to care. We walk right past the slumbering pair and leave them undisturbed.

Every kind of modern convenience you can possibly imagine in life seems to have representation here in this office. We pass by massage chairs—both the traditional ones in which you'd receive a person-to-person massage, as well as the automatic electric ones you'd find in a specialty store or in an airline shopping catalog. A few more steps, and now we pass by a glowing, multi-colored, bubbling oxygen bar, like something straight out of a Las Vegas casino.

Based off what I either see through open doorways, transparent glass walls, or on the label placards outside of closed doors, this floor also has a gym, a locker room, a yoga studio, a basketball court, a racquetball court, four conference rooms, two dozen 'study nooks', a nursing room for mothers, a smoking lounge, an arcade, a pet relief area, a communal dining room cafeteria complete with mammoth banquet tables and a kitchen twice the size of the one in the juice bar from before, and—

"Laser tag?"

I stop dead in my tracks as I read aloud the black and white sign next to a closed door on my right. It's impossible to discern from here just what kind of room waits on the other side of this door in terms of size and scope, but I can't imagine how a full-fledged laser tag arena could feasibly exist there.

Then again, *everything* I've seen so far completely defies conventional wisdom, logic, and explanation. There's no rhyme or reason when it comes to how all this stuff fits here or how any of it works or exists simultaneously. It melts my mind just trying to figure it all out. What kind of mad scientist dreams all this up… and how does anyone amass the kind of fortune necessary to bring it to life?

Signals. That's right. Signals is how all this gets paid for.

Nolan eyes the room we've stopped outside with a sadistic grin.

"You betcha, bud. Excellent way to burn calories, relieve stress, and work out any 'office tension' you might have with some of your colleagues. Don't you think?"

Clear as day, I get a mental image of Nolan sprinting up and down neon ramps in a haze of blacklights and artificial fog, sweating and screaming and styling himself a bona fide space commando. Only in my vision, he's playing at some rundown spot in the Valley that also has air hockey and a claw machine, he's shooting up a bunch of pre-teens who've gathered for a birthday pizza party, and he's utterly embarrassing himself in front of their mortified parent chaperones.

The fantasy brings a smile to my face that Nolan notices right away and reciprocates.

"Hell yeah, brother. Looks like I got me another tag aficionado."

Whatever helps you sleep at night, 'brother'.

"Definitely."

It's the best I can give him as we move on.

After a while, I notice that we've circled back into the original area we started in with the glowing white double doors and the piles upon piles of discarded shoes. I'm a bit confused. If he meant to give me a tour, he didn't describe a single thing or a single place we saw. The only time he even said a word out loud was when I mentioned the laser tag room. Otherwise, everything that I took in was simply that: stuff that I took in myself as we were walking.

We also didn't speak to or even acknowledge a single person along the way. I made eye contact with individuals here and there and gave them a cursory nod or smile, and most of them gave me a nod or a smile back. But Nolan didn't stop to introduce me to anyone. In fact, he didn't even talk to anyone at all but me, not even casually as we passed by.

He turns to face me as we move back into the same spot where we first left our shoes behind. His expression looks expectant, excited even. It's clear that he wants me to say something, but even if I knew what it was, I'm not sure I'd give him the satisfaction.

"Well, Ethan Birch, *Director of Development*. Did you notice anything?"

What kind of question is that?

"I mean, I noticed a lot of things. Are you asking about something in particular?"

Nolan looks annoyed and impatient.

"Did you notice who I introduced you to?"

Is this a trick question?

"You didn't introduce me to anyone."

He lifts his index finger, points at me, and taps the side of his nose twice.

"I told you we were gonna go in and meet all the *important* people, didn't I?"

My heart does a little somersault as I peek at the two or three individuals around us who are well within earshot. They don't seem to notice, or if they do, they don't outwardly react. But it still turns my stomach and makes my cheeks flush hot with embarrassment. How could he possibly think something like that—let alone say it out loud inside the same workplace occupied by his peers?

Thankfully, Nolan doesn't give me any more time to either articulate my true thoughts or to cover them up with a bullshit response. He takes me by the shoulder and starts guiding me toward one of the conference rooms we'd passed by earlier on his 'tour'.

"Well, that's exactly what we're going to do now. You're like the Jews in the Old Testament. And I'm like Moses. I'm gonna part the Red Sea of all the nerds and engineers and freaks who get off on Fortnite and Anonymous tweets, and I'm gonna bring you to the Promised Land. You ready, bud?"

I try my best not to make eye contact this time with any of the people we pass by, because I don't want to be considered guilty by association before I've even met any of them yet.

Nolan throws open the door to the conference room with a bang and leads me inside.

It's actually not all that different in here than the room we had at VitaLyfe—although we only had that one conference room, and they have at least four of them here at Olympus. The major difference is that anyone could look into the conference room at VitaLyfe through the custom glass walls, whereas this one has regular opaque walls shutting it off from the rest of the open floorplan office.

Around a large, ovular table in the middle of the room are twelve black rolling chairs, only three of which are occupied.

One of the occupants is a young man who looks like he's fresh out of college, or maybe even high school. He's got a mop of shaggy black hair, dark, rectangular glasses, and pink acne splotches on his cheeks and forehead. This guy's also a little pudgy. His black 'Slayer' rock band t-shirt strains against his torso in a few places and in a way that's decidedly different from Nolan's clothing situation. He also wears a gigantic digital watch strapped tightly to his wrist.

Next to him is another man, but this one is quite a bit older. He doesn't look as old as the man I saw with Nolan at the tiki bar—the man I presume to be Dr. Richard Charon—but he definitely looks older than me or Nolan, I'd say. Maybe he's in his forties or early fifties somewhere. He has bright blue eyes, thinning blonde-brown hair, and a scraggly salt-and-pepper beard. And he's scratching at a small stain on the sleeve of his beige sweater.

Across from this pair on the other side of the table is a striking woman sitting alone in her row of rolling chairs. The first thing I notice is that she has sleeves; and by that, I mean she has tattoos all up and down both arms. Some are black and white, and some are full of color, but the only common denominator is that she's covered on both sides from wrist to shoulder. If she has more ink than what's already exposed along her arms, I can't tell, because she's wearing some kind of sleeveless black tunic that covers her torso. She certainly doesn't have any on her neck or face.

Her skin is a pale ivory, though not quite as white as Nolan. This woman's eyes are dark and black, her eyeliner is dark and black, her eyebrows are dark and black, and her hair is dark and black. Clearly, 'dark and black' is a kind of theme for her.

Nolan plops down into an empty seat beside this young woman and gestures grandly at all the empty chairs around the table.

"Here we are at last, Mr. Mai Tai. Welcome to the

inner sanctum of Olympus, the creative nexus that keeps the whole machine whirring morning, noon, and night. This, my young Padawan, is *the core*."

I take the closest seat to the door and sit down as casually as I can. First days are tough anywhere, but with Nolan as my shepherd and apparent point-person, I'm trying my best not to let this one be brutal.

The woman next to Nolan extends her hand out to me and I shake it.

"Hey, there. I'm Portia, director of content. Nice to meet you."

Director of content; that definitely sounds like a department I'll be working a lot with as director of development.

The young man across the table jumps up from his chair before I have a chance to respond to Portia. He leans out across the table and extends his hand, which I grab and shake. His palm is extremely sweaty.

"Hi! Bingham Grant, but you can call me Bing. I'm director of engineering. Welcome aboard!"

He pumps my hand up and down enthusiastically and smiles like he's just won a contest.

"I didn't know we were hiring still. You're not here to take my job, are you?"

Bing lets out a small, nervous laugh and looks around the room for confirmation, but it isn't there.

I smile at the kid, because I can remember all too well what it felt like to be fresh-faced, bright-eyed, and bushy-tailed. Confident as hell that I was going to make something magnificent out of my life, but also secretly terrified that I wouldn't ever amount to anything. Maybe that's where he's at right now too, or maybe not. Either way, I can at least put his concern to rest.

"Don't worry, Bing. I don't know the first thing about engineering, so you're safe and sound. My name's Ethan Birch, and I've been hired as director of development."

There's a sort of snort that comes from my right as the man with the thinning hair and scraggly beard looks up from his shirt stain to stare at Bing, then Portia, then back at myself.

"Nice. Way to break the ice there, Mr. Birch."

He lets out another short snort of a laugh.

"For real, though, what are you here for?"

I smile back at him, wondering exactly what he means. Maybe this is some kind of joke, or perhaps a weird hazing ritual? Whatever it is, it's already becoming awkward as all get-out.

The man in the beige sweater is still staring at me with a big stupid grin plastered on his face, but his eyes are growing wild.

My own smile flickers.

"I... I'm not altogether clear, if I'm being honest, on what *exactly* I'm here for as it pertains to Olympus. Last Monday, I interviewed with Isla Charon, and she emailed me back saying I'd be coming on as the director of development. Not exactly sure what that means in terms of where the app is at right now, but I can assure you, I have tons of relevant experience when it comes to getting a project off the ground—"

"*Shut the fuck up!*"

The explosion from across the table takes me by surprise—and I'm not alone. Bing jumps in his chair and flits his eyes into the faraway corner of the room.

Beige Sweater perches forward in his chair with his gaze leveled at me. He's about to snarl out something when he turns instead to stare at Nolan with a demented smile painted across his face that seems to be fast dissolving right before our eyes.

"Is this some kind of sick joke? Huh? What the fuck is this?"

I also turn to look at Nolan, who's leaning back in his chair with his hands folded behind his skull and his elbows fanned out wide. He shrugs and smirks at the man but otherwise doesn't say a word.

"Answer me, you pasty ginger fuckboy. What's going on?"

Nolan's jaw twitches as he scratches what would be an eyebrow on most normal-looking human beings.

"I don't know what you want me to say, Chuck. I guess... we have two directors of development now? I dunno. You know I don't call the shots."

He turns to say that last bit to Portia as he gives another comically large shrug.

Portia stares down at the table in rigid, defiant silence. Bing squirms and looks like he'd rather be anywhere else than here. Chuck alternates glowering at me and glowering at Nolan, his face turning deeper shades of crimson by the second.

Just when I think the tension in the room is about to burst and I ought to try and say something to stop it from happening, the door is thrown open. In come Isla and Dr. Richard Charon, arm-in-arm, laughing and speaking in a foreign language I've never heard before. The door shuts behind them as Isla spies me.

"*Ethan!* I'm so glad you've come."

She rushes over. Before I can rise from my chair to greet her, she's already bent over and doling out light kisses on either side of my face.

Chuck has no problem rising from his chair on the other side of the table.

"Richard! What the fuck is going on here? This guy says he's director of development?"

Charon looks taller and gaunter than I remember him from the bar, but otherwise, he's very much the same. He still has the full head of silver hair pulled back into a tight ponytail that dips like an oar between his shoulder blades, and he still has the thick, woolly eyebrows, the swooping moustache, and the oiled beard coming to a sharp, daggered point beneath his chin.

Just as he was that day at Shangri-La, he's also still dressed from head to ankle in black: black blazer, black button-up shirt, and black slacks. The back of a large, black cell phone peeks out from above the breast pocket of his jacket.

All the black ends at his ankles, though. Just like his wife—and just like almost everyone here—he's barefoot. And apparently, he's either too confident or too eccentric to be self-conscious about his bony, skeletal feet with their long, knobby toes and cracked purple toenails.

Charon stares down the impressive length of his bulbous nose. Countless broken blood vessels crisscross every which way over the protuberance in pink, red, and violet. His coal-black eyes narrow into sharp slits that seem prehistoric somehow. I find myself thankful I'm sitting on this end of the table and not on the other, where he smolders his ferocious gaze into Chuck. Charon takes a deep breath in and licks his thin, chapped lips before speaking, and when he does, his voice is slow, halting, ancient, and terrible.

"This... is the end of the line, Charles. Do not act

surprised... because no one here will believe it. Just collect yourself... and go... and that will be that."

Chuck is visibly quaking. I can see thoughts and emotions firing rapidly through his brain as his manic eyes search Charon for clues as to what he should do next. Betrayal, panic, hurt, and hysteria are written all over his face.

Charon doesn't move a muscle. He just looms large in his thin, towering frame, his hands calmly burrowed in the pockets of his slacks, his hollow furnace eyes unblinkingly boring holes into Chuck's desperation.

Isla glides soundlessly to Chuck's side and lays her long fingers on his trembling shoulder. It's not a move that any sane person would make, I think—not with all the obvious visual cues of rage, confusion, and rancor Chuck is exuding right now.

But for some strange reason, the gesture seems to work a kind of spell. Chuck begins to shake less and less violently until it finally subsides altogether, and then he's still. Tears well up in the wrinkled corners around his eyes, and his expression morphs from crazed, indignant fury into something soft, piteous, and mournful.

Isla coos in a voice just above a whisper.

"*Chuckie*. How do you want to be *remembered*?"

She gently spoon-feeds that last word on a warm current of air directly into his ear. And I watch spellbound as the last vestiges of Chuck's anger—and his pride—crumble before us. Tears break free from the dams of his wrinkled flesh. But again, Isla is there with her magic fingers, lightly brushing them away from his weathered cheeks in a tender way that seems almost motherly.

This grown man struggles to contain the heaving cry

that wants to break free from his body. Through jerky breaths, spittle, and a quivering jaw, he attempts to sputter something out.

"I—I—I don't want—to—to go…"

Isla's fingers slide like snakes down his craggy face and around his neck until she's worked her whole slender arm about Chuck's shoulders. She slowly pilots him away from the table and guides him toward the door, keeping her eyes, her voice, and her body on him the whole entire time.

"I know, Chuckie. I know. It's all going to be all right. It's all going to be all right."

She quietly sings this refrain to him as she uses her free hand to open the door. Expertly, Isla guides him out of the room and off to who-knows-where. Chuck's stifled whimpers are only finally cut off when the door swings shut behind them.

CHAPTER SIX

Silently, Charon drifts like a wraith to the head of the table, pulls back a chair with a gnarled hand, and floats down into it. Even sitting down, he's absurdly tall. I can't quite believe my own eyes.

Bing is studiously focused on cleaning his glasses on his shirt. Portia is no longer staring down at the table; instead, she's now staring at the door where Chuck and Isla just vanished, her expression enigmatic. Nolan lets out a low whistle to no one in particular.

Charon speaks.

"'And yet… to me… what is this quintessence of dust?'"

He says it to no one in particular before breathing in slowly and then moving his keen gaze like a searchlight across each of our faces in turn. I've never heard anyone speak quite the way he does—in such a bizarre, entrancing, calculated fashion; filled with pregnant, awful pauses that both command your attention and make you squirm in your own skin at the same time. It's hypnotically horrifying and somehow inhuman. But it works, because it demands your full concentration.

"Anyone who thinks that was easy for me… is

gravely mistaken. Charles Henry had been with this organization for eleven years. Without Charles, there is no Signals, there is no Olympus… and there is no Richard Charon. His… retirement… does not come easy."

My heart quickens as Charon's eyes come to rest on me.

"Fortunately, we already have a replacement waiting in the wings to help facilitate a smooth and seamless transition. Ethan Birch comes to us as the former chief operating officer of VitaLyfe, the third-fastest-growing, all natural, fruit-infused, bottled water company in the country. Graciously, he has agreed to take a lesser position here with us… in the hopes of hitching his wagon to a bigger, brighter, and better star."

He shifts his focus onto Nolan.

"Let us all take great pains not to let his sacrifice be made in vain. Ethan is only here because he is under the same impression that we are all under right now… that Olympus is going to change the very way we *function* as a society. Let us pray we do not betray that belief."

Charon rotates to Bing.

"Bingham. Where are we with the build-out?"

Bing leans forward in his chair and fiddles with his watch, alternately meeting Charon's eyes and glancing down at the watch face like it's a teleprompter.

"Good, it's good. The bones are all there now. Everything's in place. Now it's just a matter of filling in the connective tissue."

Charon rests his elbow on the table and reaches for his beard, pinching it between his thumb and forefinger and stroking downward slowly, over and over again, staring at Bing all the while.

"Bones and tissue are good. Skin is better. How long before we have a prototype?"

Bing searches for the answer in his watch, smiling and sweating and stammering as he tries to buy more time.

"Well, um, that's—that's a good question. It's obviously a much bigger undertaking than what any of us have ever done before, so there's definitely been some growing pains along the way. We're actually making some good progress when you consider–"

Charon interjects.

"Bingham. Enough. Just answer me three questions... and then I will let you go. Are you ready?"

The young engineering head looks anything but ready; and yet, he nods all the same.

"Question one. Does your team still have everything it needs here to be successful?"

Bing nods again, this time more enthusiastically.

"Oh, definitely. We're definitely–"

"Question two. Do we need to alter any of the dates we give for the TrendBeat interview on Friday?"

This time, Bing shakes his head.

"No... No, I think we should be good on those still–"

"Question three. Do I need to be concerned we might not have a beta test ready as scheduled by Christmas?"

Bing isn't as quick to nod or shake his head this time. He opens his mouth, hesitates, and glances down at his watch. After a few moments of what looks like serious consideration—and perhaps even calculation?— he peeks back up at Charon, his expression grim but determined.

"No, sir. You needn't be concerned about that."

Charon studies him carefully while Bing just glistens under the old man's gaze.

Brutally long, uncomfortable seconds pass by until Charon finally draws a sharp inhalation of breath through his nose.

"Good."

He swivels his attention back to Nolan.

"Nolan. I want you to take Ethan with you on Friday. Get him acquainted with Elle… and then do the interview together."

For the first time since I met him, Nolan looks crestfallen instead of cocksure.

"What? Richard—wait, *what*? The TrendBeat interview?"

Charon nods.

Nolan is absolutely aghast.

"Really? I mean, why? With all due respect, I can handle it myself."

He looks and gesticulates at me frantically.

"No offense, but he just got here! He doesn't know anything about what we've been doing or what we have planned. I mean, he said so himself just a few minutes ago before you walked in here. No offense, but I don't think–"

Charon holds up his palm. Nolan immediately goes silent.

"Nolan. My friend… this is not a request."

The old man lets that sink in a second before continuing.

"Nothing needs to change. You will still be the one conveying all the proper information to Elle… just like I will still be the one giving you all that information ahead of time. Nothing is different. I am just sending Ethan along for a sort of… crash course in how we do things here. He is only meant to be both a fly on the wall and a sponge, but he can also be an additional resource… should you need him, that is."

I barely know Nolan, but I already know him well enough that I can guess I'll be treated one hundred percent as a fly on the wall and zero percent as an additional resource during whatever this interview is.

Charon waits patiently for Nolan's acquiescence. Dejectedly, Nolan gives him a cursory nod of understanding while still staring up at the ceiling like a sulky teenager.

Charon's lips twist beneath the swooping moustache.

"Good."

He rolls the chair back away from the table and ascends to a standing position. The others take that as their cue and do the same, so I follow suit as well.

"Bingham. It seems you clearly have plenty to attend to. We will not keep you any longer."

Bing tries to put on a confident smile, but it's not very convincing.

"I appreciate that, Richard. Thank you."

He backs away from the table a little too quickly and trips over the legs of his chair. I reflexively reach out a hand to catch him from falling, and he steadies himself, laughs, and gives my arm an appreciative pat as he speeds toward the door.

"*Whew!* Good looking out, dude—I mean, Ethan. Uh, thanks!"

He scurries out of the room to go back to work.

Charon hovers slowly around the perimeter of the

table past the three of us remaining.

"Ethan. If you would be so kind to meet me in my office in half an hour, I would very much appreciate the opportunity to get to know you better. Until then, perhaps Portia could show you around. The two of you will be working together intimately over the next three months. And Nolan... how about you come with me?"

Charon slides an arm around Nolan's shoulder and guides him out the door. I can't fight the strong sense of déjà vu I get from watching the two of them exit like that. When the door closes behind them, I turn to face Portia, who is staring blankly back at me.

Please, don't let this be awkward. I've already had enough of that for one day.

Without any provocation, she suddenly gives me a crooked smile and cocks an eyebrow.

"Hell of a first day, huh?"

Relief washes over me at once. Maybe, just maybe, she'll be a perfectly normal, down-to-earth person... who just happens to work at this funny farm.

I laugh appreciatively.

"Is it always like this?"

Portia groans.

"Honestly? Yes. But it's not always bad. If that makes any sense? Most of the time, it's actually kind of amazing."

She gives me the crooked smile again.

"It's never boring. I'll say that much."

I'm still pretty flabbergasted by everything that's just happened. As if this place itself wasn't crazy enough with all the botanical ceilings, grass floors, and luxurious amenities, that whole episode with Chuck was unnerving.

Portia reads my mind.

"I've never seen him fire someone like that, though, if that's what you're asking. Don't get me wrong— they've let plenty of people go since I got here. But normally, it's a much quieter affair. Like, *much quieter.* As in, one day, there's somebody new sitting at your friend's desk, and your friend's just… disappeared."

I cross my arms in front of my chest.

"What—you mean, literally? Literally disappeared?"

Portia laughs.

"Literally disappeared as in 'missing persons?' No, not like that."

She mirrors my posture, crossing her arms in front of her chest and looking at me quizzically as her head tilts to one side, black hair tumbling over that shoulder.

"Just, 'disappears' as in they don't work here anymore, and they don't seem all that interested in returning your calls or texts. Or basically being friends anymore."

I can't tell if she's speaking in generalities or if she's being super specific and personal. It sounds like she's talking about a particular person, but she could also be talking about multiple coworkers. I'm having a hard time getting a good read from her on any of this.

"Do you think they're being silenced somehow?"

She laughs again.

"I don't know, man. They'll send you an NDA along with all your other paperwork tonight. Word to the wise: you've never seen or signed an NDA like this one before. My dad's a corporate lawyer at a major firm, and even he said he'd never seen anything like it. Suffice it to say, if the CIA and the Illuminati had a baby, and if Facebook and the Church of Scientology had a baby, and then if those two babies met each other and *they* had a baby, that baby would be Olympus."

It's my turn to laugh. So far, Portia is everything I wish Nolan had been from the start.

"Do you mind if I ask you a question?"

She considers me carefully.

"Technically, you just did, and I don't. So, I guess you may as well go ahead."

Clever.

"Do you like working here? Like… everything's on the up-and-up? And you don't have any regrets or anything?"

Portia nods slowly and sucks on her lower lip.

"Ah. I see where this is going." Another crooked smile; another cocked eyebrow. "It is all a bit much, isn't it? The lavish outer space/jungle rainforest office, the hush-hush mentality, all the cameras, the egos, the bare feet…"

I can't help but look down as she says it, and when I do, I'm surprised to see that she's actually wearing black laced-up Converse sneakers. She wiggles them up and down, which of course immediately brings my attention back up to her face, and I blush.

"Yep, that's me. What a rebel, right?"

Her tone is wry but not unfriendly. At least she's not verbally reproaching me for getting caught. After spending most of the morning with Nolan, I'm still a bit on guard.

Portia continues.

"To answer your question: yeah, I do like working here. I love it, actually. I've never worked somewhere with so little bullshit and petty drama. It just doesn't exist here. Outside of maybe a few bad apples—"

"More like oranges."

I dip my chin toward the chair Nolan was using earlier to accentuate my meaning, and I can tell from Portia's smile and her eyes that she immediately understands.

"Right. A few bad oranges. But honestly, all the weirdness and culty vibes aside, what's not to love? The checks are fat, and they always clear. The perks are innumerable. The work itself is stimulating, challenging, important… and it's never tedious. No one's micromanaging you or breathing over your shoulder. You saw how Richard talked to Bing back there, right? That's Olympus in a nutshell. He holds everyone accountable, and he's certainly not afraid to scare the living fuck out of you sometimes with his whole old-Jesus-crossed-with-steampunk-Gandalf persona. But he also ultimately leaves us alone if we tell him everything's under control. Even when it isn't."

She says that last bit in a hushed voice and with a conspiratorial wink.

"Got any more burning questions you need to get off your chest? I feel like it's almost time to take you to Richard and we haven't even left the conference room yet. Guess I'm the world's shittiest tour guide."

I can think of at least one person we both know who's worse. And though I'm eager to get an actual tour of the Olympus office and to meet some of the other people here, I'm also thoroughly grateful to be getting this kind of inside scoop from Portia. As much as I initially like Isla—and as much as I initially dislike Nolan—neither one of them has been as blunt, transparent, and easy to talk to as Portia is being right now.

I do have one last question for her; at least, one last question for now. It's one that I probably would have forgotten about entirely today if it weren't for something she said earlier.

"Portia, something you said earlier—you mentioned cameras. We didn't have any at my old office. Granted, we also weren't a multi-billion-dollar tech company working on a revolutionary new app, either. But they had me sign a release form downstairs. Do you know what that's all about?"

Portia smiles mysteriously.

"Why? You shy about being on camera? Afraid your acting skills aren't cut out for Hollywood?"

I smile back at her, even though I'm not particularly amused by this subject matter. Maybe she's empathic enough to pick up on the fact that I'm serious, because she instantly drops the cheekiness.

"I've actually never had the balls to ask Richard directly about it. Different people will tell you different things, depending on who you ask. Usually, the answer has something to do with security; as in, the cameras are there for our own safety or for *their* own safety, so there's a record in case anyone tries to steal something. Whether that something is a computer or a purse or *an idea.*"

I open my mouth to speak but Portia holds up her index finger to stop me.

"Wait a minute. I know. None of this addresses them using your likeness however they see fit, right? That's what you were going to say?"

It was.

"For that part, it kind of goes back to the whole idea-stealing thingy. You may have noticed Richard had his cell phone riding shotgun in his jacket pocket with the lens facing out. That's not an accident; he's recording *everything*. Some people even say that Castor and Pollux—sorry, their two dogs? The black Great Danes?"

"I met them in my interview."

"Okay, cool. Some people even say that they have tiny little cameras and microphones wired into their collars. Now, I think most of this stuff is conspiracy theory office gossip. But it does all trace back to that release form. The thinking is that everything we do and everything we say while we're here should be considered valuable and potentially marketable… at least according to our mutual friend, Agent Orange, the marketing whiz kid."

Portia leans in closer to me.

"Maybe a software engineer says something to her friend during lunchtime that ends up getting used as our product tagline. Maybe one of the security guards whistles something while taking a dump, and that becomes our commercial jingle. Maybe that slightly intrigued, slightly confused, slightly frightened expression on your face right now makes such a lasting impression on Richard when he watches the tape of this encounter later on tonight that he ends up using it in our brand kit somehow. I don't know."

The idea that Richard or anybody else could be watching us now or later is enough to make the new expression on my face mostly frightened and mostly irritated.

Portia shrugs and starts moving toward the door.

"Then again, maybe the whole thing's one big reality TV show. Or something like The Truman Show. Did you ever see that movie with Jim Carrey? That was my friend's theory, at least… the one who 'disappeared', as it were, and who is no longer my friend now, I guess."

There's a hint of pain she tries to quickly bury in her voice as she says it, and I get the feeling there's more to this story that she's leaving out. It doesn't matter, though, because Portia's evidently decided that our time here is at an end.

"Come along, new guy. I have to show you something other than the most boring room in the whole building."

She briskly leads me around most of the places I've already seen now; only Portia actually does me the courtesy of conversing as we walk. She points things out, explains how things work, and gives me practical, insider advice—like when's the best time to use a massage chair, or when's the worst time to visit the gym.

Portia also offers up warm but simplistic introductions between me and anyone else whose paths we happen to cross during the tour. While she doesn't go out of her way to take me to anyone's desk or introduce me to anybody in particular, she still seems to know everyone, and everyone seems to know her. I get the sense she's genuinely liked by the people we come across.

Finally, we arrive at a massive wooden door. It's the only door I've seen on this entire floor so far that doesn't have a label placard positioned beside it.

The door itself is a beautiful work of art that is ornately carved to depict a rather graphic, chaotic scene. It looks like some kind of battlefield. I can make out soldiers that look like centurions scattered about with horses, spears, swords, bows, arrows, and shields. Some are fighting, some are running, some are riding, and some are dying. The majority of this action takes place on a plain that encompasses the whole lower half of the door.

But the upper half is a starkly different scene. Most of the area up there is comprised of a towering mountain that is lined with trees, clouds, and the occasional goat or ram. Still, it's fairly nondescript... until the very top. At its peak, a dozen or so massive beings hold court, each several times larger than the diminutive soldiers far, far below them. Some of these beings watch the action down below with interest, while others casually converse with one another, eat, drink, or kiss.

"Olympus."

Portia says it plainly, without inflection or emotion, as she looks upon the great door. Then she turns to face me.

"I'm sure Richard's expecting you. Best not to keep him waiting. I'll see you around, partner."

She gives me half a wink and walks away.

I take another look at the mythological scene on the door before cautiously rapping my knuckles against it. Some time passes without any answer. I knock again, more forcefully this go-around. More time passes. And still, no response. It seems I just can't catch a break today with the doors in this building.

Tentatively, I reach my hand out and place it on a twisting handle made of oak and iron. What's the worst thing that could happen anyway?

I immediately think of Chuck, of course. But I decide to try my luck anyway.

The handle moves all the way down, and with a solid amount of pressure, the heavy wooden door glides inward on a soundless hinge.

Inside, the room is dark. Very dark. Most of the light

I can see is what I've let in with me by opening the door. Otherwise, there seems to be no natural light in here coming in from the outside. If there are overhead lights, floor lamps, desk lamps, wall sconces, or more of those cool stalactite lights from the lobby lounge area in here, none of them are turned on.

"Ethan. Close the door… and have a seat."

Charon's voice emanates and echoes out from everywhere within the room. I'm not entirely sure where it came from. Nor am I sure where I'm supposed to sit. It's pitch-black in here as I close the door behind me.

Slowly, softly, faintly, I begin to make out a tiny flickering flame in the distance straight in front of me. Perhaps it's unwise, but I begin moving toward it like a moth drawn to the light. There's really no other alternative for me anyway, unless I want to just sit down in the dark right where I stand. As I draw nearer, the flame illuminates the wick it twists on, like an exotic dancer weaving atop a waxen candle stage.

With a gasp, I jump back as I glimpse a disembodied head floating high above the candle. I recognize it immediately as Charon, but that does nothing to quell the abject horror that rears up inside me unannounced and uninvited within the darkness.

As my eyes continue to adjust and let more of the dim candlelight in, I see now that he's seated on the ground behind the candle. Dressed as he is in all black, it's impossible to make out anything other than his ghostly head floating high above the flame. The light catches his cheekbones and his great monstrosity of a nose, but not much else, losing itself in the thick woven fibers of his hair and his beard. I'm somehow convinced that even if his eyes were open right now—and they're not—they wouldn't catch the fire either.

Charon sucks a long breath in through his nose as his eyelids flutter like bat wings and finally open. I was right. Not only do I not see the reflection of the candle in his pupils, but I can't even see the whites of his eyes. They're just two black balls of pitch set in sockets of taut skin.

"You prefer to stand?"

I probably would, honestly, given how creepy this situation is. But it's clear he wants me to sit, so I do so. I try not to think how weird it is that I'm sitting on the floor in the dark across from my new boss with only a small candle burning between us, but I'm completely unsuccessful.

Charon takes another ragged breath in and then out of his nose.

"Good."

His voice is deeper and hoarser than I remember it half an hour ago in the conference room.

"Ethan. Do you meditate?"

I shake my head. "No."

Charon studies me carefully in the gloom.

"That is a shame. Are you religious?"

This line of questioning is doing nothing to make me feel more comfortable right now.

"I'm not, no."

"Spiritual?"

I hesitate. Where is this going? Charon waits for me patiently.

"I don't know how to answer that, sir. It's sort of complicated for me, I guess."

Charon smiles. It's actually the first time I can remember seeing him smile. There's something vaguely vampiric about it.

"As it should be for all of us."

He breathes in again and closes his eyes. The silence is just as heavy as the darkness around us. I wait in terror for whatever comes next, until finally, and only when he's fully ready, does he breathe back out again.

"Ethan. Will you allow me to be completely transparent with you?"

There's an irony there, considering he's anything but transparent sitting here bathed in black across from me. I still nod my head.

Charon opens his eyes again in that peculiar, fluttering, bat-like manner.

"I know."

Either his eyes are even darker now, or the lids around them didn't open as wide as they were supposed to this time.

"I know… everything."

He lets his words hang in the air like smoke.

"I know who you are… and where you came from… and I know *why*… you came from."

I'm definitely beginning to wish I'd either stayed standing or I'd left the door ajar at least. Probably both, actually.

Charon keeps his hollow furnace eyes fixated on me.

"I know how to take a risk… but I also know *when* to take a risk. And when it comes to finding and cultivating talent, I trust more than just my own intuition. Are you following me so far?"

I actually think I am. Even if I don't want to be. And as much as I think I can see where this is going, I'm also realizing that there's no way it can end well for me.

I can barely croak out a meek affirmation.

"Yes."

He breathes.

"It does not matter to me that you lost your job. It also does not matter to me that you lied about it twice now... first to Nolan, and then to my wife."

The floating head inches closer.

"What does matter to me is if you *truly believe* that I would not seriously look into a person before bringing them aboard any project... let alone one as important and precious to me as this. Do you understand?"

My entire life comes crashing down in ruination.

"I do understand. And Dr. Charon, I am so incredibly sorry for not explaining everything that happened at VitaLyfe. That first time, at the bar, I didn't know who you were, or what any of this was—"

Charon's great upturned palm materializes out of thin air in front of him.

"Ethan. Enough. There is no need for that. It is all behind us now anyway. You are here... because you and I both want you to be here... and that is all that matters."

I can scarcely believe what I'm hearing.

Mere seconds ago, I thought I was getting exposed, humiliated, fired once again, and quite possibly even murdered in here. Now, not only is my boss telling me that he knows my shameful secret and he doesn't care; he's also telling me that he hired me for this role in spite of it.

Moreover, the revelation that he didn't just pluck me at random from a Hollywood tiki bar and offer me this job and its accompanying salary without thoroughly vetting me first actually comes as a great relief. That was one of my biggest hang-ups with this whole situation to begin with: the notion that none of it made sense, and that it all felt too good to be true. That's what I've been trying, albeit unsuccessfully, to impress upon Allie this whole time.

To be sure, the whole hiring process has still been extremely bizarre. But at least now, after my conversation with Portia, and especially in light of this disclosure from Charon himself, the ground I'm standing on feels a bit more safe and solid; if no less strange.

"Thank you, Dr. Charon. Richard. I sincerely appreciate it."

Charon's palm descends back into the murky depths and is lost to sight once more. It's amazing how little overall my eyes have adjusted to the darkness in here. I still really can't see anything other than the candle and Charon's head suspended above it.

"Ethan. Two more things… and then you may go."

I sit and wait patiently. He can keep me here in the dark—both literally and metaphorically—all day long, if it means I still get to keep this job and bring home a 'fat paycheck' for Allie and our baby that's growing inside her.

"First… stay close to Portia, both this initial week and then well beyond. She will be able to get you up to speed with everything you need to know to hit the ground running. And Ethan… just so you know, she and Chuck were very close…"

I'm not exactly sure what that's supposed to mean, but I nod my understanding and acknowledgment anyway.

"Second… I made it out to seem earlier like you will

be a passive observer during Friday's interview with TrendBeat. That is not entirely true. The reality of the situation… and I expect that you will keep this strictly between us… is that my confidence in Nolan when it comes to this matter is… tenuous."

Charon again inches his face closer to mine.

"That is not meant to disparage his character. I love Nolan like a son… and I trust he has only good intentions as far as me and this company are concerned. Fortunately or unfortunately, however, I also know his strengths and weaknesses as a person inside and out… and I fear he is not ideally suited to this particular task. I would go myself… but I have a prior engagement on Friday that I can neither cancel nor miss."

"They won't reschedule with you?"

It's not really my place to ask that question, but it also feels like he's opening up to me a bit right now, and it makes me more daring.

Charon's head moves from side to side.

"Ms. Maguire is a busy woman. Apparently, even my own considerable charm has its limitations."

He gives me a twisted smile this time that's half conspiratorial, half lecherous, and wholly unpleasant. Thankfully, it's gone just as quickly as it comes.

"Ethan. I hope my fears are misguided… and Nolan relays my messaging as clear and crisp as if I were physically there myself. But if you should sense any miscommunication or… trouble… on his part, I hope you will feel emboldened to intervene on my behalf. You may have spent considerably less time here than he has, but your prior experience and expertise qualifies you to make whatever course corrections you deem necessary. Again… only should you feel the need."

As much as I'm flattered and a bit surprised by this early show of trust, I still can't imagine a world where Nolan calmly and professionally accepts any intervention on my part. The only question is whether or not I should bring that hesitation up now to Charon. He seems like he's really making an effort to connect with me, letting me into his meditation sanctum, or office, or whatever this place is, and being so honest… and even somewhat vulnerable.

I decide to speak up.

"Not to overstep my boundaries here, but are you sure Nolan would be open to any of this? He didn't seem particularly enthused about the idea back in the conference room."

The skin around Charon's face tightens in the shadows.

"You need not worry about that. I spoke with Nolan just now in private, and he understands… the complexity… of the situation. He knows you have my blessing to do as you wish… and he will respect that."

I'm still not altogether convinced, but if anyone can get through to Nolan and rein in his ego, I'm sure it's Dr. Richard Charon.

A low hissing sound comes from Charon now. His eyes have closed again, and it looks like he's slowly exhaling through a cracked crevice in his thin lips.

"Ethan. Thank you. You may go now."

Even if we've just had a breakthrough, I'm not exactly keen to stay and hang out any longer than I have to in here.

"Okay, thanks. Thank you."

Getting to my feet again is even harder since my legs have long since fallen asleep. I get the pins-and-needles feeling in them as I try to shake out the stiff muscles and move away from the candle and back toward where I think the door might be. Like a blind man, my hands reach out and sweep back and forth in front of me in the dark, grasping timidly for anything solid and somewhat familiar.

My fingers finally make contact with what feels like heavy velvet. It surprises me at first and I draw my hands back in alarm, but then I reach back out to give it more of a lasting touch.

I'm running my hands up and down some kind of giant curtain. Maybe this is what he uses to cover the windows and keep the sunlight out? I wonder if he always sits alone in here like this in the dark or if it's only while he's meditating. Obviously, I hope it's the latter.

Moving along the width of the curtain, I finally find the flat, solid surface of a door. There's really no guarantee that this is the same door I came in through, but I'm going to take a chance and say that it is.

I locate a handle, and I'm just about ready to let myself out when I think of one last thing to say to Charon; or rather, to the darkness where I believe Charon to be. The candle has already disappeared from my field of vision. Maybe he blew it out.

"Dr. Charon—Richard, thank you. Thank you, again. For your understanding… about VitaLyfe."

A moment passes in silence. I wonder if he's going to answer me at all. I wonder if he's asleep. I wonder if he's transfigured into a vampire bat, and he's hanging upside-down from the rafters of the ceiling right above my head. That last thought is exponentially more chilling than funny.

From the thick nothingness, a hoarse whisper finds

its way to me.

"'Do not judge, and you will not be judged. Do not condemn, and you will not be condemned. Forgive… and you will be forgiven.'"

I have no idea how to respond to that, so I just give him a polite smile in return. It's only after I've opened the door, slipped out, and shut it firmly behind me that I realize there's no way he could have seen me smile in the dark. But it's too late to go back now, even if I wanted to—and I most certainly do not. So, I shuffle off to go find Portia instead.

CHAPTER SEVEN

Where the hell is Nolan?

I'm sitting in the middle of a busy coffeeshop in West Hollywood trying my best not to look stressed out. Although with every passing minute that ticks off my watch, that gets harder and harder to do.

The plan was to meet here thirty minutes before our meeting with Elle Maguire. We agreed half an hour was enough time to allot for traffic, find parking, order a couple drinks, and get settled in before the interview.

In my mind, we'd even have a bit of time left over to review Charon's notes together. It was also my way of planning to reinforce the notion that I'd be a full participant in this meeting if I wanted to be, which I do.

Now, it seems increasingly likely I might be the *only* participant in this meeting on our end—and I'm not the one with Charon's notes. I'm trying not to think that way, but it's difficult.

I've seen a picture online of what Elle looks like, and I'm keeping my eye out for her. I also told the barista hostess at the front that I was expecting two more people to join me, and I gave her their names and my name. All I can do now is hope and pray that Nolan makes it here before Elle does.

My cell phone is in one hand, and there's a dirty chai latte in the other that has long since gone cold and is now half-empty. I keep glancing at the screen of my phone like some kind of social media or technology addict, thinking any second now I'm going to see I've missed a text from Nolan saying he's parking or walking up.

At what point do I take action? And, on that note, what kind of action would that even be?

Earlier this week, I saved two new phone numbers in my contacts: one that belongs to Nolan, and one that belongs to Portia. I've tried calling Nolan three times already and gotten his voicemail each time after a lengthy period of ringing. At least it *seems* like he's not purposefully ignoring me or screening my calls.

I haven't tried Portia yet. And honestly, I'm not sure if I should. For starters, this doesn't really concern her. She's not a part of this interview with TrendBeat, and I know all too well how much she's already got on her plate. I really don't want to bother her unless it's absolutely necessary.

And although this situation is quickly venturing into 'absolutely necessary' territory, I'm also not convinced she can really do anything to help me. Unless Nolan is there at Olympus with her still, and he somehow got detained or forgot about this interview entirely, it's not like she has some other way of getting in contact with him.

I also know that if I call her, there's at least a decent chance that word gets back to Charon that Nolan's not here. And as much as I don't care for Nolan on a personal level, I still don't want to screw him over professionally or get him into serious trouble if I can help it.

It's 1:50, though. He was supposed to be here twenty minutes ago, and he's not answering my calls or my texts. I have to try Portia.

She picks up after the first ring.

"Miss me already?"

"Ha—yeah, I wish. Is Nolan there with you?"

"He's not. Isn't he supposed to be with you?"

I sigh.

"Yeah, that's where he's supposed to be, but he's not here. I've tried calling and texting him, and I'm not getting an answer. The interview's in ten minutes."

"Shit."

There's a brief pause on the other end of the line.

"I mean, I don't know. I can check and see if he's lurking around here somewhere, but I know he knows about it, obviously. Maybe he's just stuck in traffic, and his phone died or something?"

My heart freezes ice-cold in my chest. From my vantage point at this shaded patio table, I see a woman step out from the backseat of a car and onto the sidewalk in front of the coffeeshop. I can't be sure, but she looks an awful lot like the pictures I've seen of Elle. She's carrying a messenger bag over one arm, and plus, she just *looks* like a journalist.

"Oh, fuck. I think she's here."

"Elle Maguire?"

"Yeah."

Pause.

"What do I do? I don't have Richard's notes."

"You and Nolan went over them though, didn't you?"

"We talked about it yesterday but not in any great

detail."

I'd hardly even call it a conversation, either. It was basically just Nolan reciting the talking points one-by-one like he was practicing a speech on me. I'm not even sure if he let me speak once during it, and I certainly never laid eyes on the actual notes.

At this point though, my hand is forced. The woman disappeared inside and could be coming out here any second now. I have to get Charon involved.

"Portia, can you ask Richard to send me the notes directly? You can tell him the truth or lie or whatever you think is best. I just need to get a copy, like, right now."

There's another brief pause on her end.

"He's not here, Ethan. He and Nolan went to lunch together, and I haven't seen either one of them since."

Fuck. How is this happening, and why am I the only one who's getting screwed for it?

"Ethan? Do you want me to talk to Isla and see if she can call him or something?"

My brain is humming. I can see a shadow moving toward the other side of the patio door.

"Ethan?"

Think, think, think…

The door opens and the woman with the messenger bag walks through it and out onto the patio. I raise my hand and wave to get her attention. She sees me, smiles, waves back, and starts heading in my direction.

"She's here. I gotta go."

I hang up the call and push back my chair to stand just as she arrives at my table.

"Hi! Are you Elle?"

The woman drops her bag into an empty chair and

shakes my proffered hand.

"Hi! I am indeed. Now, are you Nolan or Ethan?"

Just be cool and stay calm.

"Ethan. Nolan's running a little late, but he should be here any minute now."

Elle nods.

"All good; no worries. I'm actually going to go in and use the ladies' room and grab a tea, then, before we get started, if that's all right?"

Thank God.

"Absolutely. Take your time."

She gestures toward her bag.

"Okay if I leave this here with you?"

"Of course. I'll be here."

She smiles appreciatively and ducks back inside through the door. I already have my phone in my hand and the number dialed by the time she disappears from view and the door shuts behind her.

Portia picks up.

"Is this a booty call or a butt dial this time?"

"Stop it."

"Let me guess. It wasn't her."

"No, it was. It is. She's using the bathroom and getting a tea."

"Well, that's a lucky break."

Portia laughs. I do not.

"So, what do you want me to do? You want me to try and track Isla down and have her call Richard?"

I run my hand through my hair.

"*Oh, God.* I don't know. I don't want to rat him out, but I also don't know what else to do…"

"On a scale of zero to one hundred, how confident are you that you can do the interview by yourself?"

I grimace.

"Maybe—I don't know, maybe a thirty-three? It really depends on what kind of questions she asks. I feel like I know most of the major talking points; or at least the ones Nolan went over yesterday. Not so much the different dates or any of the finer details."

"Just remember that December 25 is Christmas and that's when we plan to launch the beta. Think Santa Claus, elves, baby Jesus…"

This time, I do laugh in spite of myself.

"You're not helping."

"I'm sorry."

She pauses.

"So, is that a yes or a no on Isla?"

I'm honestly at a loss. I don't want to make an enemy of Nolan, and I'm almost positive that's what'll happen if it gets back to the Charons that he didn't show up today. But I also don't want to embarrass myself—or, more importantly, embarrass Olympus—by saying something that isn't right during this key interview. I've absorbed a ton of information over the past five days already, but I'm also still in my first week on the job. It seems ludicrous to be the appointed media spokesperson on Friday for a company that I just joined on Monday.

Then again, Charon trusted me enough to send me here in the first place. He also made it perfectly clear that I have full license to speak freely with Elle.

Of course, Charon only gave me that license because he assumed Nolan would be here. We all did.

"Ethan?"

I check the front of my phone again. Still no missed calls or text messages from Nolan Best. It appears that

I'm on my own.

"Don't say anything. I'll handle it."

"You sure?"

The surprise in her voice is palpable.

I take a deep breath.

"Not really, but we'll see. I appreciate all your help."

"Anytime. Go get 'em, tiger. And just remember: Santa Claus, elves, baby Jesus."

"Thanks."

I hang up the phone just as I hear some kind of commotion behind me and turn around.

A sweaty and disheveled homeless man is loudly panting and grunting as he heaves himself off the sidewalk and rolls up and over the wrought-iron fence that separates the coffeeshop from the street. He hits the ground in a crumpled heap as patio onlookers stare and somebody gasps. With a guttural groan, he pushes himself up to his feet, sways, takes in his surroundings, and spots me.

Of course, it's not a homeless man at all; it's Nolan.

"There you are!"

His voice is way too loud, even for being outside. He staggers over to the table, yanks out a chair with a hideous scraping sound of metal on concrete, and collapses into the seat. His shirt is two different shades of blue because of all the places he's sweat through it, and his face is bright red and covered in a wet sheen.

"Where's Elle? Is she here yet?"

Nolan's eyes are white and wild as he rolls his head around in every conceivable direction. He's slurring his words and licking his lips manically. It's clear that he's either drunk or high, or both.

I steal a quick glance toward the inside of the

coffeeshop to make sure she's not on her way out. It's impossible to see fully inside, but at least she's not there at the door as far as I can tell. Some of the people around us have gone back to their conversations or computers, but most are still staring apprehensively at Nolan and probably thinking some of the same things that I am.

I try my best to keep my voice down, hoping he'll take the hint and do the same.

"Nolan, where've you been? Are you drunk?"

Nolan audibly scoffs at the question… and sprays me with spittle in the process.

"*Please!* I'm good, okay? I'm fine! Where's the girl?"

Right on cue, Elle walks up to the table with a tea in her hand and a surprised look on her face.

"Hi there! Are you Nolan?"

I open my mouth to speak, but Nolan beats me to it as he clambers up out of the chair to a standing—actually, more like swaying—position.

"Yes! Yes, I am. Are you Elle?"

He sticks out his hand and it sways just like he does. She catches it with what I think is a justifiable degree of apprehension.

"Yes, I am."

Elle looks at me and looks back at him. I can tell she's trying so hard to remain professional.

"Why don't we have a seat?"

She breaks from his grip, sets her tea down, picks up her messenger bag from the chair next to me, and sits there herself. Gracefully, she does this while simultaneously placing the bag in the chair to her left where Nolan's standing. I'm sure the subtlety is lost on him, but it's obvious to me that she's trying to give herself a barrier there.

It works. Nolan doesn't seem fazed in the slightest as he moves over to take the only open chair left at our table. He collapses into the seat on my right with a sigh that sounds so pleasurable it's profane.

My heart breaks for Elle Maguire. She goes inside for just a minute to pee and get a drink and comes out to find this train wreck waiting for her outside. I wonder just how often this sort of thing happens to her. You'd have to imagine that working as a Hollywood journalist, it might actually happen quite a bit. It's probably just an occupational hazard that comes with interviewing pop culture icons and celebrities—most of whom are, of course, notorious for their addiction issues. She's probably interviewed numerous people under the active influence of one thing or another over the span of her career; though I doubt she expected she'd have to do so today.

Elle's a professional, though. She sets her cell phone on the table and starts recording our conversation while deftly removing a notebook and pen from her bag at the same time.

"Should we get going? I know we're getting started a little late."

It's obviously an admonition aimed at Nolan, but it flies completely over his head. He's presently alternating his focus between staring at Elle—and not in the appropriate, attentive way that he should be—and wiping perspiration from different parts of his body.

Elle's not waiting to get a reaction though. As Charon foretold, she's a busy woman. Plus, she's probably starting to get an idea of where this interview could be headed.

"All right, then. It's a shame Dr. Charon couldn't be

here himself today, but he assured me I'd be left in good hands."

She starts writing in her notebook.

"Just to confirm now, I have Ethan Birch—E-T-H-A-N-B-I-R-C-H—as director of development, and Nolan Best—N-O-L-A-N-B-E-S-T—as director of marketing. Is that correct?"

I nod.

"That's right."

"Just make sure my name is first."

Nolan practically drools the words out as he tries to give her a wink.

"If you—how you write it. Just—just I should go—I should go first. I've been here since the beginning. He just got here."

There's a world where I'd be offended by him making that kind of casual dig at me in front of a complete stranger—especially one who works for the press. This is not that world, though. More than anything, I'm embarrassed. And honestly, growing more alarmed by the second. Every time Nolan blinks, it seems to take him a little bit longer to get his eyes open again. And even seated, he's found a way to keep swaying precariously like a palm tree in a hurricane.

Elle's withering leer speaks volumes.

"I'll make sure to make a note of that."

She doesn't.

"So. Let's talk Olympus. Everybody always wants a sequel, but so few of them ever live up to the original, and almost none ever surpass it. What should we be expecting with Olympus? Is this 'Signals Part II,' or 'Signals Reimagined,' or is Olympus its own thing?"

It's clear she's addressing me and me alone. But I at

least want to give Nolan *a chance* to answer first. Whether or not he remembers it, this is supposed to be his rodeo. As far as he's probably concerned, I'm just here for moral support and to interject pearls of wisdom based on my own prior experience should a natural opportunity arise. He's also the one with Charon's notes; I know they're saved on his phone, because we briefly went over them together yesterday.

Nolan's making no move to either speak or take his cell phone out, though. His eyes are closed, and his nostrils are flaring as he breathes heavily through them. There's a decent chance he's asleep, as his torso doesn't seem to be rocking quite as much as it was before.

I turn back to Elle. She's leaning forward, pen to paper, rigid, her unwavering intention locked squarely on me. If she's fazed at all by the person sitting across the table from her, she isn't letting on yet.

It looks like I'm going to be a whole lot more than just a fly on the wall or a sponge.

"Sorry, um—yes, it's definitely its own thing. There *is* a dating component to Olympus. But that's only a very small piece of the overall puzzle. We are using the Signals platform, though, for that. So, essentially, anyone who has Olympus will also get Signals by default. It's the same Signals engine, just streamlined and compartmentalized so it fits into the larger system."

Elle mostly keeps her eyes on me as she listens and writes, only occasionally glancing down at her pen and paper. She's still utterly ignoring Nolan, who hasn't moved much save for a steady decline of his chin toward his chest.

"I'm confused. Olympus is a dating app then, or it's not?"

I sigh and look down. A ladybug is crawling along the lid of my latte. I watch as it inches its way down the mouth hole and disappears.

"Yes… and no. People who are looking to date can certainly do so on Olympus, and that's where the Signals integration comes in. And just like on Signals, you can also search for things other than romance, whether it's for friends in the area, friends far away, new pen pals, work connections and networking, or just people with similar interests or hobbies. It's designed to offer the full range of social interaction all in one place."

Elle takes a quick sip of her tea.

"Forgive me, Ethan, but this all sounds exactly like the latest version of Signals. What's the difference?"

She's polite, but it's clear that she's also growing impatient. I'm sure that Nolan's behavior put her on edge from the beginning, and I'm not really telling her anything she doesn't already know. After all, she's been there every step of the way in covering the birth and maturation of Signals through numerous interviews with Charon over the years.

If I had his notes—or even if Nolan had just pulled out his phone and opened them there before passing out—this whole episode would be playing out so much smoother. Charon knew exactly what words and phrases he wanted used for this TrendBeat feature.

Just how mortified—or how irate—is he going to be when he reads it? Will he callously discard me the same way he did Chuck? And will Nolan also get unceremoniously tossed aside with me, or will he get a free pass, since Charon views him like a son?

Elle is still waiting. Even if it's not the correct answer, I need to give her an answer all the same.

Whatever the consequences are later, I can't control that now; best to just try and explain it to her the same way Portia explained it to me.

"Imagine that instead of having dozens of apps on your device that do all these different things, you just had one app that could do all of it for you. All the social networking you'd ever need, but also all the day-to-day functions, too. Things like photo sharing, banking, transferring money, listening to music, streaming video, reading the news, tracking your health and fitness, whatever… it's all in one place, and it's all connected seamlessly and fluidly. All those components are in perfect sync with one another, and everything's in constant communication internally.

"Now imagine that it's also adaptive and self-improving. So, if you're following a podcast on Olympus that's all about cross-fit, for example, the app is designed to learn from that and begin catering content specifically for you to improve the overall UX. And not just in the app, but in your life, as well.

"Maybe it recommends nearby gyms that might be a good fit for you, or it scans the internet and finds the most relevant exercise and diet plans and collects them as pooled resources for your viewing. It updates your grocery list with the kinds of foods and supplements you, specifically, should be taking, given your current physical condition and desired results. It makes online shopping recommendations for shoes or clothing or workout gear that are uniquely tailored to your body type and experience level. It compiles other informative articles for reading, podcasts for listening, video tutorials for watching. It creates unique music playlists designed to raise your heart rate to the perfect target level while doing certain exercises.

"And without you ever having to lift a finger to do the groundwork of a search, it connects you socially with other cross-fit enthusiasts, and then categorizes and groups them accordingly for you. So, if you want to see only people in their twenties or thirties that live within a twenty-mile radius of you and who also love cross-fit, you can. If you want to see only *single* people from that same group, you can. If you want to see only people from that same group who also vote Democrat, believe in God, don't have kids, listen to Nirvana, eat vegan, don't like cats, and play online backgammon, you can find them. And then once you've found them, you can do anything and everything you want with them. And all of it, all of this, *everything*, can take place in just one place."

Elle has been feverishly scribbling at her notepad during my monologue. It feels like I've been rambling, but hopefully, it wasn't nearly as meandering as it felt.

With Elle's attention momentarily focused on her writing, I steal a quick glance over at Nolan. There's no question that he's asleep now. His chin is completely flat against his collarbone, his eyes are closed, and there's a thread of drool hanging from the corner of his lip. Perhaps he's having a bad dream, because his forehead is wrinkled up like he's trying to concentrate on something.

Elle sniffs and looks at me with a raised eyebrow.

"Well, it all sounds very grandiose and ambitious. It also sounds like a nightmare from the tech side. You really have coders who think they can make all this happen? Let alone make it actually fit on someone's phone once it's all put together?"

It's a good question. And it's not one I can definitively answer.

The correct answer is the same answer that poor Bing gave Charon on Monday. But I'm not convinced that even Bing's convinced this is all going to work out in the end. The more time I've spent with Bing-the-boy-genius the past few days, the more I get the feeling that as brilliant as he is, he could be in way over his head with this particular undertaking.

"That's what our engineering team is working on. It's a massive group of people; I'd say at least ninety to ninety-five percent of our workforce, honestly. The stuff that these guys—and girls—can do today just blows me away. It's a whole art form unto itself."

Elle doesn't look convinced, but she lets it go for the moment.

"Assuming this army of coders can make magic happen, what's the planned release date?"

Santa Claus, elves, baby Jesus…

"We're hoping to launch on Christmas Day."

Again, she cocks a skeptical eyebrow.

"Hoping?"

"Excuse me: 'planning'. Or—we are. It's happening, I mean. Ready or not, here we come."

I laugh, perhaps a bit too nervously.

Elle smiles patronizingly.

"That's terrific."

She briefly consults her notes.

"So, all these functions—the music, the video, the photo sharing, etcetera—are these all apps within an app like Signals? And if so, are they going to be made available as individual downloads themselves for those who don't want the whole Olympus experience, or are they only available through Olympus, or what?"

So far, so good on being able to answer all her questions. How adequately, I'm not sure. But at least I've been able to speak on them and give her the substance of an answer each time.

"We're not completely trying to reinvent the wheel here. Over the years, Dr. Charon has built up some pretty strong working relationships with other tech companies and brands. If there was an opportunity to team up with an existing partner we could integrate with for a specific aspect of this project, and it made sense for both sides to do so—like using Spotify for music streaming, for example—that's something we pursued and then hooked in with our API.

"If, however, such a partnership didn't make sense—either because the relationship wasn't there already or because the app could be seen as a competitor, like Facebook—then we just created that function ourselves. And, in those instances, we wouldn't really have any motivation to release them separately, since it would only take away from the total number of people downloading and using Olympus every day."

Elle takes another sip of her tea.

"You could say the same thing about Signals though, couldn't you? If Olympus is designed to do everything that Signals can do and more, why should anyone even bother downloading Signals in the future?"

I shrug.

"That's for the individual consumer to decide. Maybe some people are just looking for a dating app or a social networking platform and nothing else. Personally, I think you'd be a fool not to download Olympus anyway just because of the sheer *magnitude* of everything that comes with it. But at the end of the day, Signals remains a profitable brand enjoyed by hundreds of millions of people worldwide. If we end up cannibalizing that brand down the road, we'll re-evaluate our current stance. But for now, they don't have to be mutually exclusive."

Elle takes a moment to finish writing whatever she's writing before putting the tip of her pen to her lips.

"Okay. So, again, *assuming* you're able to make all this happen, what's the advantage to using Olympus? I understand that you're trying to create 'one app to rule them all' here, but what's the actual selling point? Less visual clutter on our screens? It sounds like instead of having a bunch of apps do a bunch of different things and take up a bunch of space, you're creating one app that does a bunch of different things and still takes up a bunch of space in the end. What's the difference?"

It's only after I've taken a sizeable swig of my cold, watered-down latte that I remember the ladybug that crawled into it. Oh well. Too late now.

"Olympus isn't only social networking and all the daily functions and cross-integrations I've described. Yes, it's designed to be a kind of 'master app' like you alluded to, but it's also unique in that it's kind of a—well, for lack of a better word—kind of a club. Or, a secret society, maybe—that's not so secret—but that's still extremely exclusive.

"This is where some of the monetary aspects come into play beyond just run-of-the-mill advertisements and in-app purchasing. Everything I've described so far is free to access for anyone who downloads the app, but there are also different membership levels and tiered perks that users can opt into after they're onboarded, some of which are more expansive and valuable than others. But it's all up to the individual user to decide just what kind of rewards and opportunities they want access to. No one is forced into anything they don't want."

Judging by her facial expression, Elle's skepticism seems to have given way to curiosity and perhaps even outright intrigue.

"What kinds of rewards?"

I smile at her.

"Honestly, without trying to sound too vague or evasive: anything and everything you can probably imagine. Early access to ticketing for concerts, sports, and other events before anybody else. VIP access and other benefits once you get there. Free, guaranteed admission to bars, nightclubs, trendy restaurants, pop-up art shows, you name it. Discounts on hotels, airfares, cars, clothing, jewelry, tech. Other incentives like cashback and a built-in points system that rewards your spending and activity with further perks and points of access to exclusive content and events."

Elle laughs.

"It sounds just like a credit card!"

"Sort of. There's certainly that aspect to it, and it is set up to encourage people to link their bank accounts and pay through Olympus with a digital wallet. But this is also a membership card in a way. The overarching idea here is that we're giving people a tool and a lifestyle aid that can do it all. Instead of dividing their time across a hundred different insufficient and unsubstantial apps, they can consolidate it in one single space and call it their forever home. And, if they're interested, that place can also dramatically improve their quality of life in every conceivable arena imaginable."

Elle looks up from her notepad.

"For the right price."

I shake my head.

"Free of charge to all users right from the very beginning. I think even the most hardened cynic would have to admit that we're revolutionizing a number of industries all at once, while simultaneously making modern civilization both easier and more accessible in the digital age. And all for free. Everything else I mentioned that comes at a cost is optional, but even that will pay for itself a million times over when you weigh those minor expenditures against the worlds of possibilities they immediately unlock."

Elle leans back in her chair a bit, crosses her legs, and gives me an appreciative look.

"Well, aren't you the perfect salesman. Quite the wordsmith, too. I can see why Richard likes you. You both just love talking yourselves off about how your big, revolutionary ideas are going to change the world."

I'm a bit taken aback. Her tone is sincere, but what she's actually saying falls just short of being hostile.

"Excuse me. I'm not trying to 'talk myself off'. I was just under the impression that you came here to learn more about Olympus, and—well, that's exactly what Olympus is."

Elle immediately dons an apologetic mask as she packs the notepad and pen away in her messenger bag.

"I meant no offense, Ethan. I've covered Richard long enough to know better than to doubt him. If I sounded skeptical or cynical, it's only because it's my job to question the things that people tell me. And usually, I have to sift through a river of bullshit to find the nuggets of truth I can actually write and publish."

Elle hits a button on her phone and pockets it before standing up and pulling the messenger bag up over her arm. I also rise to my feet. None of this action seems to bother our redheaded companion, who still sits slumped forward in his chair, drooling slightly on the sweat-stained collar of his shirt.

"I'm assuming you know then, Elle, that none of this is bullshit. I might be one of the newer members on the team, but I've also seen enough already to know firsthand that all of this is very real, very immediate, and very exciting."

Elle Maguire takes her tea in one hand and extends the other for a parting handshake.

"I don't doubt it for a second. Like I said, far be it from me to ever hedge my bets against Richard Charon spinning straw into gold where tech is concerned."

She gives me a knowing wink.

"I just think it's cute how he's already got you drinking the Kool-Aid, that's all."

Elle starts to walk a couple steps toward the patio gate before turning back to me.

"Thank you for the time today, Ethan. I'll be in touch if I need anything else. Oh, and I hope Nolan gets to feeling better, too."

She tosses her cup into the trash before exiting through the gate onto the sidewalk and then walking out of view up the street.

CHAPTER EIGHT

I'm not quite sure how I feel about what just happened. Without the benefit of listening to the playback recording of our conversation or reading any of Elle's scribbled notes, I feel like I handled myself quite well, especially given all the chaos and confusion that preceded the interview. I was never at a loss for words, and none of her questions felt out of reach. She even called me a 'wordsmith' at the end of the interview.

She also called me a 'salesman', though, and politely but unapologetically insinuated I may be full of bullshit and already drinking the company Kool-Aid.

It is what it is, though. What's done is done. I need to get Nolan out of here before he gets us both kicked out. It's a wonder no one's said or done anything up to this point, although I guess he didn't really do anyone any harm after he passed out in his chair. Other than me, of course.

"Nolan. NOLAN!"

I try shaking him several times. His head jerks around on his neck but largely remains loose and unresponsive. If it wasn't for the sound of his heavy breathing, it'd be easy to assume he was dead.

After an embarrassing amount of shaking,

prodding, poking, and subdued but forceful shouting into a hand cupped over his ear, he finally starts showing signs of real life and movement again. Nolan mostly keeps his eyes closed, but he does allow me to help him into a standing position.

Once we're vertical, I can tell right away that there's no way he's going to truly wake up. Whatever he's got in his system still has him knocked out for the most part, and it's a wonder I can even keep him propped upright with his arm slung over my shoulders.

Doing my best to ignore the stares from all the other café patrons around us, I half-walk, half-carry him out through the patio gate Elle used earlier. It's not an easy task. He's essentially dead weight on my side, and he's anything but thin and frail. In fact, Nolan's never seemed denser to me than right now as I drag him out onto the West Hollywood sidewalk.

I have half a mind to just leave him out here. It'd be all too easy to slide him down into a bush or a bus stop bench nearby and just speed off in the opposite direction. Hell, I might not even have to run. It's a Friday afternoon in broad daylight on a busy city street. There'd be nothing suspicious about it. Passersby would take one look at him and assume he's either homeless or passed out from overindulging—which is true—and walk right on by without a second thought.

It's only basic human decency that keeps me going and towing him along at my side. Well, that, and the fact that Elle Maguire at least knows Nolan made it to the interview, and also knows that when she left us, we were still seated together. I'm not sure how close she actually is to Charon, but if it got back to him that Nolan was last seen in my company and that I abandoned him, that's not exactly a great look on my part.

No one says a word to me as I lug this unconscious man down the street. People stare, sure, but no one actually says anything. At long last, I see the Jag parked up ahead at a meter that's flashing red. No ticket on the dashboard, though, which is a relief. I fish my keys out of my pocket and unlock the doors in advance to try and make getting Nolan in easier.

It helps, but not by much. I still have to sort of throw his dead weight into the passenger seat. Once his legs and feet are all inside and the seatbelt's strapped across his chest and lap, I close the door behind him and walk around to the driver's side.

What's my plan here? I've spent so much time just trying to get him out of the coffee shop and into my car that I haven't really given any thought as to where I'm taking him. My original plan was to go back to work after the interview. But what am I supposed to do with Nolan? I can't carry him into the office like this. But I also can't just leave him in my car, either.

"Nolan. Nolan! Wake up. WAKE UP!"

This is ridiculous. Honestly, what I should be doing is filming this and keeping it for blackmail. The next time he calls me 'Mr. Mai Tai' or says something crude or demeaning, I could just pull up the video and effectively silence him on the spot.

"NOLAN! Where are we going? Am I taking you to work, or am I taking you home?"

Not that I even know where his home is. Maybe he's got a wallet hidden somewhere with a driver's license and an address on it. Considering how skin-tight his stained jeans are, you'd think I'd be able to see it on him. It could be just a money clip though, or something with the ID and a few credit cards and not much else. Or maybe he has that stuff in his cell phone case somewhere.

I'm rummaging around his pants pockets, trying my best to minimize the actual physical contact between my hands and the feel of his legs beneath the fabric, when he lets out a gurgling sound that's new.

"Nolan. Nolan, wake up. It's Ethan."

His eyes are still closed, but the gurgling sound continues. Should I be worried that he's swallowing his tongue or choking on his own vomit right now? I lean down lower to try and get a better vantage point of whatever it is that's happening in his mouth.

"*Ughh... ghh... ghh...*"

With a great deal of disgust, I reach over to try and pry his jaw open a bit, because it *really* looks like he's choking from here.

Immediately, he sprays yellow-grey chunks of vomit across the windshield, dashboard, and floor of my car. It's only thanks to my quick reflexes that I'm able to jerk my hand back in time to avoid the sickening explosion.

"FUCK!"

I let out a furious exclamation and punch the steering wheel with the hand that came so close to getting thrown up on. My knuckles hit the horn and the car lets out a loud beeping momentary blast.

I'm not sure if it's the horn or the puke, but Nolan finally seems to be stirring.

"*Ughh... where am I?*"

"You're in my car, motherfucker, and you just threw up all over it!"

Another groan. His eyes are still closed, but he's working his lips like he's trying to talk. Bits of puke and saliva still dangle from his cheeks and chin.

"*Ughh…*"

I'm very close to throwing him out onto the street. Even Charon would have to understand why after everything that's happened.

"Where am I taking you, Nolan?! You can't go back to work like this."

He actually has the gall to turn away from me and get into a kind of seated fetal position like a child. With a clunk, his sweaty, freckled forehead hits the passenger window.

I would smack him, but I don't want to get his sick or his sweat on me.

"NOLAN! DO NOT fucking pass out again! Where are we going right now?"

"Home…"

"Where is that?"

"What?"

"WHERE IS HOME? WHAT IS YOUR MOTHERFUCKING ADDRESS?!"

Silence.

That does it. I'm throwing him out on the curb. I take my seatbelt off and start to open my door when I hear him mumble something. It kind of sounds like he maybe said 'Mulholland'.

"What?"

"Mulholland."

"Mulholland Drive? That's where you live?"

"Yeah."

You've got to be kidding me. I pull out my phone and load a maps app.

"Where on Mulholland do you live?"

And, next question, how much is your salary?

It takes me asking the question three more times and flicking his left ear repeatedly to finally get a street address. I say it back to him twice to make sure it's accurate and not just gibberish he's spewing out. Nolan slurs his words again, but at least the sequence of numbers doesn't change when he gives it back to me. It will have to do.

We drive in miserable, putrid silence. I keep the air conditioning on full blast and the windows rolled all the way down. Truthfully, it's probably neither safe nor legal the way I drive with practically my whole head stuck out the driver's side window, but that's what I have to do to maintain my own self-composure and suppress the constant urge to vomit myself just from the smell of my car right now.

Mercifully, it's a very short trip from the coffee house in West Hollywood to the location he's given me up on Mulholland Drive, the famous winding road that looks out over all of Los Angeles from high above the hills.

I still can't believe he actually lives up here. We pass not one, but two celebrity home sightseeing vans stuffed full of tourists. Even if Nolan makes several times over what I make, I still can't fathom how he'd be able to afford a house up here. These are all multi-million-dollar mansions owned by the stars.

Whether or not he actually lives at the address we're headed to, I make up my mind to leave him there. If anyone asks afterward, I can honestly tell them that I drove Nolan to the exact location he gave me for his residence. It won't be my fault if it turns out he didn't know what he was talking about or if he doesn't have a way to get inside once we're there. Leaving him at the gate or at the front door is more than generous at this point after everything he's done to me these past couple hours.

We pull up next to a property that supposedly matches the address he gave me in my phone. Like most of the houses up here, you can't really see much from the street. Everything is buried behind gigantic, manicured hedges, shrubs, trees, fences, and walls. This house seems to have all of those features and qualities outside, too, plus a long row of cameras angled in various directions along the top.

I creep my car along the perimeter until we finally reach a gate that presumably stands as the only way in or out.

"We're here."

I say it as much to myself as I do to Nolan before cutting the ignition and clambering out from my seat. The sooner I can get out of this car, the better. I have no idea how I'll be able to stomach this stench the whole way home, but I guess I'll just have to deal with that problem in a minute here.

The street is quiet save for the occasional vehicle that passes us by. I suppose most people who live here are either at work or at home. It's really too hot to be out walking around right now midday. Plus, there's not really a sidewalk to use. Mulholland is notoriously windy and dangerous for motorists and pedestrians alike— primarily at night in the dark, sure, but it's still no picnic in the day.

I purposefully ignore the fact that Nolan still has his sweaty forehead pressed up against the glass when I open the passenger door. When I do, his whole upper body falls out. If it wasn't for the seatbelt strapping him in, he'd probably tumble completely out of the car and land flat on his face. It's a fantasy that summons an immediate smile and makes me feel just a little bit better about this whole situation.

That pleasant feeling is quickly dispelled when I start having to navigate his vomit-soaked body to get him unbuckled and pulled up out of the car seat. I hold my breath as I loop a couple arms around his chest, drag him backward up to the gate, and then drop him in a stinking heap at its base.

I'm wiping the sweat from my forehead with the back of my arm when I hear a woman's voice coming up from behind us.

"Excuse me! What are you doing?"

I spin around to face a blonde woman pulling two lunging dogs back on their leashes.

"Ethan!"

Isla Charon's whole demeanor changes instantly, going from a bristly concerned citizen—and rightfully so—to a bubbly lifelong friend. She runs up the last several yards that separate us and hurtles into my body, enveloping me in a big grizzly bear of a hug that just might choke the life out of me if my heart doesn't give out first from complete surprise and shock.

Castor and Pollux, the two Great Danes, sense the shift in their master's mood just as quickly as it happens. The dogs excitedly lick at me from either side and pant profusely, their cavernous mouths gaping as they lap at my legs with bright pink tongues.

"What the devil are you doing up here? And who's this you've got with you? Is that Nolie?!"

I gently pat her on the back and eventually manage to break free of the hug. It takes a few more backward steps for me to get clear of the dogs, though. Isla helps when she finally realizes what's happening and decides to rein them in by their leashes.

"Isla! Hey, hi! This is so weird, running into you. What are you doing here?"

She laughs and gives me a look like I'm utterly insane.

"What am I doing here? What are *you* doing here? I *live* here."

That really sends me for a jolt.

"Wait… what? I thought this was where Nolan lived?"

"It is."

Isla laughs again and shakes her hair back from her face.

"Oh, darling, if you could see your face right now; it's positively precious. It's Richard and my home, but Nolan's been staying with us here for a while."

Her eyes move over to the prostrate form lying on her metaphorical doorstep, and she shakes her head slowly.

"*Tsk, tsk.* Looks like you boys did some celebrating after the TrendBeat interview, I see."

I blush.

"No, no, not at all, actually. We just came straight here from that. No celebrating."

Isla looks confused.

"What happened, then?"

As much as I may have wanted to initially avoid this conversation, there's no getting around it now. Not only did Nolan show up late and out of his mind to his own interview, but he also ragged on me to Elle, passed out in front of her, slept through the entirety of our conversation, and then threw up all over my car. And if all that wasn't reason enough to tattle on him, he also verbally directed me to drop him off at the Charons' house, and now Isla's here in front of it asking me about what happened. It's time for the truth.

"Honestly, I don't know. Between you and me, he showed up like this to the coffee shop. We were supposed to meet half an hour before the interview to go over Richard's notes and our strategy, but he never showed up. Elle got there first, and I was ready to start without him when he staggered in like this."

I briefly debate and ultimately decide not to offer up any personal opinions on what could be the root cause of his behavior. After all, it's pretty obvious, and Isla's not blind.

"Isla, I ended up doing the interview by myself. I think I did a good job, but I can't be sure. Nolan's the one who had all your husband's talking points prepared. Maybe Richard could reach out to Elle when he gets a chance, just to make sure everything he wanted in the article gets communicated? I'd hate to be the one responsible for anything missing."

She lets out a long sigh and turns toward Nolan.

"Whatever are we going to do with you, Nolie?"

After a moment, she swivels her focus back to me.

"If there's anything missing, it sounds like you'd hardly be the responsible party for that problem, darling. Nevertheless, I'll make sure and speak with Richard just to see how he wants to handle Elle. Thank you for bringing the matter to our attention. And for your honesty."

I nod. We both look over at Nolan, watching him breathe and bake under the bright California sun.

"Of course. Can I help you take him inside? It looks like you've got your hands full."

Isla's eyes flit between her canine companions, each sitting silent and dutiful at the end of a leash on her flanks.

"Well, aren't you sweet! No, I believe I can manage. Once the lads are inside, I should be able to handle old naughty Nolie here myself."

She drops her voice to a conspiratorial whisper and leans her face closer.

"Believe it or not, this isn't the first time this sort of thing has happened. Maybe I should leave him out here just a spell. A little sunshine might do the boy some good. What do you think?"

A little sunshine might leave this boy red as a lobster.

But I nod, smile, and eke out a chuckle.

"Absolutely. Well, if you're sure you've got it, I guess I'll be on my way then. Have to get back to the office before Portia sends out a search party. Have a nice weekend, Isla."

The hug I give her is significantly more awkward than any hug she's ever given me, but there's nothing I can do about that now.

Isla beams, nonetheless.

"You do the same, darling."

I'm halfway to my car when I turn back to her.

"Isla, if you do get Nolan all tucked away and everything before Richard gets home, maybe you could just tell him that we *did* go out for a drink or two after the interview? He doesn't really need to know everything that I told you about what happened. Not unless you think he does, that is."

There's no logical reason I should still be sticking my neck out for this guy. But for some reason, I just can't help it. I'm going to be a dad soon. I need to start acting like the best possible man I can be. Maybe that's the reason that even after everything he's done, I still don't want to see Nolan get into any serious trouble over this.

Isla reaches for the keypad on the front of her gate. Castor and Pollux stand on either side of Nolan and stare down the barrels of their enormous muzzles into his face.

Are they guarding him, or are they sizing him up?

Their master finishes tapping in the code with her long, slender fingers, and the large, iron gate starts to slowly roll open.

"Don't worry, darling. It will be our little secret."

CHAPTER NINE

Charon and Isla must have orchestrated this plan for our weekly meeting well before any of us arrived, because without any preamble, explanation, or warning, Isla just stood up, opened the magazine in her hands, found the right page, and started reading aloud. I only realized what was happening seconds before it began when I noticed Charon's scowling profile on the publication's cover beneath the title wordmark.

My original understanding was that the article wasn't supposed to be published until at least the November issue of the monthly magazine, and maybe even the December edition. More than a full month had passed since the interview, but no one had said anything to me about it coming out now in late October.

I'd asked Charon if he'd had a chance to call up Elle and add anything I may have forgotten to the story. He admitted he'd been in contact with her, but only to suggest they delay the feature's release in order to shave off some of the time between the publication date and the actual launch of Olympus itself.

Evidently, either Elle flat-out ignored that request, her editors couldn't honor it, or Charon changed his mind. Of those three options, I easily figured the last one to be the likeliest.

Isla's been reading aloud now for several minutes, and I've done my best to construct a neutral facial expression that hopefully masks some of the beaming, overflowing pride I feel within. It's difficult swallowing the urge to let my eyes wander hungrily around the room so I can check in on everyone's reactions, and I've already glimpsed a good deal of them.

Portia is resting her chin on her hand and watching Isla speak with a slightly amused expression that looks just a bit surprised to me.

Nolan is glowering at a corner of the ceiling across from him with his arms folded tightly against his chest.

Bing is smiling and rapidly bouncing his knee beneath the table, occasionally giggling at random intervals in the article while picking his fingernails and glancing feverishly at his watch.

Charon sits completely still in his chair and just stares at me unblinkingly.

Isla's face is a poster of pure satisfaction as she savors the taste of each and every word she pronounces to the room.

"'Despite his youthful appearance and relative newness to the tech sector, Olympus's director of development, Ethan Birch, carried himself with all the moxie and confidence you'd expect from a much more senior player in the game. Right away, it was obvious why Charon would choose someone like Birch to be his latest disciple.

Even still, I found myself initially a bit dubious of some of the more ambitious claims and promises made concerning Olympus's apparently limitless potential. And yet, each and every time and without fail, Birch addressed my skepticism head-on before proceeding to politely dismantle it with patient but implacable conviction.

By the end of our interview, I found myself utterly convinced that everything he had just shared with me, astounding and incredible as it may be in theory, wasn't just planned to happen—it was destined to happen.

And why not? Playing off the mythological aspects of the Olympus moniker, it only makes too much sense that its creator, Dr. Richard Charon—widely viewed as the preeminent titan of his industry—chose such a name for the kind of herculean undertaking that would be worthy of the gods.'"

Isla lets the weight of Elle's words hang in the air for a moment as she closes her eyes and drinks it all in. Softly, slowly, she folds the magazine shut in her hands with a gentle reverence, opens her eyes, gives me one of her trademark smiles, and then melts back into her seat.

Charon, who has been a statue since his wife first stood up and started reading the TrendBeat article, finally moves. He shifts forward in his chair to rest two elbows on the tabletop and begins dragging his crooked fingernails through the length of his long beard, starting high up on his whiskered cheekbones and running all the way down until they meet at a point.

"Well done, Ethan... and well done, Nolan. I doubt I would have said anything differently had I been there myself. This is exactly how I envisioned everything unfolding."

I can't help but blush. Portia gives me a tiny thumbs-up that only I can see from across the table. Meanwhile, Nolan's face looks as red as I imagine mine to be right now—though I'm sure for a very different reason.

Charon isn't done though.

"My only criticism… and maybe this is more question than criticism… is about the first paragraph in the very beginning. Perhaps I misheard, but it sounded like we listed our public release date as being Christmas Day. Am I mistaken?"

There's an awful sudden silence in the room that I don't immediately understand. The only real sound is Bing's knee bouncing up and down and the repeating little squeak the movement elicits from his chair. As it so happens, Bing is also the first one to break the silence with his voice.

"No, that's what I heard as well."

He lets out another weird giggle sound that's mainly just air before shaking his head and grinding his teeth together.

Isla's brows are furrowed as she flips through the magazine until she finds the page in question. She reads for a second in silence, then closes the magazine, looks up at her husband, and gives him a small nod.

Charon's fingers stop combing down his beard.

"Ah."

This silence is worse than the first one. Even Bing's knee stops its incessant bouncing and comes to stillness. I glance over at Portia for a clue as to what's happening, but her eyes are locked on Charon, and there's a shadow of fear over her face that I don't think I've seen before.

As a matter of fact, it seems that everyone's attention is on Charon now, whose own eyes seem to have rolled up into the back of his head. Even if I wanted to ask him what's wrong, I think I'd be too afraid to do so at this very moment.

If I can't get a read on what's happening from Portia, my next best bet is Bing. Telepathically, I try to ask the director of engineering what exactly is going on right now and why it feels like someone just sucked all the oxygen out of the conference room.

It's no use, though. Like everyone else in here, his focus is magnetically sealed on Charon. Even without his gyrating leg, Bing looks like he's short-circuiting on the inside. His cheek keeps twitching, and he's still noticeably mashing his teeth and breathing funny.

Charon finally speaks again.

"Bingham... this issue of TrendBeat hits the racks tomorrow. It goes live online later tonight."

Bing's knee starts pumping again as Charon hisses.

"Tell me that we can make this... adjustment... happen."

All of the faces in the room move now from Charon to Bing. The twenty-year-old tech prodigy has his shaggy black head in his hands when he lets out the giggle-cough-thing again.

"Oh, man..."

I can see his jugular vein throbbing in the side of his thick, wet neck.

"*Man.* This is a—this is a three-week jump, we all understand that, right? So—so, instead of twelve and fifteen, we're talking nine and twelve now, right?"

Charon's chin dips, almost imperceptibly.

"That is correct. Will it be a problem?"

This time, Bing actually gets out more of a solid laugh as his head slowly transitions from shaking horizontally to shaking vertically in a kind of crazed bobbing motion. He sucks down air, wipes his forehead, checks his watch, sighs, looks back across the table at

Charon, then looks down at his fingernails. With trembling hands, he starts picking and peeling at the skin around his cuticles.

"No. Nine weeks? To get a beta test ready? No. No problem, I mean. We—we can do that. We'll do it. Whatever. Umm… we can… we'll make it happen."

There's a dawning thought in my brain of what may have just happened. And if I'm right, it's all my fault.

Well, it's also Nolan's fault, really. But unlike a month ago when I was the one who had to directly suffer the consequences for someone else's mistakes, this time it looks like Bing is the one who's going to have to unfairly take the brunt of a costly error that's no fault of his own.

Charon licks his lips and studies Bing another moment, then places his veined hands on the table and pushes himself up to a standing position.

"Good. I will leave you all to it, then."

Without another word, he drifts around us and disappears out the door.

Isla stands, picks up the magazine, and follows in her husband's wake. Just before she reaches the exit, she pauses, looks down at me, smiles tenderly, and lays the copy of TrendBeat in front of my hands on the table.

"You still did a magnificent job, darling. Don't you fret."

She ruffles the hair behind my ear affectionately, then walks out of the room herself.

The four of us who are left sit in silence for a second, save for the sound of Bing's knee rapping up steadily against the bottom of the table.

I'm the one who breaks the loaded quiet this time.

"Bing, listen, I'm so sorry. I don't know what

happened–"

Nolan cuts in with a sneer.

"I know exactly what happened. You told Elle we were *releasing to the public* by Christmas instead of just *launching the beta* by Christmas. That's what happened."

He has to be out of his mind.

"Really? Really, Nolan? You really wanna go there right now?"

He shrugs, folds his hands behind his head, and leans back far in his chair.

"To the victor go the spoils, both the good and the bad. You want to take all the credit? Go ahead. But you'd better be ready to take some responsibility, too, when shit hits the fan."

I jump up out of my seat.

"Shit would have never hit the fan in the first place if you hadn't–"

But I stop myself mid-sentence. I've kept the truth of Nolan's condition that day to myself for weeks now. Outside of Isla, no one else knows—not Charon, not Bing, not Portia. Nolan and I have never even talked about it. When I saw him the Monday following, it was as if nothing had happened.

Granted, there have been plenty of moments over the past month where I've wanted to say something. Not necessarily to Charon, and not necessarily even to Bing or Portia, though I've grown close with both of them.

Mainly, I've wanted to say something to Nolan. Every day, he's acted the same way toward me: condescending, spiteful, mocking, jealous. I've been waiting for the moment where he's going to push me too far and I'll be forced to reveal just how miserably fucked-up and worthless he was during our 'joint interview' with Elle Maguire.

Well, maybe this is that moment. Maybe he wants an excuse to feel that his position has been threatened, and his exalted status as Charon's prized lapdog is in jeopardy. Maybe he's itching for a fight, and he's just waiting for me to make the first move so he can properly retaliate.

Nolan stares me down from his seat, still reclined and making every effort to appear nonchalant and unfazed.

"If I hadn't what? Go on, Mr. Big Shot Magazine Star. Mr. *'Moxie'*, Mr. *'Implacable Conviction'*. What do you wanna say?"

I actually might just say it right here and right now. But then Portia stands up and lays a hand on my shoulder.

"Guys. This is beyond stupid. You both need to cool it."

Before either of us can respond, Bing jerks back in his wheeled chair, stands, and starts moving toward the exit.

Portia's eyes follow him with concern.

"Bing, are you okay?"

Bing turns his head back over his shoulder and answers all of us and none of us as he reaches the door.

"Me? Yeah, I—I'm just gonna–"

His voice trails off as he throws his weight into the handle and then spills into the hallway and out of sight.

Portia looks back and forth between Nolan and me.

"I'll go make sure he's okay. *Do not* fucking fight each other. Okay? We all have enough problems as is right now; we don't need any more."

She waits expectantly until she gets an affirmative

nod from me and some kind of pouty shrug from Nolan; it wouldn't be enough for me personally, but I guess it is for her.

"Good. Behave like men, not like boys."

Portia gives us each another threatening look, squeezes my shoulder with her fingers, and then hurries out the door to go find Bing.

Nolan watches her leave. Like, *really* watches her leave. It just makes me hate him all the more. For the good of my own career, though, I swallow my fury and move toward the door myself.

"You think you're such hot shit. Don't you?"

His voice stops me dead in my tracks as I put my hand on the metal handle.

"You've got this whole superiority complex just because you're the shiny new toy in town. You don't think I get that? You really think I haven't been there myself? I was the child prodigy once, too. The golden boy; the apple of his eye. Back when we did Signals. Let me give you a little piece of advice you didn't ask for, bud: soak it all in, and enjoy it while it lasts. Because sooner or later, you're gonna be sitting right where I am. And I promise you, I will be there that day to tell you I told you so."

I give him a pitying look over my shoulder.

"You owe me a hundred dollars for throwing up inside my Jaguar. I'll email you a copy of the receipt I got from the detailers."

For once, Nolan actually seems at a loss for how to respond, which was exactly my hope. I turn on my heel and walk out the door and down the hallway to my office.

While it's nowhere near as cavernous as Charon's

office, you could probably still fit two of my old office at VitaLyfe into my new one here at Olympus.

Highlights include a remote-control-operated, glass-covered, 'living' standing desk filled with succulents and river rocks; an ergonomic chair that may actually be more comfortable and more luxurious than the California king Allie and I share at home; a small but surprisingly accommodating sofa sectional for guests; a well-stocked mini-fridge of drinks and snacks that magically seems to replenish itself each day; and—my personal favorite—floor-to-ceiling window walls with breathtaking panoramic views of Los Angeles.

In keeping with the rest of the Olympus office, the floor is almost entirely covered in lush, green grass, and the ceiling is a verdant cornucopia of tropical hanging plants, vines, and flowers, with soft, golden, ambient lights interspersed and artfully camouflaged amidst the leafy foliage. There are cameras up there, too, of course, but at this point, I've pretty much forgotten they're even there.

Work is difficult for me today. It's hard to stay focused on any particular task with all the events of this morning still fresh and percolating in my head. And even though I know this situation isn't really my fault, I also know that it kind of is.

Considering I received absolutely zero help from Nolan, I didn't have Charon's notes, and I'd been with the company for less than five full days at the time of the interview, it's frankly miraculous I managed to come off sounding intelligent and informed at all. Truthfully, I'm a bit surprised the only real mistake I made was this date mix-up.

That said, I completely understand the shitstorm

I've just created for Bing. Yes, it was only one mistake, but that one mistake effectively vaporized three weeks of time from our rollout schedule. I'm no coder, but I've spent enough time around Bing and some of the other engineers in this office over the past month to get a sense of just how truly ambitious and unprecedented this project really is from the technical side of things.

Needless to say, losing a full quarter of the time they have left to come up with a product we can beta test probably isn't going to go over very well with anyone. I just hope they won't all blame me.

But of course they will. Even if Bing is nice enough not to reveal exactly what happened, anyone who picks up a copy of TrendBeat or searches for it online can read the story for themselves. And while Nolan's name does appear at the beginning of the article—*after* mine, I might add—he's never mentioned again thereafter.

Though surely no one would believe I'd have the power to cut three full weeks from the build-out schedule myself, right? They'd have to know that any edict that crazy and significant would need to come down from on high; from Charon himself and no one else. Even if they didn't assume that right away, I'm sure they'd either figure it out eventually, or Bing would let them know.

There's a light knock at my door before it pops open a crack. Portia sticks just her head through, like she's one of The Three Stooges or some kind of vaudeville comedian. It's a particularly goofy look, given the fact I can still see the rest of her body on the other side of the glass wall.

"Quit watching porn on the company computer!"

She yells it loud enough that anyone walking nearby

in the hallway will definitely hear her, but I laugh anyway. After exaggeratedly glancing in both directions behind her, Portia elects to come all the way in, closing the door as she does so.

"Oh, yeah. Some people definitely just heard me, in case you were wondering."

She crosses over to my desk and flicks me playfully on the earlobe. After I swat her away, she shuffles over to the sectional and dramatically collapses into the cushions. Portia then swings her black Converse sneakers up on top of the sofa ledge and presses the rubber soles flat against the glass wall behind the couch.

I don't know when she started doing it, but it wouldn't surprise me if this habit started well before I ever got here—as this used to be Chuck's office, after all. And while I do find the pose charming in its casual ease and comfortability, I also find it consistently challenging on my end to avoid seeing more of Portia's chest than she probably intends me to when she lies like this on her back.

Right now, the upside-down face below that chest is giving me a wicked grin.

"So, Ethan. Inquiring minds want to know: did you and Orange Crush behave yourselves after I left the room, or did the dick-measuring contest get physical?"

I lean back in my chair and rub at my temples.

"*Ughh.* He's a real piece of work, isn't he? I'm trying. I know it might not look like it all the time, but I really am trying. He just makes it so hard. I honestly think he wants me to hit him sometimes, I really do."

Portia wiggles the toes of her shoes against the glass and watches her feet.

"Oh, one hundred percent. That's exactly what he

wants you to do. And it's all the more reason not to give in and give him that satisfaction. Remember that."

She's right. But of course, it's also easy for her to say. If Nolan antagonizes her the same way he does me, I've never seen it myself or heard about it from her.

"How's Bing? I feel terrible."

Portia stops tap-dancing on the window.

"Umm… not great, honestly. If you wanted to go and see him, it probably wouldn't be the worst idea in the world. He's doing his best to project confidence while selling the change to his troops, but you can tell he's really shaken up by it. I don't blame him."

I lean forward in my chair.

"Do you blame me?"

"No, not at all. You said Nolan showed up late but ultimately in time for the actual interview, right? If that's the case, he should have been able to correct any misunderstandings about the dates. Right?"

Even inverted, her probing look makes me a bit uncomfortable. Sometimes, I wonder if she knows the truth—whether because Isla told her, or just because she knows Nolan well enough to suspect what actually happened.

Either way, I'm not about to say anything outright unless she does first. Tensions are already high enough as is between me and Nolan without me choosing to rehash his dirty laundry at work.

I get up to my bare feet like a prisoner preparing for the gallows.

"Where is he?"

"Who, Nolan?"

"No. Bing."

Portia lets her legs fall back down flat on the

cushions with a heavy sigh.

"If I tell you, you have to promise me not to give him any shit about it. I mean, you totally can one day in the future, but just not today. I'm not sure he'd be able to handle it."

"Of course, I won't. Where is he?"

She lets out another heavy sigh, and with a dramatic flair, begins to roll her lithe, tattooed body up off the sofa and back to a slumped standing position.

"Come on. I'll show you, actually."

Of all the weird and magical rooms in this office building, I have to admit I'm more than a little surprised when Portia leads me to a door with 'Nursing Room' labeled on the placard outside.

"Really?"

She nods.

"Really, really."

Portia then points a finger of warning in my face.

"Remember: no jokes. Not today."

I try to shoo her away.

"I know, I've got it. Thanks."

She gives me another dramatic finger-point and a stern frown, pats me on the back, and then walks off to leave us alone. When she's gone, I knock lightly at the door.

"Bing? Bing, are you in there?"

Silence.

"It's me; it's Ethan. Can I come in?"

More silence.

"Hello?"

I think I hear soft footsteps approaching the other side of the door, and then comes the unmistakable sound of a deadbolt being drawn out of place. After another second or two, I try the handle, and it opens easily.

Inside, the room is small and dark. From the light outside in the hallway that spills in, I can see that there's a recliner chair and a side table set up next to it with a lamp on top, but the lamp is turned off. It takes my eyes a minute to adjust to the dark.

Bing is seated in the chair, which he has extended to its full reclined length. His bare feet dangle over the edge of the chair bottom in midair, but otherwise, his entire body is cocooned in the wide, plush embrace of the recliner.

Once I feel like I can see well enough not to run into anything in the small room—not that there's all that much to run into—I amble over to the wall opposite the chair and slide my back down against it until I'm seated on the grassy floor.

"Hey, Bing."

"Hi, Ethan."

His voice doesn't immediately sound sad, at least. He just sounds tired. And, strangely, old. Maybe it's just my imagination, but the pitch of his voice seems to have dropped a full octave.

"How you doing?"

It's a ludicrous question to ask, given the circumstances that brought us here, and I regret it at once.

Bing is too nice to call me out on it, though. Whereas Portia would answer with sarcasm and Nolan would answer with contempt, Bing just answers with honesty.

"Not too whippy, I have to admit."

"I'm sorry to hear that, buddy."

I try to make out what his face looks like in the darkness, but it's pretty much impossible.

"Bing, would it be okay if I turned that lamp on? It's so dark in here."

There's a soft click as Bing reaches over toward the lamp and illuminates the room himself. When he's done, he slides back fully into the chair and tilts his head up toward the ceiling. I'm not positive, but the faint red streaks running up and down his plump cheeks make me think he's been crying. His eyes are closed now, though.

"Did Portia send you in here to cheer me up?"

"No. No, Bing, not at all. I asked her where you were because I wanted to come see you myself."

I swallow hard.

"I wanted to apologize. For what happened earlier. With TrendBeat. I hope you know it was never my intention to screw you over like that."

Bing lets out a sharp exhalation and covers his face with his hands.

"Yeah, dude, *what was up with that?* Not trying to point fingers here, but how can something like that even happen? Neither you or Nolan noticed you guys got the date wrong?"

What can I tell him? Even if I told him the truth about Nolan being incapacitated and me handling the interview solo, it wouldn't change the fact that I still gave the wrong date to the magazine.

"Honestly, Bing, no. Neither one of us noticed. It came up just once and it was in the midst of a much longer, more complicated explanation of Olympus and all that it's meant to do and be. I had it in my head all along that Christmas Day was the date I needed to remember, but I just forgot to clarify that it was for the beta test and not for the final release. I'm not sure what else to say, other than I'm sorry. I am so incredibly sorry I put you in this situation. And if there's anything I can do to help, you just need to let me know what it is, and I'll do it."

He peeks open one eye to look at me from behind his thick, rectangular glasses and between the fingers of his hand.

"You think you can figure out a way to compress a couple terabytes of complex data into a single packaged app that can fit universally on any device?"

My jaw drops as I do my best to give him a playful smile.

"Is there anything *else* I can do to help, besides that?"

It works. Bing breaks into a smile himself and then even a sharp cackle of a laugh that slowly grows into a steady cough. His face reddening, he doubles over in the chair as spasms rock his body. I make a move to stand up and help him, but he waves me off with his hand before bringing it back to shield his mouth. When the coughing fit finally subsides, he digs a shiny wooden box out of his pocket that immediately looks familiar to me.

"What is that?"

I jerk my head in the direction of the object.

Bing's eyes dart up from the box and meet mine. Bizarrely, he looks a bit suspicious now.

"What, this? You don't know what this is?"

I shake my head no, and Bing's eyes grow wide.

"Really? No one's given you Viaticum yet?"

A callous snort erupts from my nose before I can stop it.

"You've got to be kidding me."

Bing doesn't smile or laugh.

I don't want to offend him, but I just can't help myself now.

"Why are you taking Viagra at work?"

This time, he does laugh, and it's more of the same from before; a weird cough-giggle-laugh that he has to fight for control over.

"No, no. Not Viagra. That's a good one, though. *Viaticum*. You know… Charon's obol?"

Bing's eyes glint behind his glasses as he sits and waits for a light to go on in my head that just isn't coming. When he finally realizes that, he goes on.

"Well, if Richard hasn't talked to you about them yet or given you any, then I don't know if it's my place to be the first one. Let's just say that these here are kind of like brain boosters. That's what I call them, at least. My little brain boosters. And I'm going to have to up the dosage now, thanks to you and Nolan."

He opens the gleaming case and shakes out a couple of the thin, circular, white pill-things into his open palm, then throws them back into his mouth and swallows with a gulp.

"What are they exactly?"

Bing's pudgy face could be sheepish now, or it could be suspicious again. Maybe a bit of both at the same time, actually.

"What, you're some kind of narc now, too? Come on, man, I can't take much more of this today."

He extends the glossy container in my direction.

"Want to take a look, or a sniff, or whatever else it is you need to do? They're completely legal and completely harmless. I only take them because they help me concentrate and think outside the box so I can solve unsolvable problems. You know… see things that weren't there before."

My curiosity gets the better of me as I move up onto my knees, reach forward, take the small pillbox, and look inside. There are maybe two dozen more paper-colored disc capsules in there, each about the size of a silver dollar.

"I guess you're welcome to try one, if you want. Just don't tell anybody I was the first person to give you one. I think it's sort of Richard's thing."

"What's in it?"

Bing shakes his head.

"I don't know. Some big mystery. Apparently, Richard has an old business partner or an old college roommate or something who works in natural supplements and vitamins, so I think he gets massive quantities of them for free."

I hand the box back to Bing and get to my feet.

"Hey, if they help, I'm all for them. Well, Bing, I really wish I knew more about what you do. Maybe then I could actually help you right now."

He wiggles his way forward to the edge of the recliner and allows me to assist him up and onto his feet again. When he's fully vertical, Bing bestows on me the sad, knowing smile of a martyr.

"I know you do, Ethan. And I really wish you could, too."

Then he gives me a quick pat on the shoulder to try and dissipate some of the somber mood.

"It's all right, dude. I'll figure it out. We all will. Don't worry so much."

He tries to laugh again as we move toward the door, but he's unsuccessful. And once we're outside, his demeanor instantly changes. Bing looks around to make sure no one's noticed us coming out together from the nursing room, gives me a curt nod, and then takes off at a brisk pace back toward his office without another word.

I watch him disappear before turning and moseying back to my own office.

There's that same feeling again inside me, just like the one I had immediately following the TrendBeat interview. It's a weird combination of pride, relief, concern, and uncertainty. I feel like I've completed what I set out to accomplish, but at the same time, I'm afraid I haven't really done or said much of anything at all.

When I get back to my office, I discover with a shock that Charon is in there waiting for me. I don't see him at all as I first walk in. He's dressed as he always is in all black, and, seated in the charcoal sectional, he blends in perfectly with his surrounding environment like it's some form of natural camouflage. It's only after I'm halfway across the room to my desk when he clears his throat that I jump back a full foot in surprise.

"*Jesus*—Richard! I didn't see you there."

"Apologies for startling you."

Charon runs his tongue over his lips.

"How is our director of engineering doing?"

I take a seat behind my desk.

"Bing? Did you—did Portia tell you?"

He crosses one long leg over his knee.

"I try to make it my business to know as much as I can at all times about those I employ. How is he?"

Am I ever going to escape this feeling that I'm some kind of informant on my coworkers?

"He's—he's doing better. We had a productive

conversation. I think he'll be all right."

Charon's face darkens.

"You think… or you know?"

How does he expect me to answer that?

"I think if anyone can figure this out, it's Bing. I have complete faith in him."

Now, Charon looks amused.

"Do you now? Such unwavering belief in someone you just met a month ago?"

What is this we're doing right now?

"I'll admit I'm still learning the ins-and-outs of the technical side of things here, so maybe I'm not the best judge. But I do know that Bing works as hard, or harder, than anyone else I've met so far. From everything I've seen, heard, and experienced, I think he's brilliant."

The old man strokes the tip of his beard between his thumb and forefinger.

"I think so, too."

His gaze drifts away from me until he's staring out at the city around us through the clear glass walls. A news helicopter flutters by and Charon tracks it with his eyes like a predator on the prowl.

"What do you think of Portia?"

"What do you mean?"

I'm immediately aware that my office door is wide open.

"I mean: what do you think of her? How is your relationship?"

"It's great. I've stuck close to her, like you suggested, this past month. She got me up to speed extremely quickly with everything. She's my go-to person whenever I have a question, and she always seems to know the right answer."

"Portia… is very resourceful… and extremely valuable to this company. It pleases me to hear that you two work together so well."

He doesn't look particularly pleased as he studies the swerving path of the helicopter with a dour expression on his face.

"What about you and Nolan?"

Here we go…

"We're good, too. He's—he's definitely helped during this transition, as well."

Charon shifts his focus back to me.

"I only ask because I sense a great deal of tension between the two of you. Am I incorrect?"

Even though I've been here now for several weeks, it still amazes me just how much Charon stays in tune with everything around him. For an old guy who spends most of his time either holed up alone in his office meditating or out and about Los Angeles in private meetings with other tech moguls, entrepreneurs, and visionaries, he always seems to have a preternatural awareness and understanding of things he shouldn't.

I hesitate.

"Nolan and I are fine. I think—I think sometimes, the way he does certain things, or says certain things, it's maybe not the way I would do it. But then again, maybe he feels the same way about me. Anyway, it's nothing we can't work through. Nothing we haven't been working through already, even."

Charon's black eyes are hard as flint.

"Was TrendBeat one of those 'things' he did that you would have done differently?"

Does he know? I try to search for some further sign or indication that he's referring to what I think he is, but his face is inscrutable. He also shows no outward signs of elaborating anytime soon.

"Yeah, I would say so."

I can't tell if he's giving me permission to reveal something he already knows about or if I'm just imagining everything. No matter how much Isla seems to like me, there's really no reason to believe she wouldn't tell her own husband the truth. For all I know, I've been harboring Nolan's secret unnecessarily for weeks.

Charon studies me for a long time before speaking again.

"Interesting."

I try to think of something else to say, but nothing springs to mind, so I just sit in silence, feeling the enormous, oppressive weight of his judgment on my person, and wonder when or if this moment will ever end... until finally, it does. He rises from the couch like a towering plume of smoke billowing up into the atmosphere.

"Isla and I have a place together... a cabin out in the middle of the desert in Death Valley. We go there sometimes when we need to gain perspective... or find deeper clarities beyond the scope of what the city can afford us. I wonder if it would be of some use to all of us right now."

He waits. I guess he wants a response from me?

"You mean, like a retreat?"

Charon's lips twist into a warped, crooked smile between the bristling hairs of his beard and moustache.

"'Retreat' implies a backward movement. What I am talking about now is making a bold forward advancement. To make profound changes in your life, you need either inspiration or desperation. I believe that one or both of them will come to us if we do this now… all of us… together."

I hope my smile isn't as outwardly incredulous as it feels to me from the inside.

"You don't mean 'now' like 'right now', though, do you?"

Charon's smile flickers away and is replaced by a stone mask of grim solemnity.

"What better time than right now? Our problem is fresh and new… our solution should be fresh and new. Perhaps a change of scenery is exactly what young Bingham needs to find his answers. It may also serve to strengthen your relationship with Portia… and mend your relationship with Nolan. The cabin… much like the desert that surrounds it… is a strange and wondrous place."

He's clearly not joking about any of this.

"Umm. Well, I'd need to talk to Allie first, obviously. I take it this isn't the kind of thing I can bring her on?"

Charon shakes his head slowly.

"With all due respect to your wife, Ethan… this is more of an emergency work trip taken out of sheer necessity… than a vacation getaway for executives and their partners."

I blush at his implication. Frankly, it makes me a bit angry, as well. It's easy for him to say such a thing when he already works with his wife, and it's also not lost on me that, as far I know, Bing, Portia, and Nolan are all single. Certainly, none of them are married, at least.

As is increasingly the case these days though, I'm not really in a position to say no. And definitely not to

Richard Charon of all people.

"I understand. Do you know how long you think we'll be gone for, though?"

Charon goes from grave to disinterested in a heartbeat.

"As long as it takes. Ethan... this is the other side of unlimited PTO and flexible working hours. You and your wife... you both understand that, right?"

We both fully expected there would be some late nights and occasional sacrificed weekends, but I'm sure neither one of us expected impromptu—and indefinite—desert excursions on a Monday. Still, what choice do I have?

"Of course."

Charon's voice lightens a bit.

"Good. Take the rest of the day to go home, talk to your wife, and pack whatever you believe is necessary. I will speak to the others and arrange cars to pick everyone up at two. That should be enough time to get us all there by sunset."

But will it be enough time to explain exactly what's happening to Allie? I'm not so sure that even I understand what all is happening. Besides, she's at work right now. Do I really have to have this conversation with her over the phone? Call my pregnant wife and inform her I'm leaving in the middle of a workday to go on a desert trip with my coworkers and I have no idea when I'll be back? How exactly does anyone do such a thing?

None of this is Charon's problem, though. Without another word, he drifts out the door of my office and disappears, leaving me alone with only my thoughts and these breathtaking panoramic views of Los Angeles to keep me company.

Paradise has a price, I suppose.

CHAPTER TEN

It takes four phone calls, two texts, and one voicemail before Allie finally gets back to me. The clock on my cell reads 1:46 p.m. when the screen changes, and I see her name appear above a selfie photo of the two of us taken during a day hike up at Griffith Observatory. I pick up the call and immediately switch her onto speakerphone so I can keep my hands free to continue this frenetic last-minute packing.

"Hey. Thanks for getting back to me."

I'm terrified to hear what her voice is going to sound like right now. While I made sure to specify in my texts and in the voicemail that this wasn't an emergency, I did also warn her that she probably wasn't going to be very happy with what I had to say.

"You didn't leave me much choice. Sorry I couldn't call you back sooner."

Her tone isn't overtly antagonistic or annoyed; she just sounds a little stiff and stilted.

"No, don't be sorry at all. I know I'm calling you at work."

My heart's beating irrationally fast as I remind myself that we have gotten through exponentially more trying episodes than this one could ever amount to be.

"So, what's up? Why have I been warned not to flip out on you?"

Divert the blame right away. Let her know it's not your fault.

"Richard wants me to go out to Death Valley for work. It has to do with the TrendBeat interview."

There's a lengthy pause on the other end of the line. I listen for anything that might clue me in on her reaction, but it's really just silence.

"The interview you did last month."

Was that a question or a statement? Does it matter? Why do I care? It's not important.

"Yeah, with Elle Maguire."

Another pause. What is she thinking right now?

"What about it?"

I open a dresser drawer to grab underwear and socks, although I have no idea how many pairs to bring, since I have no idea how long I'll be gone for.

"Um... well, I made a mistake in terms of when I told her that Olympus would be ready. I accidentally cut out about three weeks' worth of prep time."

Fuck it; I'll just take everything. I scoop it all up in my arms and carry the precarious load over to my suitcase.

"It's not really my fault, to be honest. Remember that Nolan's the one who showed up to the interview drunk and on drugs or whatever."

Of course, the two suitcase pouches I have designated for underwear and socks aren't big enough to contain everything that I own. By the handful, I stuff as much of it in as I can fit.

"What does any of this have to do with Death Valley?"

Good question. I'm still wondering the same thing.

"To be honest, I don't really know. Apparently, the Charons have a cabin or something out there. Richard thinks it could be useful for us if we all go out there and brainstorm a solution together. I guess he thinks getting away from the city for a while and locking us all up in the desert will force creativity or inspiration or something to strike. I don't know."

The pouch zippers just barely work as I pick up everything that wouldn't fit and carry it back to the dresser.

"Obviously, none of this was my idea."

She's definitely not making it easy on me with these lengthy pauses. A lesser man might assume the connection had been lost or intentionally severed on her end, but I know my wife better than that.

"When are you going?"

There's no easy way to say it. I close the drawer extra gently.

"Now."

"*Now?* Like, right now?"

I move back into the room and touch my phone screen to check the time.

"Yeah, like, in five minutes or so. I guess Richard's sending a driver to pick me up at two. To be honest, I'm kind of figuring all this out on the fly myself, obviously. I don't even know what kind of car I should be looking for, or who it is that's driving me."

My toiletries are up next, but something tells me I need to stop and wait here for a second to see what she says.

But that's the problem. She's still not saying anything. Maybe five seconds go by, or maybe five minutes. My heart has moved up into my throat and it still hasn't slowed down a bit.

"Hello? You still there?"

I touch the screen again to make sure the connection hasn't been lost or cut off, but it hasn't.

"Al?"

"What?"

"Well… are you mad at me?"

"I don't know what I am yet. Stunned, I guess."

A text message from an unknown number pops up on my phone. It reads simply: *'I'm here.'*

"I know this is a lot to take in. And again, I can't stress enough to you that none of this was my idea. Richard's basically forcing us to go–"

"How is he *forcing* you to go? You're telling me that in the middle of a workday he just suddenly commanded his entire staff to follow him out to his cabin in the desert and everyone just said yes? That makes no sense."

What am I forgetting still? I haven't had time to check the weather there yet, but I went ahead and grabbed fistfuls of both t-shirts and sweaters just to cover all my bases. There's also a heavy jacket, a pair of jeans, a pair of dress slacks, a button-up shirt, nice shoes, and pajama pants all stuffed into the suitcase. Beyond deodorant, toothpaste, and a toothbrush, I don't know what else I should bring. I have my laptop, a notebook, and a pen buried in there somewhere, too.

"It's not everybody; it's just a few of us. The main, important people. You know, the core. Nolan, Bing, Isla. Portia."

The text reappears on the screen and it forces me into my bathroom to get those final toiletries. I think I can hear Allie sigh, but I can't be sure, since my phone's in the other room now.

"Are you mad at me? Because like I said, I don't really have a choice here."

"Please stop saying that you don't have a choice here, Ethan. Richard's not holding a gun to your head. He can't force you to do anything you don't want to do."

Hurriedly, I dump the bathroom items into the suitcase, flip the lid over, lean my weight down on it, and use both hands to drag the grumpy zipper all the way around its edge until somehow the monstrosity manages to close.

"I thought we talked about this already. You told me you understood it was an unconventional job with unconventional hours."

"This is not 'unconventional'. This is insane. How long are you even going to be gone for?"

A call waiting notification with the unknown number from the text lights up my screen.

"I don't know."

"You don't know?"

I swear under my breath as a quick peek out the bedroom window reveals a black town car idling at the curb.

"Look, I'm sorry, but this is what *you* wanted. You pushed me into this. I wanted to wait—I asked you if we could wait—and you said no. Remember? You were the one who said I'd been 'dealt a great hand' and that it was 'the start of something special'. Remember all that? Well, this is a part of what comes with that. This is what it costs. This is the other side of unlimited PTO and amazing health insurance and a ridiculous salary and all the other perks and bells and whistles that we've been enjoying. You knew what we were getting into when we signed up for this."

I grab the suitcase roughly by the handle and flip the light switch off. I'm halfway down the hall corridor before I hear Allie's voice, and it reminds me I've left my phone behind on the bed.

"No, Ethan. This is not what I signed up for. I don't think it's what you signed up for, either. Did you even read those articles I forwarded to you?"

The poor driver is calling me again. I can see his number flashing across the screen a second time as I retrieve the device and carry it out with my free hand, dragging the bloated rolling suitcase behind me with the other.

"What articles? You're not talking about those subreddit links you sent? Are you?"

"Did you read them?"

From our front door entryway, I can see that the driver has now stepped outside his car and begun maneuvering up the sidewalk to come fetch me. I open the door to give him a wave and let him know that I'm here while simultaneously gesturing apologetically at the phone. He nods his understanding and looks visibly relieved just to see that I'm home and ready to go.

"Hold on a second, Al."

I switch off speakerphone, bring the device to my ear, and mouth 'thank you' to the driver as he takes my suitcase from me. This conversation is teetering into dangerous territory now that I'm no longer alone. Even with Allie off speaker, I'm still extremely conscientious of what this guy might be thinking about what he's hearing me say on my end, so I step into the back seat and close the door behind me as he loads the suitcase into the trunk.

Momentarily alone, I try to speak quickly but quietly in an urgent hush.

"*Articles?* Those aren't articles. Online message boards filled with Looney Tunes gossiping about secret societies, sex parties, and cover-ups for *fucking murder?* Come on, Al. Those aren't articles; those are conspiracy theories spouted off by a bunch of whack-jobs who are probably just pissed Richard's not out, like, saving the whales or the rainforests."

"What about the blog I sent to you? That guy Charles who used to have your job? Did you read that one? He sure didn't sound like a whack-job."

There's precious little time left for this conversation as the driver closes the trunk and circles round toward his door.

"He got *fired*, Allie. I saw it with my own two eyes. Chuck is the living, breathing definition of a disgruntled former employee who's just trying to get back at the people who let him go."

"Oh, really? Well, then, why is his blog gone?"

The driver opens his door and clambers inside. I flash another apologetic smile at his reflection in the rear-view mirror, but he doesn't seem to pay me any mind as he gently eases the car away from the curb and out onto the road.

My volume drops substantially.

"What are you talking about?"

"His blog is *gone*, Ethan. Like, vanished off the face of the Earth. One night, it's all there, dozens of posts and photos and links and testimonials. And then, the next morning, *nothing*. No domain name, no posts, no record of it ever having even existed anywhere. And this is the *internet* we're talking about, where there's always a record. But there's *nothing* out there anymore. It's all just *gone*."

"It sounds like he had second thoughts about airing his dirty laundry for all the world to see."

"Or it sounds like someone *made* him take it down. Or maybe even took it down for him without his permission. This company, these people—they *control* the internet. Do you have any idea how many different corporations the Charons have been linked to?"

Unfortunately, none of this is a new conversation. I'm not sure when it started exactly or what caused her to start drinking this deep-web Kool-Aid concoction of fake news, private forums, and tabloid propaganda bullshit, but for days now, all she wants to do is regurgitate the latest nonsense she read online and then pass it off to me as fact. Honestly, I'm getting sick of it.

"Enough. I didn't call you to go through all this again."

"So, why did you call me?"

"I called you to let you know about this work trip. And to ask if it was all right for me to go on it."

"Are you asking me or are you telling me?"

My mouth falls open, but nothing immediately comes out.

Apparently for Allie, it's just enough silence.

"You're already in the car, aren't you?"

What can I say to that? I'm not about to lie to my wife.

"I have to get back to work."

"Allie…"

"Be careful out there."

"Allie… Allie? Hello? Allie?"

When I look down at the screen this time, she really

is gone.

Outside my window, the midday sun beats down upon us as the driver merges expertly into northbound freeway traffic on 'The One-Oh-One'. His eyes are glued to the road in front of us, and I wonder just how much he's heard from up there. I also wonder how much he really cares about any of it. Clearing my throat, I decide to try and find out.

"Sorry about all that."

His crisp blue eyes glance up to the rear-view mirror to meet mine.

"Hey, no worries, Mr. Birch. Feel free to do whatever you need to do back there; don't worry about me any. I'm Eric, by the way; your driver today."

"Hey, Eric. I appreciate that. Thank you."

He returns his attention to the road.

My phone buzzes. Thinking it might be Allie, I glance down at the screen, but instead, I see a new text message from Portia. When I open it, a photo appears of her dirty black Converse sneakers pressed up against the glass of what looks like a car window. Two seconds later, an accompanying message comes through that reads *'Adventure awaits. Are you ready?'* I close out the text window and look back up at the rear-view mirror.

"I'm sorry about making you wait back there. I didn't expect that call to last so long."

Eric doesn't bother meeting my eyes this time when he answers.

"None of my business, Mr. Birch, but I appreciate that. Like I said, do whatever you gotta do back there. Just pretend I'm not even here."

None of it feels exactly natural; Eric calling me 'Mr. Birch', me pretending like he's not even there, two strangers driving out into the desert together in the middle of a Monday afternoon. But if I've learned nothing else since I took this job, it's that I need to appreciate these moments for what they are and recognize the fact that most people in the world would absolutely *kill* to be where I am right now, getting paid obscenely well to stretch out in the comfy backseat of a luxury town car destined for a desert cabin getaway in Death Valley.

Eric asks me if there's something in particular I'd like to listen to. When I tell him no, he asks if it's all right to turn the radio on. I nod magnanimously and make it clear I'm up for whatever he wants in terms of music genre, talk radio, or anything else. Soon after, we're cruising along to 90s hip hop and R&B classics, and suddenly I don't feel so bad about not feeling bad about this trip.

On a whim, I twist beneath the seatbelt, lift my feet up in the air, plant my sneakers against the window glass, and take a picture of them on my phone. I send it back to Portia and let her know that I, too, am ready for whatever comes next.

CHAPTER ELEVEN

For the past hour, my main source of entertainment has been watching the outdoor digital temperature reading on the town car's dashboard slowly climb upward in degrees. That's what happens when your driver makes it clear he's not a conversationalist, and you run out of games to play and things to look at on your phone.

By 5:15 pm, the temperature outside read ninety degrees. By 6:15, it was ninety-four—a full twenty-degree swing from what it was in L.A. when we left four hours ago. Eric's been keeping the car's air conditioner pumping at full blast, though, so neither one of us has anything to worry about from in here.

Still, I'm just starting to wonder whether it's worth asking the biggest road trip cliché of all time—"Are we there yet?"—when we suddenly veer off the highway and venture out onto an unmarked dirt road.

Even through the darkened glass of the backseat windows, I can see the distant horizon shifting and shimmering in the heat. This is not the kind of place you'd ever want your car to break down in.

After another twenty minutes or so of traveling along the dirt road, we turn onto another dirt road, this one also unmarked. Steadily, we climb up higher and higher along the winding way, straining against gravity and all common sense to try and get as close as possible to the burning sun peeking out above a desert ridge.

Somewhere and sometime along the journey, we drive past a plain, chain-link fence that's split wide on either side of this road. Eric slows the car a bit and continues on at a reduced speed. I wonder if we've just turned onto the Charons' private property.

Maybe five minutes later, my suspicions are further strengthened as a hazy structure in the distance starts to come more fully into view. At first, it's little more than a mirage, but the closer we get, the larger and more defined it grows. Eventually, there's no denying the building for what it is: a solitary cabin left out in the middle of nowhere, isolated and alone, but looming unmistakably just in front of us now—all darkened, dirty blocks of deep brown wood and sand-polished stone.

Eric slows the car to a stop about fifteen yards or so from the front door. There's no driveway or garage; it's all just dirt. Here and there, that dirt is broken up by a cactus, a thorny bush, an overgrown weed, or a boulder. It's impossible to distinguish what may have been placed intentionally from what's just always been out here since the dawn of time.

We do seem to be the only car out here, though. Am I the first one here? And if so, what do I do now?

The temperature outside hopefully has leveled off at ninety-four, and the sky looks like it could be near sunset; it's hard to tell through the tinted windows.

Eric leaves the car running.

"Do you need any help with your bag, Mr. Birch?"

I only have the suitcase in the trunk, so I should be

able to manage on my own. I'm confused, though.

"That's all right, but thanks, Eric. Aren't you staying, too, though?"

He gives me a wolfish grin in the rear-view mirror.

"That's a negative for me, Mr. Birch. Dr. C puts us all up in Vegas on the Strip every time we have to make the trek out to the cabin. It's actually even closer to here than L.A. That's why everyone always jumps at the chance to drive if it's the cabin."

Four hours with this guy and he barely says more than a few words to me. Now that we're finally here and he's apparently just dumping me off, he decides to open up and show some actual human enthusiasm and personality. Go figure. I guess Vegas will do that to you. Also: 'Dr. C?'

"Good for you."

Just try to play it off like you knew this was the plan all along.

"Don't lose too much money."

I immediately hate myself for sounding like someone's parent. Disgusted, I release my seatbelt and reach for the car door handle. And then, against my better judgment, I rotate back around to face him once again.

"This is my first time coming up here, actually. I'm not the first one here, am I? It's just that I don't have a key or anything to get in."

Eric flashes a super-white smile again at me, but I can tell that it's forced. He's obviously impatient to get back on the road and get off to whatever trouble awaits him in Sin City, and he's doing his best to hide it; he's just not doing a great job.

"Everyone else has already been dropped off, Mr.

Birch. We're the last ones. The door should be unlocked though, so you're good to go."

I nod and swing the car door open. It's like opening a portal into hell as the heat blasts me back in the face. Somehow, ninety-four degrees just doesn't quite do the air outside justice. The heat index has to be much, much higher. Either that, or I'm already woefully underprepared for this adventure, and I only just got here.

I turn back to Eric a second time and give him a low whistle.

"Wow. Definitely hotter than I thought it'd be out here for October. Jesus."

He gives me a polite nod and fidgets with something on the dashboard; maybe the air conditioner dial.

"Yes sir, Mr. Birch. It'll cool off by evening though, don't worry."

I hope to God he's right.

"One more thing, Eric. Do I just—am I just supposed to call a number or something to reach you when I'm ready to be picked up? Or how does this work? Like I said, this is my first time here."

It looks like it's taking every ounce of Eric's self-restraint and professional decorum not to just drive off and leave me here in a cloud of dust. His knuckles are as white on the steering wheel as the artificially brightened teeth in his manufactured smile.

"It's all taken care of, Mr. Birch. When Dr. C wants us all to come back, back we come. Don't worry so much. You're going to have a great time."

I'm not convinced, but I also don't know what good will come from me getting back in the car and demanding that he take me back to L.A. Besides, I've already made up my mind to lean in and make the most of this whole adventure. There's no point in turning back now.

"Thanks, Eric."

I swing my body out of the car and head for my suitcase in the open trunk. The *second* I grab it and shut the door, Eric puts the luxury sedan in drive, loops around, and begins the solo journey back down the way we came and off toward what I'm quite certain will be a long night of drunken debauchery.

I watch the black car grow smaller and smaller along the unmarked dirt road until it finally melts into a hazy mirage in the distance and then disappears altogether from view.

It's actually not so bad out here once you get used to it a bit. That first moment of direct exposure coming out of a comfortably air-conditioned leather car interior was brutal, don't get me wrong. But standing here now in the stillness of an arid alien landscape, I feel as if my body is already starting to adjust to its new environment.

I'm no expert, but it does seem like sunset is imminent. The sky is still mainly blue every which way, but you can tell it's beginning to ponder a transition to pink and purple in a couple faraway places.

I unbutton a couple of the top buttons along my shirt, roll up my sleeves to my elbows, grab my suitcase, and continue the rest of the way across the dirt 'front yard' and up the faded steps leading to the thick wooden front door of the cabin.

My knuckles rap against the surface and are immediately answered by the baying of dogs… because of course. When the door opens, I have my suitcase down and I'm ready. Castor and Pollux bound up onto my thighs and throw their bodies against my stomach, slobbering and kissing and licking all over me while I try my best to fend them off.

Isla, fashionably clad in a form-fitting black kimono, only half-attempts to curb them. We both know she could cut their behavior short in an instant if she wanted to, but the dogs have grown on me over time. They know it, I know it, and she knows it, so she lets them greet me their way before she takes her turn and pulls me into a tight embrace.

"Ethan, darling. So good of you to come."

As if I had a choice. But I remind myself that I'm committed to keeping an open mind about this desert adventure, so I hug her back in kind.

"Everyone's out back by the pool already. How about I show you to your room first, and then I'll take you there?"

No one said anything about a pool. And I definitely don't have a swimsuit packed.

"Thanks, Isla. That'd be great."

It's quite a bit homier in here than I expected. After having spent so much time at the Olympus office—and after seeing the exterior of the Charons' residential property on Mulholland Drive—I truthfully expected a more extravagant setup.

The cabin interior is actually somewhat modest. The most notable feature in the main area of the room we're standing in is a beautiful stone fireplace centerpiece. Around it, there's a worn, mustard-yellow sofa sectional and a set of matching armchairs that all look like they were plucked straight from the 1970s. We walk past a small kitchen with an attached dining area. It smells like something delicious is cooking, but I can't quite place the scent for what it is.

Soon, we're passing several closed doors in a long, wood-lined hallway littered with artwork on the walls, most of it Southwest or Native American-inspired. Isla guides me from up front and her two faithful canine companions trail just behind us. She indicates certain doors as she talks and passes them by.

"This is the master over here, so that's Richard and I, obviously, should you need us. There are two guest bedrooms, one with a queen and one with two twins."

She stops walking and turns to me.

"We figured it only proper that Portia take the queen. Bing was also gallant enough to volunteer for the sofa-sleeper in the den, so I hope you don't mind: we have you and Nolie sleeping in the twins in here."

Of course. Fuck it all to hell. I do my best to muster up an appreciative smile.

"I'm good wherever you put me. Just happy to be here."

Isla beams.

"Oh, *grand!* Did you pack a suit?"

I'm assuming she means a swimsuit.

"I did not, actually. I didn't know you had a pool... or that we'd be swimming."

She laughs girlishly.

"*Dar-ling!* You're in the desert; there's always a pool. Come now, set your bags down in here and wait just a tick. I'll grab one of Richard's old suits."

She lowers her voice to that conspiratorial whisper she loves to use on me.

"He never swims anymore, anyway."

Isla skips off to the master bedroom with the Great Danes traipsing close behind her.

I open the door to the room with the twin beds and flip a light switch on. There's nothing unusual about it at all. It's just two twin beds with cream pillows peeking out from beneath patterned burgundy duvet covers, two wooden end tables with fat bedside lamps, a large wooden armoire on the other side of the room, and a small closet. On the walls, there's more 'local' artwork, but no photographs of the Charons anywhere to be found.

The only worrisome thing in here at first glance is the air conditioning unit in the window—mainly because it looks like it could be several decades old. It's currently making an awful racket as it tries to keep the room cool. The dial on the front is set to seventy-two. I'm no HVAC specialist, but even I feel like that's way too ambitious for this tiny antique piece of machinery.

Predictably, there's already a suitcase standing sentinel on top of the twin bed closest to the A/C. Lest there be any doubt or confusion, it appears that Nolan has claimed that space for himself.

I set my own suitcase down on top of the other bed and try to get into a relaxed, comfortable mindset again. It's been years upon years since I shared a bedroom with anyone other than Allie. And unless I'm forgetting someone, the last time I slept in the same room as another guy was way back during freshman year of college with Chad.

Isla re-appears in the doorway holding a pair of plain, navy-blue swimming trunks.

"I do hope these will fit you. Richard probably hasn't worn them in thirty years."

She tosses me the shorts and smiles mysteriously.

"Ethan, I don't suppose you like sweets, do you?

I've got a batch of brownies in the oven. It's sort of tradition for me to bake them every time we come up here. You did have supper now, didn't you, darling?"

I'm not sure when I could have had supper even if I'd wanted to, considering Eric showed up outside my house in his town car at two o'clock sharp. All the same, I was raised never to show up to someone's house expecting to be fed, no matter how hungry you might actually be. It's just bad manners—especially if it's your boss's house, and *especially* if his wife is British.

"I did, thank you, Isla. And brownies sound delicious. Just don't tell my wife if I have more than one."

She eats it all up.

"Oh, splendid! I'll see you out by the pool, then."

Against all odds, the swimsuit somewhat fits. Judging by the places where the drawstring appears more worn, Charon probably used to knot it quite a bit tighter than I am now, but all that matters is that I'm able to tie it off at all without sucking in my stomach.

I walk slowly down the hallway, taking in the decorations on either side as I go. Most of them are abstract works of art by painters I'm not familiar with. Unlike in my bedroom, there are actually some photographs out here in frames, but they don't seem to be of the Charons. Or, if they are, I don't recognize Richard or Isla in any of the photos that I pass by.

Eventually, I come to the kitchen. Isla is sitting with her legs crossed at the knees atop a laminate counter in her silk kimono, shins and feet dangling far below her, sipping out of a large goblet wine glass. She stares lovingly out the opened blinds of a window toward muffled sounds coming from behind the cabin.

Castor and Pollux are nowhere to be seen. For that matter, neither is Charon, unless he's out back with the others.

I watch her for a second until she turns and notices me.

"I'll be out in just a tick, darling. Run along now and play with the others."

She gives me a radiant smile that brooks no resistance, so I shuffle toward a sliding door off the main living room that leads to the backyard area and open it.

Outside, there are half a dozen different-colored rope hammocks hanging about from various iron supports and frames, a wicker dining table with a tall umbrella and eight matching patio chairs set around it, a large wood-burning firepit surrounded by an eclectic collection of folding chairs and dusty bean bags, and an ovular turquoise swimming pool bordered at each end by four brown plastic reclining deck chairs with tan cushions. Above all of this, several wispy strands of hanging electric Edison bulbs dangle against the desert sunset.

Regretfully, the first person I make eye contact with is the only person who's actually in the pool right now.

"Mr. Mai Tai! Glad you could join us, bud. Nice trunks!"

From what I can see of his body from the waist-up above the water line, Nolan is already looking very pinkish. With any luck, he'll be thoroughly sunburnt and miserable by nightfall.

The next voice I hear belongs to a woman.

"Well, look who it is!"

I follow it to the source and discover Portia sitting at the far edge of the pool with just her feet in the water.

She's wearing a simple black one-piece swimsuit that coordinates well with her jet-black hair, which she has tied back in a ponytail. It also complements the dark ink of the many tattoos spread out around her skin, a good portion of which I'm just now seeing for the first time.

The last person I notice is Bing. He's suspended in a low-swinging hammock at the same end of the pool as Portia. Although he's wearing a fire-engine red swimsuit, it doesn't look like he's gotten it wet yet. He also has a black 'Anthrax' rock band t-shirt pulled tight over his torso.

Bing boisterously waves hello.

"What up, dude! Welcome to the par-*tay!*"

It's impossible not to smile.

"I thought this was an emergency business trip?"

Nolan cups his hand and sends a small wave of pool water splashing in my direction. Before I can duck to the side, it hits me square in the trunks and immediately sends shivers up and down my body; although I have to admit, it actually feels pretty good in this dry desert heat.

He laughs triumphantly and bounces up and down on the balls of his feet beneath the surface.

"This *is* an emergency business trip. This is how we do *business* at Olympus!"

To accentuate his point, he falls gracefully backward in the water until he's floating languidly on his spine with just his face, chest, fingers, and toes hovering above the surface.

I look over at Portia.

"Where's Richard?"

She watches her feet swing back and forth beneath the rippling waves for a moment or two before she shrugs and answers me.

"He's here somewhere. Isla's making brownies, by the way."

Nolan jerks back to an alert standing position in the pool.

"Is she really?"

When Portia nods, he practically orgasms in front of us.

"*Oh… my God… yes…*"

Bing guffaws from his swinging seat in the hammock. Portia just rolls her eyes. I walk over and sit down in between them at the edge of the pool.

By now, the sky is a full explosion of sunset colors: azure blue, smoky violet, magenta, goldenrod, orange creamsicle. A pale crescent moon hangs high overhead where the sun until very recently held sole dominion. It will be dusk and then dark before long. Above us, the thin bands of electric lightbulbs grow ever more noticeable in the failing twilight.

The water is cool but not cold on my tired calves and feet. Portia bends forward and uses her index finger to flick a few droplets of pool water at my head.

"Not what you were expecting, I take it?"

I brush the wetness off my face with a smile.

"Not in the slightest. Have you been here before?"

She lifts the same finger in the air.

"Just once. Maybe about a year ago."

"What about you, Bing?"

This is an entirely different human being than the one I last encountered in the dark of the Olympus nursing room. Gone is the subdued, tear-streaked man with the puffy eyes, husky voice, and somber disposition. In his place is an energetic yet relaxed figure fresh out of his teens who is equipped with a whole new rosy outlook on life. Bing is almost unrecognizable to me as he swings himself in the hammock and chatters up at the appearing stars over our heads.

"Fellow first-timer here, Ethan; though the stories I've heard from these two are legendary!"

I glance over at Nolan, who has resumed floating on his back in the center of the pool while staring up at the sky.

"How many times have you been here, Nolan?"

For a second or two, he looks like he either didn't hear me or he's choosing to ignore the question. Finally, he spews a small fountain of pool water from his mouth and sighs luxuriously.

"*Ahh...* good question, good question. I don't remember exactly. Must have come here dozens of times during Signals. But it's been a while now, for sure."

Dozens of times? That has to be an embellishment. I don't know how long it took them from start to finish to build Signals, but it's hard to imagine they could have gotten anything done at all if they came all the way out here *dozens* of times throughout the process.

Especially if no actual work got done while they were here.

There's certainly nothing wrong with taking a trip out to the desert to get away from the city, explore nature, hang out by a pool, and eat some homemade brownies. But wasn't it Charon himself who told me that this wasn't a vacation getaway or even a retreat? I believe the exact words he used were 'emergency work trip taken out of sheer necessity'.

Needless to say, this isn't exactly what I pictured when he said that.

"So, what usually happens on these cabin trips? I

guess I thought, given the severity of our situation, we'd be plunging right in with a brainstorming meeting or something similar tonight. Is that happening out here, or inside, or tomorrow morning, or what?"

"*Jesus Christ*, Mr. Mai Tai. Why don't you channel some of the island vibes from your nickname and learn to relax and just take it easy for a second? We just got here. You just got here. And you're at the cabin now. *Let the cabin provide...*"

Bing snorts.

"You sound like a hippie."

Nolan brings his legs back down in the pool so he can stand and level with us.

"You can laugh now, *Bingham*, but you won't be laughing later when all the answers you've been searching for find you and smack you straight in the fucking face. I've seen it happen, and it's happened to me, numerous times now. More times than I can count. And don't forget that the only reason we're all even here in the first place is because of you, bud."

The complete lack of self-awareness on Nolan's part shouldn't shock me anymore, and yet it still does.

Thankfully, Bing seems to be in too good of a mood to argue with him or let it bother him.

"Man, I hope you're right. It does feel kind of magical out here, doesn't it?"

And it does. The sun is now fully set, and the sky has transformed into a deep indigo pinpricked with stars. It's been a long, long time since I saw this many stars. Absent all the city's ambient light pollution, it's easy out here to spot and trace whole constellations.

Between this sea of stars, the silver lantern moon, and all the soft-lit Edison bulbs swaying gently overhead in the warm evening breeze, the general scenery around us becomes bathed in an otherworldly yet peaceful ethereal glow. It certainly doesn't hurt either that we're the only structure for miles in any direction.

All four of us grow quiet and still as our surroundings.

Maybe I imagine it, but I think I see a shooting star streak across the blackened horizon in a sudden burst of sparkling gold and red. But before I can open my mouth to ask if anyone else just saw it too, I turn toward the sound of the back door sliding open and then shut behind me.

Isla strolls out into the inky luminescence with two trays, one in either hand. It's hard to see her at first, since she's silhouetted against the interior light fanning out from within the cabin, but by the time she makes it over to us, I notice that one tray is piled high with eight chocolate brownies and the other is ringed with four plastic cups.

"How's the water, Nolie?"

She gracefully kneels to set both trays down at the edge of the pool, dips her slender fingers into the water, and shudders appreciatively.

Nolan wastes no time in wading over toward the refreshments.

"Absolutely amazing, per usual. Just like your magic brownies and cocktails."

"Oh, *grand.*"

Isla stands back up and glides over toward the wicker dining set. When she gets there, she removes her black kimono and lays it gently on top of a chair. In the dark, my heart skips a beat as I realize she's not wearing any clothes underneath.

It's not until she's fully returned to the pool that I discover she's not actually naked; she's just wearing a nude-colored swimsuit. With barely a splash, she slips her thin, elegant frame into the water until she's standing waist-deep beside Nolan.

Isla turns and gestures at the trays.

"Help yourselves, darlings, and don't be shy. I made plenty to go around."

Bing clambers awkwardly out of the hammock and joins us at the pool's edge. Nolan already has one brownie in his mouth, another brownie in his right hand, and a drink in his left hand. Portia waits patiently as Bing reaches past her, selects a brownie and a plastic cup, and then returns back to his hammock perch with a satisfied groan. When he's clear, she grabs a drink for herself, looks down at the brownies and then back up at me, and smiles devilishly.

"Wanna split one?"

That depends. Are we splitting one because of calories… or because of something else? I'm not sure what Nolan meant a moment ago. Did he mean 'magic brownies and cocktails' as in brownies and cocktails so delicious they're magical? Or did he mean 'magic brownies and cocktails' as in 'magic brownies', plus cocktails? The former is one thing; the latter, quite another.

Even the cocktails alone are a cause for concern. Besides not knowing what's in them, I haven't had a sip of alcohol since Allie told me she was pregnant. It's not as if I've permanently sworn off the stuff or anything, but I did make a mental commitment to myself when I learned about the baby—and then when I took this new job—that I'd do everything within my power to become a responsible, hard-working, dependable breadwinner, husband, and future father. Regardless of our earlier fight over the phone, I'm not exactly keen on throwing all that away just to fit in with my coworkers right now.

"What's in them?"

Isla sinks lower in the water until only her long neck remains above the surface. Slowly, she tilts her head back and allows her hair to flow out freely behind her.

"Sugar and spice and everything nice."

She winks at me before dipping completely underwater.

When it becomes clear that she's not coming right back up, I turn to Portia instead. She's sipping at the drink in her hand when she finally notices me.

"What?"

"Are these normal brownies… or are they special brownies?"

"Special as in how?"

From his hammock, Bing gleefully chimes in between chews.

"They're not *special* brownies; they're *magic* brownies."

The rippling reflection of the pool water lights up Portia's wicked grin.

"You hear that? They're not *special* brownies; they're *magic* brownies."

"I'm serious, Portia."

She laughs.

"What? I don't know what's in them, if that's what you're asking."

Nolan kicks over to us and sets his plastic cup on the side of the pool. It's empty already. The brownie he had in his mouth is also long gone, but he still has the other one held straight up above the water like he's afraid of getting it wet.

"*Jesus Christ*, Ethan. Just take a fucking brownie already and stop being such a little bitch."

My first instinct is to reach down and pop him square in his smarmy mouth. Maybe he senses it too, because he uses his legs to torpedo himself away from us and back out to the middle of the pool, arm and brownie vertically outstretched like a periscope all the while.

Seething and lasered in on Nolan, I don't even realize at first that Isla has resurfaced and swam up right in front of me. She places a hand on either side of my knees and lets her legs drift out behind her until she's holding herself up and floating on the surface, rhythmically but soundlessly kicking her feet and engaging her stomach muscles to stay flat in this position. Her eyes are trained on me as her lips whisper right above the water line.

"Everything is all natural, of the earth, and made purely with love. There are no chemicals, illegal substances, or toxic agents in anything I'd ever offer you, Ethan. You have my word on that."

She lifts one hand from the wall, takes a brownie from the tray, and brings it to her mouth for a small bite, as if that action alone might prove that they're not poisoned.

"Trust me when I say that you are safe here. All I want is for you all to feel at home."

Even if the brownies are all natural, that doesn't mean they're not laced with something. They could have been baked with marijuana; or worse, something like magic mushrooms. The last time I smoked weed was in college, though I'm pretty sure I'd still be able to detect it if these are pot brownies. And while I've never tried mushrooms before, you'd think that would have a pretty distinct taste, too; probably something worse, even.

Portia splits a brownie down the middle and holds one half out in her palm as she lowers her voice to speak to me.

"I honestly don't know what's in them. But if it helps, I had two of them the last time I came here, and I felt perfectly fine. If anything, they kind of… cleared my mind, and made me sharper and more aware."

I'm still not convinced, and she can tell.

"Let's just start with one half each and take it from there. If you hate it, I will personally volunteer as tribute to stick my fingers down your throat and help you throw up later. But that's not going to happen, because you're going to be fine. I promise. I haven't steered you wrong yet, have I?"

She hasn't. But this certainly feels well outside the realm of normal workplace guidance.

Isla sets her nibbled brownie back on the tray, takes the last plastic cup off the other tray, sets it down between my legs, and places her hand on my knee.

"And this is just a good, old-fashioned, classic mojito, darling. Nothing unusual or untoward, but perfect for washing down sweet chocolate on a dry desert night."

Again, Bing reminds us all that he's still here from his hammock.

"I can confirm two things for you, Ethan: one, this is indeed a mojito, and there's nothing funny or wrong with it; and two, it doesn't matter what's in the brownie, because it's delicious, and I'm absolutely going to have another one."

True to his word, he rolls himself out of the hammock netting and walks over to the brownie tray. He takes one, thinks better of it, and takes two instead before shambling back to his personal happy place.

Portia snickers.

"How would you know what a mojito is supposed to taste like? You're not even twenty-one yet; you shouldn't be drinking anything at all."

Bing takes an outrageously large bite out of one of his two brownies as he lowers himself back into the hammock's loving embrace.

"Oh, yeah? How are you gonna call the cops on me without any cell service, Portia?"

They both laugh. Nolan stands alone in the center of the pool, eating his brownie in silence. Isla still floats on her stomach facing us with her feet out behind her, one hand gripping the wall beside my left knee and the other planted firmly atop my right knee.

"You're a part of our family now, Ethan. We're all in this together until the end."

She squeezes me.

"Join us."

I've never been one to succumb to peer pressure, but this situation defies ordinary peer pressure. Stranded indefinitely in Death Valley, with no service, no agenda, and nowhere to run or hide—and with my boss's wife's hand on my leg, no less—I suddenly realize clear as crystal that I don't really have a choice. And perhaps I never did.

Without another thought, I turn and take my half of the brownie from Portia's outstretched hand, 'cheers' it against her half, and the two of us each take a bite.

CHAPTER TWELVE

Bing loudly applauds behind us and yells through mouthfuls of his own brownies.

"Finally! It's about time!"

Even Nolan, his brownie consumed and his hands now free, sarcastically claps his hands above the water.

"*Bravo*, Mr. Mai Tai. Baby's first brownie. They grow up so fast, don't they, Isla?"

Isla tunes him out. She just smiles proudly, gives my knee another light squeeze, then finally relinquishes her hold on me and on the wall as she pushes herself off and out into the water.

Bing is right; this brownie *is* absolutely delicious. I take another bite and try to see if I can detect any strange flavors in my mouth that might feel like they don't belong, but there's nothing there. It just tastes like a really, really, *really* good brownie. And that's it.

Similarly, the mojito in the cup between my legs tastes just like a mojito. It's been a long time since I've had one, but everything I think I know about them seems like it's ringing true enough. I can taste the rum ever so slightly, but mainly what I'm getting is lime, mint, and carbonation. Isla is also right; it tastes just perfect for the desert.

Now that I've committed to my choices, everything quickly gets so much easier and more *fun* for me. I feel lighter, freer, and more relaxed already. It's not long before I forget why I was so reluctant and uncertain about trying any of these things to begin with.

Later, it's me, not Portia, who suggests we split another brownie. If she's at all surprised by my invitation, she recovers well. Nonchalantly, she picks up a bar of chocolate from the tray and breaks it in half in her hands. I watch as she does this, and, since I'm feeling curiously bold all of a sudden, I decide to ask her about the tattoos.

She hands me my half and takes a bite out of hers.

"What about them?"

"Well, you have so many of them. Is that… like, a choice? Or what?"

Portia laughs and considers me.

"Yes, Ethan. It was a choice. Thank you very much for asking. This didn't happen to me by accident. I wasn't walking down the street one day when a runaway ink toner truck overturned and splattered all over my body from head to toe."

I snort as I finish the last of my mojito. Some of the rum burns up on the inside of my nose.

"Ha ha, very funny. I just mean…"

"You just mean what? What do they all mean? What do each of them mean? Do I ever regret having done this to my body? What are you asking me right now?"

I can't tell if I've upset her or not. Her tone is playful, and she's doing her usual troublemaker smile thing, but the words she's saying just sound so aggressive to me right now.

"I think I'm making you mad. Maybe I should just

shut up."

"Maybe you should just finish your brownie and then get in the pool. We can't play chicken with only three people."

She stuffs what's left of the brownie into her mouth and then somersaults from the ledge into the water. Once she's sunk to the bottom of the turquoise pool, she sits cross-legged for a while, blowing little bubbles from her nostrils to help her stay down there. When she finally resurfaces with a gasping breath, Portia pulls the ponytail tie from her hair and shakes it free, then opens her mouth wide and sticks her tongue out at me. The brownie is gone.

"Ta-da! Your turn."

Even though it's only a half-portion, the remaining brownie in my hand suddenly feels monstrous. I'm not convinced I can chew up and swallow more chocolate, delicious as it is, in this dry, warm weather. I pick up my cup with the intention of using it to help me chase the dessert down… but then I remember that I've already finished my mojito.

"Bing."

He doesn't answer the first time.

"Bing!"

"Yeah?"

"Can I have some of your mojito? I already drank all of mine and I need something to help wash my brownie down."

It's hard to distinguish him clearly back there in the shadows, but I think I see him reach forward, lift his cup off the ground, set it down, and lie back in the hammock.

"Sorry, dude. Can't do it. There's nothing left. I

finished it already."

Fuck.

"Fuck."

Guess I'll just have to power through.

"Guess—I guess I'll just have to power through."

He doesn't respond, so I take another second or two to compose myself as best I can before shoving the chunk of rich chocolate into my gullet.

Somewhere in the midst of chewing, I must have either fallen forward off the ledge or decided to go in, because I'm completely in the pool all of a sudden. I'm now dancing from foot to foot underwater, tapping my hands out beside me on the glassy waves, and munching with all my might, chin upturned, and eyes glossed over staring at the stars.

Eons pass before I finish swallowing. Even then, I still taste crumbs and bits and pieces of the brownie on the inside of my mouth and stuck between my teeth. As discreetly as I can, I lower my lips to the surface, take in a small swig of pool water, swish it around, and spit it back out.

That's so much better. Immensely satisfied, I turn toward Portia, open my mouth wide, and stick my tongue out exactly the way she did.

"Ta-da!"

The only problem is that she's no longer there.

Frantically, I look around until I spot Isla standing at the far end of the pool, her palms outstretched on either side of her body with just her fingertips grazing the top of the water. There's a ton of splashing—a ridiculously unnecessary amount of splashing—and I have to turn my face away and shield my eyes from all the crashing spray.

When it finally stops, I look up again, and now Portia and Nolan are both there on either side of Isla, standing, dripping, panting, and yelling all at the same time.

"What do you mean it was a tie? I smoked his ass from end to end!"

"Are you kidding me, Isla? I touched you a full second before she got here!"

Isla laughs and shakes her head from side to side.

"A draw's a draw, my loves."

There's more cursing, arguing, splashing, and laughing, as I make my way over to them. Isla's the first one to spot me.

"*Darling!* How are you feeling?"

Nolan and Portia both turn around to face me at the same time.

I feel a bit embarrassed, like I'm suddenly on display. But the sensation passes as quickly as it comes, and then I just feel warm and *fluid* again.

"I feel... great. Fluid, you know?"

Nolan drops his jaw and lets out a loud, crass, nasal laugh, but Portia splashes water into his open mouth and then turns back around to face me.

"Good! That's great, Ethan. Are you ready for chicken?"

I don't know what that is.

"I don't know what that is. Are you talking... like, the kids' game?"

Nolan is sputtering and spitting out pool water until Isla slides an arm over his shoulders to quiet him.

"It's not a kids' game if you're still young at heart, Ethan. How about you and Portia take on Nolie and I for the first game?"

Portia's already swimming up to me.

"Come on. Go under so I can get on your shoulders."

My brain is mush; all I have now is reaction and instinct. So, I close my eyes tight and sink beneath the surface in a torrent of bubbles.

In the pressurized dark, I feel Portia place first her hands and then her thighs over each of my shoulders. Her legs are smooth and strong on either side of my face, and I start to think I kind of like it down here… especially as I realize with an adolescent glee just what parts of her body are pressed up against the back of my skull and my neck. Then I feel her tap quickly on the top of my head.

I push my legs against the floor and rocket us up out of the waves to standing. She's heavier up here than she was down below, so I instinctively grab hold of her shins below the knees to keep her from toppling over. She tucks her toes behind my back and then moves my hands further up past her kneecaps and onto her thighs.

"Hold me here, okay?"

I nod dumbly, as the ability to speak momentarily eludes me. Blinking through the water running off my face, I see that Isla is perched atop Nolan's shoulders in much the same way I imagine Portia to be perched atop mine.

"Tell us when to go, Bing!"

I've completely forgotten about Bing. Is he in the pool too? I turn around to look toward the hammock he was lying in, but he's sitting on the edge of the pool now next to the trays with Isla's discarded brownie in his hand.

"Wrong way, Ethan! Turn us back around!"

Portia squeezes my head between her thighs and taps the top of my head frantically, as if I've left us vulnerable to attack from behind or something. I'm about to explain to her that the game hasn't even started yet when I hear Bing's voice ring out through the night.

"GO!"

Caught completely unawares, I try to spin us back around, but it's already too late. Nolan closes the distance between us in a surge of water that catches me full in the face like a tsunami. I just barely catch a glimpse of the expression on Isla's face—primal, barbaric, bloodthirsty—before I feel Portia's weight pulling us both backward, up, and over into a mess of swirling limbs and bubbles.

We come up separately... in more ways than one.

"You weren't ready! You weren't even facing the right way."

I scowl at her.

"I—I didn't even know we were starting. He didn't give 'on your marks, get set.' He just yelled 'GO!'"

Isla and Nolan celebrate their victory wildly, and she stays up on top of his shoulders.

"Let's give it another round, shall we? Best two of three?"

Nolan spits pool water.

"Ha! You're giving him too much credit."

That's enough motivation for me. I shoot him the most murderous glare I can conjure up, then sink beneath the chop without another word. Moments later, I feel Portia mount me, and when she's in place and I have my hands where she wants them, I thrust us upward like a great whale breaching the ocean.

They're no match for us this time. Inspired and

furious, I charge into Nolan the second Bing cries 'go' and practically slam our foreheads together above the waves. Portia does the rest, easily dispatching Isla with her flailing fists and sending the older woman tumbling off my enemy's shoulders and into the swirling sea.

With each side having won once, both teams approach this championship bout with renewed focus and intensity. Not much, if anything, is said. We both just stand facing one another, two in the water and two in the air, and wait for Bing's signal to come.

When it finally does, all hell breaks loose. It takes all of my strength and then some to hold onto Portia as she thrashes wildly against Isla, their fingers flying through the air and grappling at each other like talons.

Below them, Nolan and I do our best to maintain solid bases and adjust accordingly, while simultaneously playing dirty by timing knees and kicks to one another's legs, feet, and groin. He delivers a particularly vicious blow to my stomach, and I double forward as the air comes rushing out of my lungs. I feel Portia tighten her legs around me in response, and something about that feeling triggers an animalistic reaction deep and powerful within me. With a last, desperate heave, I close my eyes and lunge my body into his, and seconds later, I hear whooping and high-pitched screaming as Portia pounds on my head.

"We did it! We did it!"

I open my eyes. Sure enough, Isla is down in the water now, jaw clenched tight as she smiles and nods at both of us with forced composure and manufactured restraint. Nolan is sputtering and coughing and shaking with rage.

"*You fucking cheated!* You can't do that! You can't just

spear someone like that!"

I ignore him altogether and sink low enough on my heels so Portia can disentangle herself from my shoulders. When she's off and standing beside me in the water, she grabs me by the face and kisses my cheek.

"I knew we could do it!"

There's a moment where we just look at each other. Then, Isla breaks in.

"All right, all right, you two. Congratulations. Now, it's time we switch the teams up."

A strange expression comes over Portia's face for a second before it's gone. She glances over at the wall of the pool.

"Unless Bing wants to play. Bing, you want in?"

I follow her gaze to the figure slumped down at the edge of the water. Maybe his head moves a bit upward, but then it shakes slowly from side to side.

"I'm good. You—you guys keep at it."

Portia doesn't seem convinced, but Nolan and Isla certainly do. Nolan's already swam up beside my ex-partner, and Isla glides across the ripples like a shimmer of moonlight until she's standing there dripping in front of me.

"Well, Ethan. Are you ready?"

I'm not sure I know how to answer that, so I do the easy thing and drop down below the surface. Isla is immediately on top of me, and I notice even underwater how the weight of her feels different than Portia, and how the skin of her legs and thighs feels different against the skin on my back, neck, and shoulders. Instead of a tapping on my head, Isla slides her hands down through my hair, grabs hold of some of it, and tugs me upward when she's ready.

We break the surface together to face Nolan and Portia, but they're not facing us. Rather, both of them are staring off to the side and past us in the direction of Bing. They look fairly surprised, so I decide to turn us around as well to see what's the matter.

A tall, dark figure has appeared at the side of the pool. I watch it bend slowly over the mass of another figure at the water's edge.

All of a sudden, I remember that second figure is Bing, and I want to scream at him and tell him to watch out as this towering vampire moves in on his neck for the kill. My speech fails me for the second time tonight, but it doesn't matter, because Isla's voice sails out from above me.

"Richard! You've figured it out!"

Neither figure stirs up ahead, so I take a few more halting steps forward in the water until they both come into view more clearly in the gloom.

My vampire is indeed Charon. The old man clad in black has wrapped himself awkwardly around Bing from behind, his frame bent over, and his face lowered all the way to Bing's level. He has one large hand shielding his hooked nose and his thin mouth from us as he whispers secrets directly into Bing's ear.

Isla runs her nails softly against my scalp, and magically, I know that's her signaling me that she wants to get off. I dip down underwater and let her slide over my head, and when I come back up to the surface, Portia is also off Nolan's shoulders and standing by my side.

We all just stand there in the water and watch in silence as Charon articulates the full extent of his secret message to Bing. All throughout, Bing's face never changes in the sickly blue light reflecting up from the pool's surface. But I can tell that he's listening intently and soaking in every word that he hears.

It's right around this time that I fully accept the fact that I'm fucked up.

I've been shoving the thought away and keeping it at arm's length for what feels like hours now, but it's been there all the same, knocking politely but firmly on the door to my brain and trying to tell me that something's not right, and that everything's not as it normally is and normally should be.

I shake my head violently, as if that might miraculously clear me of this condition.

It doesn't, of course, so I sink down beneath the water, hold my breath for a few seconds, try to concentrate on concentration, fail, and rise back up to the surface. I repeat this maybe two or three more times before I give up and decide to do something else above the water.

But once I'm up there, things are different. While it doesn't make any sense, the world has somehow changed already just in the short amount of time that I've been doing my weird, futile exercise in attaining sobriety.

There's a small but steady fire burning in the fire pit. Charon stands guard beside it, the dancing flames reflecting in his coal-black eyes as he pokes and prods at the logs with a metal poker. Isla is there, too, sitting in a blood-red folding chair with her legs crossed, staring into the flames. She's no longer in the nude-colored swimsuit; or if she is, it's hidden beneath the silk black kimono she was wearing earlier today. Otherwise, the chairs and beanbags around them are unoccupied.

I spin around in the pool, but no one else is in here

with me. Portia and Nolan aren't racing each other beneath the surface. Bing's not sitting at the wall or in his favorite hammock. The two trays are still there at the water's edge, but both of them are empty now.

My heart pounding in my chest, I half-swim, half-bounce along the pool floor until I'm at the end. When I get there, I hoist myself up along the edge, and like a fish out of water, I flop my way onto solid ground until I'm finally breathing heavily and lying on the side of this great big hole in the earth.

I don't know how long I just lie here for, lungs swelling up and down against my ribcage, vision swimming in and out and in and out and in and out and in again.

I know I need to do something. But what?

The air around my wet body is warm and pleasant and maternal. I look down at my torso and my legs, crunched up in the fetal position on the ground, and realize that I'm mostly dry already. It's just the swim trunks that are still wet, dark and waterlogged against my bones and muscles. I can live with that. And if I can't, I'll just take them off. It's as simple as that.

Armed with this newfound power of logic, I make it up to my hands and knees. I try to go a bit further and get up to crouching and then to standing, but neither one of them works for me. I just feel nauseous in either position, so I make my peace inwardly that wherever I need to go, I will crawl.

The heat and light of the fire beckons me closer. I drag my palms, knees, and toes along the concrete backyard patio and through dirt, sand, and darkness, until finally, I'm at the outer ring of the circle of seats. Drawing on reserves of energy, willpower, and strength

I never knew I had, I dig my nails into the filthy canvas of a folding chair and pull myself up into it.

It's a wonder the chair doesn't collapse beneath my weight or topple over, but somehow, I'm able to get situated. There's even an absurd flash of pride that comes over me as I realize I could have much more easily scaled one of the beanbags scattered around the same circle, but no—I chose the path of most resistance, and now I have a seat at the table that befits my rank and station.

Charon and Isla are both silently watching me from across the flames.

"S—sorry about that. I had—I didn't know…"

What am I trying to say? I've forgotten already.

Charon stabs at a log in the fire. Something hisses and crackles, and a cloud of glowing embers rise up and then vanish into the night.

Explain yourself, damn it. Everyone is gone. Everything is different.

"I… I wasn't… I…"

My lips pucker as I close my eyes and let out all the air that's vibrating inside my lungs in one long, jagged stream. When I'm finished, I try to talk again, but something different comes out.

"It… it wasn't my fault… Richard. The interview. I… Nolan…"

Someone is touching my arm. A hand is wrapped tightly around my forearm, and I follow it to find that Isla is sitting next to me now. I didn't hear or see her move, but she's there all the same, holding onto me and smiling, her soft blue eyes telling me that maybe everything's okay after all.

She's not the one that speaks to me though.

"I know. I know everything, Ethan. Surely, you must understand that by now?"

His voice seems to emanate from the fire itself. But I know that can't be right. And yet, glancing over and seeing his sunken face like a white skull floating in the darkness, it doesn't appear as if he's spoken at all. But I know he has. I just know.

I try not to break down and weep.

Isla's grip on my arm, the physical contact she's lending me—it should be a comfort, I know that. But it's not. Instead, it feels like she's holding me here with them, making sure I don't slip away or look away from the awful, terrible realization that comes upon me all at once and shakes my soul to its very foundation.

This was all a mistake. I never should have come here. I never should have left...

Allie.

Her face appears in the fire for me as I say her name out loud in my head, and my heart rips from the inside and spills itself out within the rotten bag of my body.

This time, the tears come unchecked and unfettered. I sob quietly in my seat.

Charon stares at me or at the fire. Isla holds onto me and occasionally reaches over to wipe away the saltwater with all the tenderness of a lover or a mother.

From the boundaries of black at the edge of my sight, Nolan emerges into the glowing sphere. He takes a good long look at me... and I let him. Finally, he moves more fully into the firelight and seats himself beside Isla with a weary sigh.

"I can't find him anywhere. Looked all over."

Isla gives him a sympathetic smile.

"You did your best, darling. That's all any of us

could ever ask."

Nolan leans forward and massages the muscles in his legs. His eyes reflect the fire. He looks different to me right now; different than I've ever seen him before.

"Where's Portia?"

They all look over at me together as I slowly realize that I'm the one who's spoken.

"Where's Portia? Where is she?"

Charon and Isla are silent, though Isla does remove her hand from my arm.

Nolan is the one who talks now.

"We went out together to look for Bing. I'm sure she'll be back soon."

My brain swells and heaves as it tries to connect the dots. Nolan looked all over but couldn't find Bing. Portia went with him to search but hasn't come back yet. Bing and Portia are missing.

Suddenly, I'm standing.

"I'll—I'll find her. I'll find both of them."

Charon looks up from the fire and studies my face. Isla reaches out and gently takes my hand.

"Ethan, darling. It's very dark. In the morning, we'll be able to conduct a proper search. If they haven't both turned back up by then… which they will."

I might be fucked up, but these people are crazy.

"Wait… what? No… we need to find them. It's… it's… what? They're not… here. That's… not okay."

I turn, break away from Isla, and stumble off around the pool and into the darkness. It's not until I'm well on my way that I think I hear a distant voice cry out something like 'stop' or 'wait', but by then, I've gone too far already.

It doesn't take long for the ambient light of the

backyard bulbs and the fire to fade away, and soon, it's just me, the stars, and the moon out here in the dark desert wilderness. My legs feel like jelly, but it does feel good to be standing and walking and moving again.

Occasionally, my brain almost seems to come back around to something I can recognize. But most of the time, it's a steaming, swirling mess of images, feelings, thoughts, and sentences, all of which appear and disappear at random intervals without any fleeting semblance of control.

"PORTIA! BING!"

I repeat their names over and over again as loud as I can. Traipsing barefoot through the darkness, my hope is that maybe this quest I'm on will set me straight again. But more importantly, I just hope that I can find my friends.

Although I can see much more in the moon and starlight than I otherwise would have assumed, it's still awfully hard to be sure of anything in these conditions. More than once, I think I see something move down in front of me or off to the side in the shadows, and I pull my naked feet back in terror, ready to run or fight or hide... only to finally coax my own nerves into continuing along this thankless journey when it's clear that whether or not something was actually ever there to begin with, it's not going to come out again to confirm its existence on command.

I wish I had shoes on. It's nothing short of miraculous that my bare feet haven't already been torn up by rocks, cacti, scorpions, snakes, spiders, or glass out here. Maybe they have, and I just can't notice yet. I try to look down as I stumble onward, but it's too dark to see if I'm hurt.

Onward and onward, I trudge through the night, alternating my calls between their two names, wishing more than ever now I'd told Charon to fuck off back in my office earlier today. Peculiarly, I also find myself thinking about a reality where I didn't get fired from VitaLyfe. I try to imagine in my mind what I might have done differently these last few years, and I play out conversations between me and Chad, and then between me and Allie… including the big ones.

Somewhere, in the midst of all these hallucinations, fantasies, and dreams, I come to a place where I can see a faint color in the distance. It might not be big, and it might not be real, but it's the first thing I've seen out here in hours that gives off any kind of light, movement, sound, or hope.

My pace quickens as I hurtle forward in the direction of this beacon, trying my best to evenly split my attention between where I'm going and where, specifically, I'm running along the ground. There's a slow, dull pain in one of the toes on my right foot now, and as I reach down to touch it and then bring my fingers back up to my eyes and next to my nose, I realize that maybe, despite my best efforts, I've injured myself all the same out here in the unforgiving wilderness. Blood is the least of my worries, though.

I pick up my speed again as the color glows brighter and brighter, until I can make out that it's fire, and before I know it, I'm running around the pool again as I close in on the very same fire pit where my search first began.

Now, however, I am truly and inescapably alone. Charon, Isla, and Nolan have all vanished. The fire burns low in the pit, and Charon's iron poker lies unattended against the side of a folding chair. The water in the pool is calm and undisturbed. If I didn't know any better, I'd say that outside of this dying fire, there's no sign anywhere that six people very recently were here.

Of course, my sense of time is also utterly destroyed. The amount of time that's passed since I first went out looking for Portia and Bing could be five minutes, or it could be five hours. Distraught, I slide back into the same folding chair that I think I sat in not so very long ago.

Everything is quiet all around me. The only sound is the occasional gaseous pop of the fire as it burns itself slowly out.

Maybe I could fall asleep out here. Maybe I do.

But suddenly, I feel cold. It's a new and remarkable sensation, considering how hot I've otherwise felt since arriving here in the desert. For the first time now, I'm conscious of the fact that I'm not just cold, I'm freezing.

I wonder just how much of what I'm feeling is real and how much is drug induced. No matter what Isla claims she did or didn't put in our brownies and our cocktails, there's no denying the fact that all of us were drugged somehow. It's the only logical explanation for the way my brain continues to stutter-step its way through the unknown and the unexplainable, and it would also explain the disappearances of Bing and Portia.

Vaguely, I wonder if this is that same Viaticum drug that I've seen Bing and Nolan take before, or if this is something different altogether. It certainly doesn't feel like a 'brain-booster' to me, if it is Viaticum.

Cold, tired, and defeated, I decide to ask myself a question. It's a simple question, in theory, but it holds great weight and significance, if you really stop and think about it.

Can I live with myself if I fully commit to sleep right now?

On the surface, there's nothing more I can do. I already went out searching for them in the dark, and—surprise, surprise—I didn't find them out there. Not only is it nigh impossible to conduct a proper search in the desert at night, but it's even harder to do it while you're tripping on unknown quantities and qualities of drugs, and especially if the people you are searching for are also tripping on those same quantities and qualities of drugs.

My memory's shot, and I could be wrong, but I *think* that I had one full brownie, split into two halves, and spaced out over some unknown amount of time, with one drink along the way. Portia did the same as me. Nolan took two brownies because he put an extra one in his mouth at the very beginning.

What about Bing, though? The tray was empty. Could it be possible that the twenty-year-old engineer under a mountain of stress took not one, not two, not three, but *four* brownies, and then washed them all down with a mojito for good measure? Isla did take a bite off the corner of one brownie, but as far as I know, she didn't have any more; she set it back on the side of the pool. And Charon came out only after all the snacks and drinks were gone.

The optimistic, naïve part of my carousel brain wants to believe that both Bing and Portia are sleeping somewhere peacefully. Hell, maybe they're sleeping inside the cabin right now. I've spent so much time out here thinking about all this and spinning out in mental circles, it never even occurred to me that maybe they found their way back while I was out looking for them.

I get up and stagger toward the back door. All the lights inside are turned off; everything is as dark inside the cabin as it is outside. Only the red embers of the fire in the pit remain; those, and the soft gold lightbulb strings, stars, and moon, of course.

Even the stars and moon seem about ready to turn in, though. The moon is further away in the sky than I remember clocking it the last time I checked, and all those constellations that were so easy to spot earlier in the night now seem lost to me in a dizzying blur of contrasts.

I try the sliding door, but it won't budge. Thinking maybe I'm just out of my mind, literally, and not pulling or pushing it the proper way, I try it again. Still, no luck.

Discouraged but not defeated, I decide to slip around the cabin and go try the front door. I can't remember if it was locked or unlocked when Isla greeted me so many long hours ago, but I do remember coming in that way at least when I first got here.

My legs are wobbly as my bare feet climb the ancient stone steps. The front door materializes like a desert oasis in front of me. I'm almost afraid to knock on it, but finally, I steel my courage and smack my knuckles against the solid wood.

Nothing. Just like at the back door, it seems like all of a sudden, no one is even here at all.

I know that can't be true, though. If they're not out back by the pool or by the fire pit, then they must be sleeping inside. Either that, or maybe Charon, Isla, and Nolan all came out looking for me, Portia, and Bing.

For some reason, I doubt that, though. It seems

infinitely more probable that there are people inside these walls just sleeping in wanton ignorance and apathy while their very friends, employees, and coworkers wander aimlessly outside in the dark and in the cold, suffering from the very same drugs that *they* provided.

This is getting absurd. If they're not going to open up the doors, then I'm going to have to break my way in. It's not something I've ever done before, or something I've ever planned to do, but if it's a matter of getting indoors where all my things are—not to mention a bed—or sleeping outside in my swimsuit in the cold with who knows what kind of wild animals prowling about… well, I'll do whatever I have to do.

I shamble off to the backyard again until I'm face to face with the glass sliding door. I knock heavily, violently, against it one more time, and wait for a response. When nothing happens, I start planning my next move. There's a small decorative boulder set off by the far end of the pool. I walk up to it, assess it, and pick it up slowly with two hands. This just might do.

With the grim determination of someone trying to survive in the wild—because that's exactly what I'm doing—I count silently in my head and then hurl the large rock at the glass sliding door.

Shockingly, it bounces harmlessly to the ground.

Undeterred, I pick it back up, move a couple steps further back, and prepare to toss it again.

This time, I really let loose with full abandon. Closing my eyes and reminding myself that entering this cabin right now is a matter of life or death, I heave the stone with all my might against the sliding door.

The glass cracks this time, but still doesn't break. It also makes an awful sound as it happens. I shuffle forward to examine the jagged line in the door... and leap backward in terror when I see Charon staring back at me from the other side.

At first, I think I'm seeing him in the reflection, and I try to spin around to look behind me. My feet trip over themselves as I fumble and fall backward onto the ground in a painful heap.

The cracked glass door slides open and shut again as the real Charon advances on me in the darkness, his face blazing with a terrifying intensity of hatred and vengeance the likes of which I've never seen before in a human being.

I back up on the ground all the way to the fire pit, and I can feel the heat of the dying ashes on the back of my scalp when I realize that he's holding a double-barreled shotgun in front of him—and he's aiming it at me.

Even though the embers are mostly out, something old and evil burns in Charon's eyes as he stares me down. From behind him in the darkness, I can see a thin, glowing ring of fire haloing around his head.

I hold up a quaking hand against the awful nightmare of the gun. How is this happening? Is he really about to kill me?

"Richard... please... it's me... it's Ethan... I'm sorry... it's me..."

Tall and terrible, Charon glares down the barrel of his firearm at my helpless being splayed out on the ground before him like easy prey. If he recognizes me, he doesn't care. Nothing in his face, body, or spirit changes from one second to the next. The very air outside reeks of pain, fury, and bloodlust.

Death finally blooms between the two of us. I close

my eyes as I either see or imagine his finger pulling the trigger, and I think of Allie and of our unborn child, and how I'll never get to be there for them.

This waiting is almost as excruciating as my imagination right now. If this is it, I want it to be over already.

I open my eyes.

He's gone.

What?

I don't understand.

Too confused and too horrified to feel even a modicum of relief yet, I pull my shivering body off the ground and look everywhere for danger.

The sliding glass door is shut. It's dark inside. No one is out here with me; at least, no one that I can see.

It's hard to be sure, but it does look like there's a jagged crack running down the back door. That *must* have actually happened.

The low embers of the fire have completely gone out. Not even smoke rises from the pit. Everything around me is still, quiet, fearful, and dark.

I stifle a sob and move up to try the back door, hoping it was all just a bad dream or a hallucinogenic vision caused by the drugs. Sadistically, though, the door is still locked.

Something finally breaks and gives way inside me. Drugged, cold, scared, confused, and tired, my weariness is the condition that wins out, and I throw myself into the same hammock that I think Bing laid in once upon a time.

Darkness overtakes me. Maybe even peace at last.

Somewhere in the bottomless midst of it all, touch rekindles my consciousness just long enough to make my eyelids flutter. Someone else is here with me in the hammock, and they're burrowing into my body now as if their very life depends on it.

No words are spoken, but somehow, it's silently understood that neither one of us plans to resist the other as we each remove what little clothing the other person has left. In the breathless dark, we slide as close together as two strangers are physically capable of.

Maybe all this happens... and maybe I'm just dreaming.

CHAPTER THIRTEEN

It's still dark outside, but it's quickly fleeting when I regain full consciousness again.

I know immediately from the smell of the hair my face is buried in that it doesn't belong to Allie. She's been using the same shampoo and conditioner for the full extent of our marriage—and maybe even longer than that. I know what her hair smells like just like I know what the weight of her in the bed feels like, what the sound of her light snoring in the morning sounds like, and what the touch and temperature of her body feels like against my own when we're holding onto each other.

This is not any of those things. This hair smells like chlorine and stale dust, the weight is all wrong, there's no heavy breathing or gentle snoring, and the body I'm pressed against is cool and foreign to me.

In a dull stupor, I extricate myself from this alien presence. She shivers slightly in the dawn breeze but otherwise remains still and silent as I carefully pull away from her and disentangle from the hammock. As difficult as it is to do this gracefully and quietly, I have all the motivation in the world, as I cannot bear the thought of actually waking her and having a real conversation right now.

When I'm finally free and back on the ground in communion with gravity, I crawl past her discarded black bathing suit and reach for Charon's swim trunks. It's far from freezing out here in the early morning twilight, but I still have goosebumps on my thighs as I hurriedly mask the shame of my nakedness with the borrowed shorts.

I can't let myself think about what may have happened. At least, not yet. Instead, I'll ward off the barrage of thoughts and questions ramming at my pounding brain by coming up with distractions and concrete actions that I can take. Maybe if I just keep moving, I can leave all this behind me, and I'll never have to face it. Maybe I can just wake myself up.

I definitely won't look at her again. Instead, I'll go inside.

If I can…

Half-formed memories come flying at me in broken flashes of imagery and sensation. There's really no way of discerning what's real and what's not. For all I know, I'm still tripping on whatever mystery substance or substances I consumed last night.

That said, I do have multiple strong associations with being locked out of this cabin. I remember trying the front door as well as the back door, endlessly hammering on both until my fists felt like they could break. There's also half a memory of hurling a rock at the glass until it finally cracked, and then seeing Charon advancing on me… and with a shotgun.

Doubt surges in at once. That last part doesn't feel real or seem real at all. There's no rhyme or reason for why Charon would pull a gun on me. Unless maybe he thought I was an intruder? Even still, I swear I remember being on the ground and backing up as he marched on me and held his aim. I backed all the way up until I ran into the firepit and singed my head on the embers.

Reaching back now, though, there's nothing funny about my hair back there or the skin beneath. No ash, no dried blood, no pain or tenderness when I rove my fingers around my scalp.

This is ridiculous. Whatever memories I think I might have of last night aren't to be trusted with any kind of seriousness. From the moment Isla brought out those brownies and drinks until right this very second, I'm choosing to disbelieve and disavow anything and everything that may or may not have happened while we were all not of sound mind.

There's an ugly, jagged line running crooked down the glass of the back door that has another idea, though. I touch two fingers to where it starts up high in a strange but beautiful amoeba-like design that could be a spiderweb or a snowflake.

Did I do this? I had to have. Unless my drug-addled brain saw someone or something else do this to the glass and then decided to take credit for it in a dream or a hallucination, the most plausible scenario is that I actually did try to break in with a rock sometime last night. And if that actually happened...

No. Don't go there. At least, not yet.

Ironically, the damaged door opens without issue when I pull on the handle now. My eyes fixate on the crack as I step inside the air-conditioned cabin interior and close the sliding door behind me.

What exactly is my plan right now, or my exact

course of action? Both feel startlingly unknown. All I know though is that I *need* action; I need to keep moving. Otherwise, I'll just be dormant and dwell in my head, and that's where all these ghosts of memories want to congregate.

First things first, I should pee. I actually kind of have to pee, so this is good; I can start with something nice and easy.

Of course, halfway down the hallway to the bathroom I get stopped by a voice from the kitchen.

"Ethan! You're up early. Can I fix you some tea or coffee?"

Isla stops me in my tracks. She's in the exact same spot I saw her in last night: sitting atop a laminate counter with her legs crossed, right next to a window that faces the backyard area. It's unsettling how eerily similar this tableau is to what I saw yesterday evening.

Only this time, the blinds in the window are closed instead of open, she's holding a mug of tea instead of a goblet of wine, and she's wearing a much more ordinary (and much more modest) floral terrycloth bathrobe instead of her silk black kimono.

"Hi. Morning. I'm just… on my way to the bathroom, actually."

She blows slowly on her tea.

"Well, hurry back if you'd like after. I'll make us breakfast and we can have a chat."

I don't think I want to have a chat.

"Sure."

It's the best I can come up with on the spot as I flee to the sanctuary of a locked restroom.

When I'm done, I take stock from the hallway and realize that all three bedroom doors are open, and each room appears unoccupied. The bed in the Charons' master is made, as is Portia's bed and the bed that was supposed to be mine. Only Nolan's bed across from mine is unmade, but he's not sleeping in it.

Cautiously, I step inside the room I tried so hard to get back into last night. As if I'm checking for a monster from a nightmare, I even open the closet to see if he's sleeping in there on the floor, but he's not.

Thankful for my momentary solitude, I lock the bedroom door and decide to change out of the dirty but dry swimsuit and into something more normal and hopefully more dignified. Briefly, I contemplate crawling into my tiny twin-sized bed and falling asleep. I have no idea what time it is, and I also don't really care, but if I slept at all last night, it was a fitful, restless, vivid sleep that afforded me no real recharge.

I have my hand on the comforter when I think better of the decision. Where is everybody? Something's off this morning. Things aren't adding up.

Eventually, my curiosity gets the best of me, and I decide to go back into the main area. I still have no desire to 'have a chat' with Isla, but I'm also wondering if I walked right past Bing in the living room on my way in just now and didn't see him.

He's not there in the den, though. If he did sleep in the pull-out sofa sleeper, he's since put it back. And yet, the old yellow couch looks completely undisturbed. There are no pillows, blankets, or sheets anywhere on or around it.

Isla has started working on breakfast. She has a carton of eggs out, and she's already frying bacon and sausage links in a skillet.

"How do you like your eggs, darling?"

I take a seat at a small, round kitchen table in the corner. Despite my best-laid plans to keep moving and stay active at all costs, I can't deny how good this feels just to sit down. I'm so incredibly tired, and my body feels like shit. There's already a full-blown headache splitting my cranium open from the inside, and now my stomach's starting to turn and grow nauseous, as well. The smell of greasy food cooking on the stove definitely isn't helping me any, either.

"Thanks, but I think I'll hold off for now, Isla… on all of it. I'm not feeling so great."

She looks surprisingly devastated by this revelation, but she only pauses for a second before continuing on with her work.

"Oh, *bugger*. I'm sorry to hear that, Ethan. Can I get you anything? Water? Aspirin? Bloody Mary?"

I just catch her wink as she says that last bit between cracking open two eggs. The very idea of tomato juice and vodka together might be enough to get me to vomit.

"Just a water would be great. Thanks."

She pours me a glass, and I swallow it in gulps. It's only when my stomach makes an ominous gurgling sound that I realize I'd better slow down or even stop altogether before we have some serious problems.

"Where is everybody?"

Isla finishes breaking the last of the eggs into a second skillet. I wasn't counting, but it seems like she used the full dozen, and I'm not quite sure why, since I already told her I couldn't handle any food just yet, and no one else is in here right now.

"Well, Portia's outside."

She's actually bold enough to raise her eyebrow and give me a quick, cutting glance over her shoulder when she says this before she slowly turns back around to the stove and continues.

"Richard took the dogs and went back already. Nolan's out for a sunrise hike, but he should be back any minute."

There's so much to unwrap here.

"Wait. Richard went back already? Back to L.A.?"

Isla nods.

"Yes. He left pretty much right after he figured everything out."

Am I really that brain-dead, or is she just speaking gibberish right now?

"I'm sorry. Figured what out?"

Isla turns again and gives me a mysterious smile.

"Our little TrendBeat predicament. That's what he was inside working on while we were all out frolicking in the pool."

Like a bad dream, I summon up a shadowy image in my mind of two dark figures at the edge of the water, with one bending around the other's neck and whispering into his ear.

"So, he figured out Bing's space issue, then? That's it? He knows how to make it all fit?"

Isla shrugs and starts scooping the eggs and meats onto plates.

"Don't ask me, darling. I'm just director of recruiting. They may as well be speaking Chinese when they start in with all that tech rubbish."

We agree on that much, at least.

"Is that where Bing is? He went back with Richard?"

Isla hesitates ever so briefly.

"Yes."

She spins around then and sets the steaming plates

down on the table—and far too close for my liking. It takes everything in my power not to instinctively turn my nose away or cover my mouth with my hand.

"Are you sure you won't eat? I know Nolie will when he gets back, and I figured maybe you and Portia both would be hungry."

There she goes again with her not-so-subtle vocal intonations and facial expressions. I lower my eyes away from her and choose to focus on the remaining water in my glass instead. I'm not about to be baited, especially not on the one subject I'm trying more than anything to avoid confronting this morning.

"I'm good for now, thank you, though. Actually, what's the plan today? If Richard and Bing have everything already worked out, there's really no reason for us to be here any longer, right? Are we calling the drivers back?"

Isla pulls out a chair next to me and sits down with her tea. The more normal seat to choose would have been the chair across the table, since it's just the two of us. But I've also come to realize at this point that normal just isn't in Isla's nature.

"What's the rush? Didn't you have fun last night?"

The innuendo practically drips off her tongue.

"Yeah. Too much fun, actually. Don't get me wrong, this was wonderful that you guys did this and brought us all out here. I just—I think if it's all the same to you, I'd rather get back home. Get back to the office, I mean. It's only Tuesday."

She coos into her tea.

"It *is* only Tuesday…"

"Right. So, there's probably plenty of work to get to. Especially with whatever new stuff Richard and Bing have on their plate now."

"*Richard and Bing* have it on their plate now."

Never in a million years did I think I'd ever find myself a job where I'd be the one trying to convince my boss to let me do more work. It just further adds to this overall sense of unnatural surrealism that's taken hold of everything since I arrived in the desert—and, to some extent, since I arrived at Olympus.

"Isla. I'd really like to get back, please. Who do I need to—how do I get ahold of Eric and tell him to come out here?"

She pouts dramatically.

"Well, if I *really* can't convince you otherwise, I suppose I could get on the landline and give *all* our drivers a ring after breakfast. The others will be so disappointed, though."

"They don't have to go, and you don't have to go, either. If you want to just give me Eric's number and tell me where the phone is, I can call him up myself."

Isla tosses her head back and laughs wildly.

"*Dar-ling!* It's not yet eight in the morning! You're mad if you think Eric's awake in Las Vegas, Nevada, right now."

I'm just about to tell her that I'll take my chances— he's probably still out partying from last night anyway— when the front door to the cabin bangs open and closed. My heart skips a beat as I prepare to face Portia, but then I remember that she's out back.

Nolan is the one who comes striding in, all sweat and stench and sunburn. He's dressed comically from head to toe in tan-colored hiking gear, including a wide-brimmed straw hat with a drawstring pulled up tight against his pink throat. If I wasn't so miserable and on edge, I'm sure I'd laugh openly at his ridiculous appearance.

When he sees me, he grins lasciviously, pulls out the chair on my other side, and plops down in a cloud of dust and odor.

"Well! Good morning, *stud*. And how are we today?"

Already, there's an extra insinuation and implication in his usual antics that I know I won't be able to tolerate.

"Not today, Nolan. I'm not in the mood."

He looks at Isla and then back at me.

"*Jesus*. Was it really that bad? I'd have thought you'd be on cloud nine this morning."

"Shut the fuck up."

"Did you just not last very long or what?"

I lurch from my chair and shove him backward in the chest. He tries to fend me off with his hands, but we both fall over and onto the ground as our chairs clatter to the floor around us. We grunt and grapple at each other, only landing glancing blows and mostly just trying to keep our faces away from each other's fists and fingers while we struggle to get up off of our sides and pin the other person down in a position where someone can do some actual damage.

It's an embarrassing fight overall, and a short one that Isla easily breaks up by literally grabbing me around the ankles and dragging me away from him.

"Boys! *Boys!* This is *absurd!* Get ahold of yourselves! *NOW!*"

I'm the first to get back on my feet. Isla helps me up while also pulling me further away from Nolan, and once I'm fully vertical and at least somewhat confident I'm not about to throw up, I break away from her, as well.

"Call Eric! And call him *now*—not after breakfast!

I'm getting out of here if I have to fucking *walk* home!"

She cries out my name a couple of times as I storm off down the hallway into my bedroom and lock the door.

Despite all the rage roaring up inside me—as well as the sick—I'm struck by how juvenile everything just felt. Fighting at the breakfast table with Nolan, Isla stepping in and separating us like a mother hen, me running off to my room and locking the door behind me; it's like some sick, bizarre pseudo-family-drama we've all just played an archetypical role in.

Except this is real. It's all too real. And as much as I keep trying to avoid it, these people are making that harder and harder to do.

I collapse on the end of my bed and let my hands rove around my face for open wounds. Though I can't feel anything right off the cuff, that doesn't mean there's not an injury somewhere on my body that I'm just not touching or seeing right at this moment.

Vaguely, I reminisce on a fleeting memory of pain somewhere on a toe—maybe on my right foot?—but when I look down to examine the appendage, everything looks fine, albeit a little ragged and dirty.

To be honest, I was in plenty of pain and psychophysical agony even before my dust-up with Nolan. Asking myself 'where does it hurt?' is a silly question, since the true answer is 'everywhere'.

I half-expect Nolan to come charging down the hallway after me and bang on the door, angling for another brawl or accusing me of messing with his stuff or something similarly infantile. But it's actually very quiet out there. I guess Isla either calmed him down or took him outside, because I don't hear either one of them anymore. Maybe she finally agreed that I shouldn't be here any longer, and she's actually calling Eric right now to come and get me.

Sitting here, being still and doing nothing, it's impossible not to let my mind wander… and that's exactly what I'm trying not to do. Again, I ponder trying to sleep. But even if I wasn't so profoundly terrified of being alone with my thoughts and memories, I'm not sure if I'd be able to. Exhausted as I am, I also feel jittery, nauseous, and sort of hollow inside. Maybe this is what it feels like to be cracked out. Hell, maybe I actually am cracked out.

Fuck it. I can't just sit in here and wait to be rescued like a fairytale princess. I'm not afraid of Nolan, and I'm not afraid of Isla. Sucking up my courage and sucking down the bile that's forever tickling the back of my throat this morning, I stand back up, open the door, and move as confidently as I can back down the hallway and into the kitchen.

Nolan and Isla are both gone. But Portia's here now. And that's a hundred million times worse. She's sitting across the table in a chair with her knees pulled up to her chest and her arms hugging her legs in close. The bacon, eggs, and sausage are all untouched on the table beside Isla's abandoned tea and my abandoned water.

Portia's wearing her black bathing suit from last night. She looks up at me blankly as I enter the room.

"Hey."

"Hey."

An awkward silence follows. This is even worse than I feared.

"Look."

She points at the plates in front of her.

"The breakfast fairies must have come and gone before sunrise this morning."

I respect her attempt at lightening the mood, but I'm not sure it's possible for me to get on her level.

"Yeah... Isla made all that. I'm not sure for whom... but if you're hungry, I think it's available."

She holds herself tighter.

"I'm not hungry."

"Neither am I."

Another awkward silence. This time, I'm the one who breaks it.

"So, I need to ask you something... if that's all right..."

"Oh, God. You're not about to make things weird, are you? If you are, then maybe you just shouldn't ask."

"I need to know though... about what happened last night."

She considers me thoughtfully for a second.

"Do you?"

"Do I what?"

"Do you need to know?"

It's an interesting question. Honestly, it's not something I've really considered. Not that I've really considered any of this.

"What are you talking about?"

Portia sighs.

"Look, I'm gonna be one hundred percent honest with you. I feel like dogshit this morning; like a freight train ran over my skull, hit the brakes until it screeched to a stop, then went back over me in reverse a second time just for funsies. If you really want to have this conversation, we can have it. But I *beg* you to let it happen later on in the afternoon or in the evening."

253

It's a reasonable request, but one I can't grant unfortunately.

"I would, but I'm leaving soon. I told Isla to call my driver and get him here ASAP. I'm headed back home."

"Oh, no. Really? Was that what all the commotion was about?"

"No, that was about me and Nolan getting into a fight. Isla had to break it up."

"No shit? What was it about?"

"It's not important. Listen…"

I decide to sit down across from her.

"Portia, I know this isn't easy. But I really do need to know what happened last night."

She lowers her feet down to the ground, leans forward, and rests her forearms on top of the table.

"Why? Why do you need to know, Ethan? And furthermore, what even is there to know? We all had a bunch of brownies and cocktails that probably had drugs in them. Things got crazy. But that's what happens when you have a bunch of brownies and cocktails that probably had drugs in them. End of story. Case closed."

How can she so casually dismiss all this?

"Umm… *no*, it's not that simple. At least not for me."

I don't know why I even bother to look around to see if we're alone still, since apparently everyone else already knows, but I do it anyway before proceeding in a barely audible whisper.

"Portia… I think we had sex last night."

She doesn't even blink.

"Okay. Well. If that happened, then it happened."

I give her a chance to keep talking, but she doesn't seem interested.

"That's it?"

"That's it."

She sees my face.

"What do you want me to say?"

"I don't know. But I figured you'd say something more than that…"

"You want me to apologize?"

"No—"

"Because I won't."

She straightens in her chair.

"I'm not going to apologize if we slept together, because I'm not even sure that we actually did. I don't know about you, but my brain is awfully foggy on just about everything last night and this morning. Once again, *drugs* and *alcohol* will do that to you."

"We woke up naked next to each other in a hammock."

"Did we *fuck* though? Do you remember that? Because—no offense—I don't. I mean, I *think* we may have. And I also think I might have just dreamt that. And then there's also a part of me that thinks maybe you're just planting the idea right now in my head and my brain is too milky and mushed up to tell the difference."

"I'm almost positive we had sex."

She thinks.

"Okay. Well, then I guess we had sex. What do you want me to do about it?"

Why is she having such a hard time understanding how this is a problem?

"I just don't understand why you're being so… cavalier about all this."

Portia's expression softens a bit.

"I'm not trying to be *cavalier* about all this. I just don't know what kind of reaction you want from me. I already told you that I don't remember all of what happened last night because we were on drugs. If you think we had sex, then I believe you. Are you worried about this making things awkward between us? Because right now—*this* conversation we're having right now—this is what's going to make things awkward between us. Not whether or not two grown adults fooled around while they were both smashed out of their minds."

"Portia. I'm married."

She shakes her head slowly and tries to muster a meek, comforting smile.

"Okay. Well, I know that. Again, I don't really know what you want me to say. This isn't, like, some devious plan I hatched to bring you out here to the desert, get you fucked up, take advantage of you, and ruin your marriage. I hope you know me better than that."

"It's just—I *don't* know you all that well. I just met you a month ago. I just met everyone a month ago. This whole lifestyle—these mysterious pills everyone's always taking, the drug brownies, spontaneous cabin trips, playing *chicken* in the pool—that's not me. This isn't me. I don't know what things were like before me with you and Chuck, but I just think we need to dial back our working relationship…"

For a split second, I see genuine hurt streak across Portia's face. And then it's gone, shuttered and replaced by a cold, hard mask of emotionless indifference.

"Wow. And here I was trying to help you feel better about things. Thanks, Ethan."

She abruptly stands.

"I don't know what you think you've heard, but

Chuck and I were collaborators, and we were friends. That's it. Not that it's any of your business anyway."

Portia pushes her chair back and starts to move past me out to the hallway.

"Portia, wait—"

"Forget it, man. Sorry I wasted both of our time."

And then she's gone. A couple seconds later, I hear a door slam and assume she's gone to be alone in her bedroom.

Do I follow her? I can't really justify doing it. As much as I may have botched this entire dialogue, going and knocking on her bedroom door now and apologizing doesn't seem like it'll help. Plus, it just doesn't feel appropriate. Not that any of this feels appropriate.

I'd go to my own bedroom instead, but I'm not sure that's a good idea, either. Not only is it right next to hers, but it's also shared with another person. And it's the same person I just attacked in the kitchen, too. I can't stay in here, though, with these cold breakfast meat smells, or I'll throw up. Ultimately, I elect to go outside and get some fresh air.

For the first time all morning, I don't feel nauseous as I spread my body out on the ground beside the pool, lie on my back, and stare up at the unforgiving blue of the desert sky. Perhaps I overreacted in my fear of being alone, inactive, and present with my thoughts. Either that, or maybe I shockingly feel somewhat better after having talked to Portia. Sure, the conversation couldn't have gone much worse, but at least I know the truth now. Amidst all the fever dreams, vision quests, and wild-eyed wanderings, there's little doubt left in my head that Portia and I actually had sex.

What do I do about that, though? What *can* I do about that? Do I tell Allie? I have to tell her. Right? I mean; I don't *have* to tell her, technically, but it's the right thing to do.

Could I live with myself if I buried the secret down deep, locked it up, and forgot all about it? Or maybe she'd understand if I told her the whole naked truth of it all: the drugs, the alcohol, the peer pressure, the power dynamics.

She wouldn't excuse it, and she wouldn't forgive me any easier, but maybe—with the right amount of context—she could at least be made to understand *why* it happened. We're too old now to use inebriation as an excuse, but add in the proper context of this bizarre company culture and the murky relationship dynamics between all the major players, and maybe that might be enough to soften the blow just a tad. Allie's the one who's been reading about all these conspiracy theories, anyway. Maybe she's expecting it at this point.

Or maybe I should just never tell her.

Neither option is easy, and neither option is appealing. In a perfect world, I'd build a time machine and throw Isla's brownies into the pool. Or I'd just refuse to eat one. Or I'd go inside the cabin, find Charon, and help him solve all our problems while the rest of them act like buffoons and degenerates.

I don't have a time machine, though. All I have is a guilty conscience and a killer headache.

Who knows how long I've been out here for, frying on the inside and on the outside, when the sound of the sliding door wakes me up from my personal hell. Please, God, say it's not Portia or Nolan. I lift my head off the hot concrete to check.

It's Isla. Glad as I am that it's not one of the other two, I'm also not exactly relieved to see Isla, either. She strolls across the expanse of the backyard area and sits down next to me, then dips both feet into the pool.

"*Ahh*. That's better."

I should probably sit up, but I'm not going to. At least lying flat on the ground, I can control my nausea; even if it's the only thing I have control over anymore.

"Isla, I'm sorry about earlier in the kitchen. With Nolan. That was uncalled for."

"What's done is done. I hate to see my boys in a row, but I also understand, given the history between them, why you'd both react the way you did."

I pause.

"The history between who?"

Isla splashes her feet in the water.

"Why, between Portia and Nolan, of course. You knew about them, didn't you?"

I don't believe it.

"No. I didn't know. They dated?"

Isla's voice is all singsong.

"Oh, I don't know if you would even call it dating. You know how it is with you young people nowadays: no boundaries, rules, or expectations."

Somehow, I feel like this should have come up at some point from someone. I'm all sorts of things right now: surprised, disgusted, judgmental, disappointed. And, more to my own personal dismay, I'm even sort of jealous. But I know that reaction is irrational, irresponsible, and dangerous, so I add it to the growing blacklist of mental items I plan to never visit again.

Isla interrupts my train of thought by cupping her palm to my cheek.

"I hope I haven't said too much."

I tilt my head to look up into her soft, kind eyes. They're even more baby blue with the full expanse of the late morning sky behind them.

"It doesn't matter. Whatever it was, I don't care."

"And why should you care, darling? You've got a lovely wife yourself now, don't you? I'm sure she'll be thrilled to pieces when she learns you came home early today, the conquering hero returning in triumph."

She rubs her thumb slowly from my earlobe to the corner of my mouth.

"By the by, I gave all our drivers a ring before taking naughty old Nolie out back for a spanking. The cars should be here any minute now, if you want to get your things together."

I sit up, perhaps a bit too quickly. I'm glad the movement breaks me free of her fingers, but I'm also not fully prepared for the sudden wave of dizziness that comes over me as my vision swims in and out.

Isla giggles.

"Steady now, Romeo. Steady."

She pulls her feet up from the water, swings herself around, and comes to stand with a long, audible sigh.

"It's a pity, actually. I had such beautiful plans for this trip. And here we are, not twenty-four hours arrived, and we're already headed back."

Cautiously, and with a great deal of effort, I battle back gravity and nausea as I hoist myself up off the ground and onto my legs again.

"No one said you had to leave. Any of you. I just need to get back myself."

She places a hand on my shoulder and smiles.

"We're family now, Ethan. Where one goes, we all

go."

I do my best to smile back at her before detaching myself and heading back toward the cabin. Halfway there, I stop and turn around.

"Isla... random question, but... you and Richard, you guys don't keep a gun out here, do you?"

Of all the hammocks, chairs, and beanbags out here to choose from, of course Isla's moved over and spread herself out luxuriously in the exact same hammock that Portia and I woke up together in this morning. She laughs.

"A gun? Richard and I are both pacifists. We'd probably shoot ourselves just trying to get the damn thing loaded. Why do you ask?"

"No reason. Strange... dream, that's all."

Isla closes her eyes and basks in the sun.

"That sort of thing will happen out here, darling. It always does."

I leave her in the hammock and go inside. There's still no sign of Nolan anywhere since this morning's altercation; he's not in our room, even though his stuff still is. Portia's door is shut. I hope that she's sleeping, and that she'll feel better when she wakes up.

There's not much to pack or get ready for my departure, since I never really unpacked to begin with. I get my suitcase all set, use the bathroom, and come out to the kitchen. Feeling brave, I pick up a piece of bacon and take a bite off the end, chew methodically, and swallow.

Well, at least I didn't *immediately* throw up. I don't want to push it, though. I finish what's left of my water, refill the glass, drink that down, set it in the sink, and make my way out to the front of the cabin, nibbling gingerly on the piece of cold bacon in my hand throughout.

It's not long before the cars start to arrive. The first driver to get here isn't Eric—this person identifies himself as Mark—but he's still more than willing to take me back to Los Angeles if I'm ready, which I am. I sit in the back seat with the air conditioning on full blast, worrying that at any second now, Isla or Nolan or Portia is going to come running out from inside the cabin to stop us and delay our escape for some terrible reason I won't be able to stomach.

But they don't. No one comes, the front door remains shut, and eventually, Mark puts the car in drive as we begin the long journey back to civilization. Mark's a bit more of a talker than Eric was, but now I'm the one who's polite, yet otherwise tight-lipped. Thankfully, it doesn't take him long to pick up on my verbal cues, and we complete the rest of the long trek back to Los Angeles in silence.

Hours have gone by when he abruptly asks if he's taking me home or to the office. To be honest, I've been wrestling with that same dilemma myself. No one explicitly said what the expectation was for all of us today. I know Charon and Bing left in the middle of the night to get back to Olympus, but I also know that Isla intimated there was no great rush for any of the rest of us to go back in.

After some internal deliberation, I tell Mark to take me home, and I give him my address. If there's one thing I know right now, it's that I'm in no fit state of mind, body, or spirit to have *the* conversation with my wife just yet. Because of that, I'm glad Allie's at work right now and that I'll have the house all to myself. *If* I decide to have *the* conversation with her—and just how redacted the contents of that conversation will be—are questions I'm simply not mentally or emotionally prepared to answer just yet.

I thank Mark for the ride when he finally idles up in front of our house. He tells me that he hopes I have 'a good one'. I tell him that I hope so, too.

Chapter Fourteen

When the town car drives away and I'm left alone and standing at the end of our sidewalk gazing up at our house, that's when it really hits me what I've done.

Some 'conquering hero returning in triumph'.

Allie's probably at work wondering why I never called last night to let her know I got there safely. Even without any cell service myself, I certainly could have asked the others if any of them had a signal. It also never occurred to me that a powerhouse tech couple would have a landline in their cabin.

In retrospect, that makes sense as well, when you consider how remote and isolated it is out there. How else did I expect the Charons to contact our drivers in Vegas? Smoke signals? Carrier pigeons?

This Death Valley expedition was already a tough pill to swallow for Allie and me because of how it was sprung on us and how it came with so few known variables. I could have done more on my end to try and make it better for us both. Instead, I took a bad situation that was already extremely combustible, and I chucked a stick of dynamite at it by getting into a fight with her on my way there.

I have no idea how well I'll hold up when I see her

later on tonight. I've been playing out that encounter over and over in my head ever since I left the cabin, and every hypothetical rendering ends differently.

In some variations, I'm able to successfully blockade the terrible truth and keep it locked far away from Allie… at least for now. In other versions, she sees it written plain as day all over my guilty face the second she walks in through the front door.

Maybe it's not too late to adopt Portia's school of thought in suggesting we might not have actually had sex. Maybe we moved in that general direction but then we both passed out, and it was only waking up naked next to one another that made me draw any conclusions.

If we'd at least woken up in our swimsuits, I feel like it'd be an easier narrative to convince myself of. It's still a terrible look for a married man and an expectant father to fall asleep next to his coworker on a business trip, but between the psychoactive substance consumption and the fabric shields that would have separated our flesh, at least it'd be possible not to immediately assume the worst.

That's not what happened, though. Whatever did or didn't actually happen between us, I know how we were when I woke up. And that's something I'm going to have to live with for the rest of my life. I just don't know how yet, or whether I should force Allie to share that heavy burden of my shame with me.

It's a long, slow walk up to the door. This is supposed to be a happy surprise, coming home early like this, after only one night away. That's the angle I need to latch onto and embrace with every atom of my being. I just need to keep reminding myself that on the surface, there's nothing awful or suspicious about this homecoming whatsoever.

This is a good thing. It's a good thing for both of us. Maybe I'll take a long shower and then a long nap. And then maybe before she gets home from work, I'll cook dinner for us. Her favorite meal, perhaps. Maybe that will do the trick.

Steadying my breath and my thoughts, I twist my key in the lock and turn the knob—and nothing happens. I repeat the motion a couple times, but for whatever reason, the door's still not opening, even though I can feel my key pulling the lock free in the wood.

Am I still on drugs, or what is happening right now? The key and the knob are both working fine like they always do, but the door's just not opening.

After half a minute of trying to figure out just what I'm doing wrong, the thought finally dawns in my brain that maybe the deadbolt's drawn. Which is odd. We never use the deadbolt. And why would the deadbolt be drawn if no one's home? Something's not right.

Slowly, I pull my phone out of my pocket, thankful that I took Mark the town car driver up on his offer to plug it in and charge it for me on the ride home. I call Allie's number and it rings, rings, rings, and then goes to voicemail. I do this a second time, and it's the same thing all over again.

There's no reason why she wouldn't be at work right now. She's at work right now, and that's why she's not picking up her phone. There must be some other explanation for why the deadbolt's drawn on our front door.

I look around our street, feeling a bit foolish standing locked outside my home in the middle of the afternoon with a suitcase beside me. I recognize one of my neighbors out mowing his lawn, and I wave to him, but he doesn't see me. Probably for the best. I try calling Allie a third time. When it goes to voicemail yet again, I pull up our messaging history to send her a text.

At the top, there are several unanswered incoming messages from her that I never received while in Death Valley, all asking whether I'd made it there safe and sound, and all imploring me to call or text her back whenever I can. The timestamps for these messages are all over the place. Clearly, the service while I was out there in the desert was even more nonexistent than I initially expected.

At the bottom, there are three images. Upon first glance, I can't really see what they are; the pictures are dark and hard to decipher. It just looks like three low-lit photos showing a blurry blob in the middle of a blue-black background.

I touch one of them to make it expand and see that the blob is actually two people. They're both naked and intertwined, this man and this heavily tattooed woman, lying together in a rope hammock. The other two images are different angles of the same scene, and between the three photos, it's possible to clearly make out their sleeping faces even in the dim lighting.

Below the third image is a 'read' timestamp earlier this morning, but otherwise, nothing in return from Allie.

I stare at the screen in abject shock, horror, and disbelief. I don't know what I'm looking at or how it even exists. This can't be real. It can't be real. I must be dreaming still or tripping. This isn't real.

But it is. It's right there on the screen of my phone,

all laid bare for me to see… and for her to see. I just don't understand it, though. Who took these? And how did they put them on my phone and send them to Allie?

My equilibrium gives out, and I quickly reach out my free hand and slap it against the door to stop from falling. All the dizziness, the motion sickness, the headache and the stomachache and the *heartache*, they all come rushing back at once as a dam breaks inside me.

I don't know what to do. What can I do? How do I fix this? I can't.

I just keep staring at my phone screen and wishing the images would disappear. Every time I close my eyes and open them again, it's all there still. I can't delete any of it and I can't unsend it. I can't make Allie unsee it. I can't undo any of it.

A new thought dawns on me. I race over to the garage and stand on my tiptoes to peer inside the decorative glass inlaid at the top. Sure enough, Allie's car is parked in there. She's not at work today; or if she once was, she's since come home early. Probably after she got these text messages; probably after she saw these pictures.

I run back over to the front door. Phone in hand, I frantically bang the backside of my fist against the wood.

"Allie! Allie!"

Over and over and over again, I hammer my bones against the wood, hoping that even if the sound doesn't bring her to me, the impact might be enough to crush my phone inside my palm until it's nothing more than tiny bits of bad glass and plastic. If I can smash it to smithereens, maybe it will take everything inside with it into oblivion, and all will be well again. Maybe I just need to splinter it up until blood starts to pour freely from my hand, and that will be enough of a human sacrifice and a true penance to atone for my sins that it will deliver me back into a state of grace.

"Allie…"

My voice breaks long before the phone does. Her name is garbled out between choking sobs and spittle as I keep beating on the door. Tears flow before blood, and there's nothing I can do to stop them. There's nothing I can do to stop any of it anymore.

"ALLIE! Allie, please…"

Through a blinding fit, I turn my phone hand around, and now I'm battering the screen against the wood in time with my screams. Harder and harder, I pound the evil machine into my front door, until finally there are other sounds besides the impact and my splitting voice yelling out her name, and then there are sharp stabs of pain all over my fingers and hand as either the bones inside break, or the skin gets ripped open and blood finally comes oozing out.

"Please, Allie… Allie, please… Allie…"

Something moves on the other side of the door; I see it through the glass at eye level. At first, all I can make out is a figure coming around the corner from our living room.

Ever so slowly, though, Allie comes fully into view. Our eyes meet as she draws nearer, and seeing that my wife who never cries has clearly been doing it plenty is enough to bring out a new wave of water from me. She moves close enough that I could reach out and trace the outline of the vein in her right temple if we weren't separated by this block of wood and glass. Her jaw is clenched, her nostrils flare as she breathes, and I can see that she's quivering all over as she looks me dead in the eye and lifts her cell phone up to the glass. I have no choice but to once again look upon what I've been trying so hard to destroy forever.

"What is this?"

Her muffled voice sounds husky from inside. She waits for a response, but all I can do is sob.

"What is this?"

I can't. I don't believe this is happening right now.

"Al... I... I..."

"What is this?"

The look on her face alone is enough to banish me straight to hell.

"Please. I—I'm sorry, Al, I..."

My legs feel like they're about to give out. I paw at the doorknob like a beast.

"Please... just let me in... please..."

I've never seen this kind of anguish; not from her before. She's holding it all down and holding it all in like she always does, because that's just the kind of person she is, but this is different. It's seeping out in cracks that only I can see, because only I know where to look for them. No one knows her like I do, and no one loves her like I do... and I'm losing her. It's happening right in front of me, and there's nothing I can say or do to stop it.

"Al... please, Allie... just let me come in..."

Her pink-brown eyes glaze over as she lowers her phone down and away from the glass until it's buried in her pants pocket, right below her belly where our child is growing.

"No."

Spasms rock my body as my breath and tears spill out onto the glass.

"Please... please, Allie..."

Allie shakes her head.

"No."

She stares into me for another long moment, and then she starts moving away.

"Allie! Allie, no, please! Please don't! Don't leave me... Allie... *please!"*

The further she gets from me, the louder I scream and pummel the door.

Something finally snaps inside me. Everything changes. Maybe it's pure, raw desperation. Whatever it is, it comes surging up from a dark, hidden place deep inside me, this dangerously old yet dangerously new thought and feeling.

"It's not fair! I forgave you!"

She stops just long enough to give me the courage to continue.

"With Chad! I *forgave* you!"

I can't tell if what I'm feeling is rage or agony anymore. Maybe it's still just desperation. But there's also a kind of catharsis that comes from recognizing the balance and equality in our relationship now. We've both strayed and made our mistakes, terrible as they were. I forgave her. Now she will forgive me. It's only fair.

Allie's standing just as still as before. I need to know that she is hearing me right now.

"It's the same thing. It's the exact same thing."

She turns back in my direction and there are fresh tears brimming up behind her glasses. But there's something different there, too. It's as if I've just stabbed her in the heart all over again; only this time, I twisted the blade.

"Get out of here. Go. My family are on their way.

Leave now… or I'll call the police."

She says it loud enough that I can hear her.

And then she's gone.

"Al! *Allie!* Allie, come back here! *Come back here right now!"*

The ground surges up to meet me as I fall sliding down the door, crumple, and collapse.

"It's the same thing… it's the same *fucking* thing… why can't you see that…"

There's nothing left to do but cry. So that's what I do. The only thing that I can do.

I keep waiting to hear the lock get pulled and the door swing open. All I need is a chance. If she has a change of heart, takes pity on me, and comes outside or lets me come inside, I can tell her the whole truth. I won't leave anything out. I'll tell her everything I know, every single detail, no matter how difficult it is for her or for me or for both of us. And together, we'll get through it.

Because that's what we did when this was her. When she was the one who came to me in tears begging for my forgiveness, begging me not to leave her, begging me not to leave VitaLyfe, begging me to talk to Chad, to talk our way through this, to stay professional, to stay realistic, to stay unemotional, to move forward, to move past this, to forget about all of this, to treat it like a mistake, a brief lapse in judgement, a freak anomaly never to be spoken of again… I did all of that and so much more, and I did it simply because she asked me to. Because she needed me to. I did it all for her.

And she can't even *listen* to me right now or hear me out? She can't even stand still for two seconds on the other side of the door in the house that my money paid for and listen to my explanation of what happened? She can't hear me out on how I was *drugged* in the desert and how everything that happened wasn't even my choice or my desire? She, of all people, after what she did and who she did it with, can't even *listen* to me?

By now, the desperation and the agony are long gone. Only the rage remains, and rightfully so.

Allie's not the only one deserving of it, though. She may be a hypocrite, but she's not a sadistic, manipulative, vengeful *fuck* who casually decides to destroy another person's life just out of jealousy and spite. Someone had to take those pictures and then knowingly send them to my wife from my very own phone. And I know exactly who that someone is.

It's time to get up. Slowly, I claw my way back up the door, pulling myself up by my own doorknob with my good hand. The other hand is swollen, bruised, and tender, and there's dried blood around my split knuckles. I can move my fingers enough to assume that maybe they're not actually broken, or if they are, at least they're still usable.

Miraculously, my phone is in a similar state. The screen is shattered everywhere, and the hard case protector is missing whole chunks of metal and plastic from the shell, but it looks like it still works somehow.

First things first, I need to get out of here. I don't think Allie would really call the cops on me, but I also can't set about fixing anything if I'm stuck inside a holding cell.

Moreover, coming face to face with Allie's sister, mother, or—God forbid—her father would only make things worse for every party involved right now. Unless she really wants me to go toe-to-toe with them—and I'm fairly confident they have no idea their precious Allison has a sordid history of skeletons in her own picture-perfect closet—I'm better off tackling that subject matter another time when I'm not in such a compromised emotional state myself.

Throwing my suitcase in the trunk of the Jag, I get in, start the engine, and back out down the driveway. While I don't know where exactly I'm going yet, I do know exactly whom I'm going to see.

I can't help it though; I stop and idle for a minute or so out front of our house, hoping and praying that maybe, just maybe, I'll see Allie come to the door, draw open a curtain at a window, or even just materialize like a shadow on the other side. For better or worse, right or wrong, I realize that I'll take anything I can get right now; any indication at all that she heard my car start and came to see what's happening and maybe is realizing now that yes, we both fucked up, and yes, that means we should both be forgiven.

When it's clear that none of that is happening, I plant my foot on the gas and lurch off down the street.

That's all right. It's all all right. I'll be back, Allie. Don't worry. I'll be back. Even if you can't see right now that this is just karma's sick, twisted way of balancing the scales, I'll come back for you. I'll be the bigger man; the bigger person. Let me take care of this first and right this wrong, and then I'll come home, and you'll realize that we were one and the same all along. We're both flawed; we're both people. That's what makes us great. That's what makes us *us*.

But first: Nolan.

CHAPTER FIFTEEN

I call his number five times in rapid succession and get his voicemail five straight times. After the fifth strikeout, I pull off onto a residential street in Hollywood and put the car in park for a minute.

He could realistically be anywhere in the city right now. There's even a chance he could still be in Death Valley. Isla did say she gave all their drivers a call though, so I'm assuming everyone left the cabin not long after I did. If that's the case, he's most likely either at the Charons' or at work.

But which one? I could hit both places. Obviously, it'll be easier for me to look for him at Olympus than it will be at the Charons' private residence on Mulholland, considering I only have immediate access to the former.

There's another solution that could help save me a trip, but it involves doing the one thing that any marriage counselor worth their salt would surely tell me not to do in this very moment and time. In light of everything that's already happened this morning though, I decide rather quickly that I don't really give a fuck anymore.

Of course, there's no guarantee she'll feel the same way, or that she'll even pick up the phone. That's why I'm surprised when she does after just a couple of rings.

"I only picked up because I'm *assuming* this is work-related. Tell me I'm right or I'm gone."

"It is. You guys aren't still out there, right? I'm looking for Nolan."

Portia pauses.

"Why?"

"I just need to talk to him, and he's not picking up his phone. I promise it's work-related."

Her voice is soaked in suspicion.

"What about?"

"Portia, please. It's important. All I'm asking is if you know what the plan was. Are you all coming into the office today, or is everyone going home?"

She hesitates again before finally answering.

"I can't speak for him, but I know Isla told both of us that we should take the rest of the day off to recharge and recuperate. I'm guessing that's what he did. Why? Where are you?"

"Recharging and recuperating. Thanks, Portia."

I end the call abruptly. Confident as I am that I'd be able to find my way there on my own, I decide to play it safe and pull up the Charons' home address in the search history of my maps application. Plugged in and ready to go, I set off on what my phone tells me will be just a twenty-minute drive. I do it in fifteen.

Déjà vu. It's right around the same time of day now as it was when I first came up here and parked in front of this massive shrub and camera-lined fence. On that occasion, I wanted nothing more than to get away from Nolan and make him someone else's problem. This time, I want nothing more than to get *to* Nolan and make him *my* problem.

Now that I'm here, I need to figure out a way to get

in. Or at least a way to get him to come out. I try calling him again as I pace outside my car in front of the Charons' property, but there's still no answer. At this point, I've memorized his stupid voicemail greeting.

'Where are you?' I type the words out and hit send on the text. An electric yellow sportscar comes flying around the bend and whizzes past me in a cloud of dust. I just don't understand how more people aren't dead every day on this stupid road.

Maybe it's my imagination, but the cameras seem to be following me as I move like a caged animal back and forth outside the high fence. I suppose it's not that absurd to think they're all motion activated. For no particular reason, I wave like a lunatic up at the one closest to me. Nothing happens. Of course nothing happens. What did I expect would happen?

Still, something about the soulless black camera lens peering down from above fills me with a sudden rage. Wildly, I scan the ground for a suitable weapon, find a rock about the same size as the one I used on the back door of the cabin last night, and hurl it at the camera with all my might.

"Say cheese, *motherfucker!*"

It's even more satisfying than I could have possibly imagined. The stone smashes the camera head-on, and the whole thing explodes in a shower of sparks and sound. There's a small puff of black smoke that follows, and when it clears in the breeze, the camera is hanging precariously by little more than a few exposed wires and mechanical tendrils.

One down, another dozen or so to go.

Something happens though that stops me. There's a gentle motoring that starts off to my left, so I follow the noise to its source and discover with astonishment that the tall property gate is opening all on its own. I haven't touched the keypad and there's nobody else here, but suddenly there's an entrance forming where before there was only an obstacle.

Did I do this? There's no way my knocking out a security camera with a rock would have anything do with this gate opening… which means that either someone's coming out, or someone's inviting me to come in.

At first glance, no one seems to be walking up. I watch and wait for something to happen, alternating my focus between the path on the other side of this gate and the cameras that are still working on either side of the fence, all of which are pointed at me now. After a few moments of absolutely nothing happening, the soft motoring sound starts up again, and slowly, the gate begins to roll back along the guided track as it closes.

With one last look up at the cameras, I make a decision to step over the threshold. Seconds later, the iron gate clangs shut behind me.

Now that I'm in here, there's nowhere to go but forward, so I start down a cobblestone path. On either side of me, gigantic green hedges, each perfectly shaped and manicured, prevent any kind of spatial awareness on my periphery. There's the path in front of me and the path behind me, and that's it. I wind along this never-ending tunnel of green, waiting for that magical moment where everything will spread open up ahead and I'll stop feeling like a rat stuck in a maze.

Even in broad daylight, there's something hypnotic and disorienting about this walkway. I can conceptually understand the necessity for privacy among Hollywood's elite and the rich and famous, but making your houseguests wander aimlessly this far and for this long in between towering walls of impenetrable vegetation just feels… peculiar.

Surely, the Charons don't use this path every time they come or go, do they? There must be a back entrance, maybe a garage or an alley tucked away on the other side of the property that's known only to them. I can't imagine them doing this whole Queen of Hearts routine every day, no matter how eccentric they are and no matter how much they love their plant life.

After what feels like centuries have passed, the hedges finally start to grow apart from one another and fan out into a delta of leaves and multicolored cobblestone until at last, I come to a house—if you can even call this a house. Words like 'house' and 'mansion' just don't do this structure justice. The most accurate word I can think of is 'castle', as ludicrous as that seems, because that's much closer to what this massive monument really is and really looks like, even from here.

I simply don't know how things like this exist in the middle of Los Angeles. Take a picture of this building, put it on a postcard, and slap any number of European locations on it in typescript below—Scotland, Ireland, England, France—and nobody would ever be the wiser. Yet here it is, a towering castle in the Hollywood Hills off Mulholland Drive.

Now I understand why it felt like I had to walk a mile or two just to get here; from the road, you can't see any of this. Somehow, the architects or the property designers—or perhaps the Charons themselves— managed to lay everything out just perfectly so that you'd never know this monolithic citadel was tucked away on the other side of those great big hedges and that long, iron gate where I parked my car.

The walls of the building are grey... I think. It's hard to tell because of all the overgrown ivy and moss climbing up everywhere. Honestly, they might be more green than grey when looking at it all with a naked eye and from a distance. It's a fact that doesn't surprise me in the slightest, given what I know of the Olympus office.

There are windows dotted here and there along the stone walls and tucked amidst the dense foliage. Absurdly, I count at least *three* chimneys spiking out from different places high up above the battlements. There's also a magnificent turret looming above everything on the far end.

Immediately before me, the cobblestone path spreads out in several different directions like a grid, crisscrossing a bright green lawn. There are marble benches at some of these intersections, but the vast majority of the space is wide open. It's not hard to draw parallels between the landscaping and layout here with those same components in the office at Olympus.

It's the statues that really set this place apart from Olympus, though. The yard is positively littered with them—all different sizes, shapes, colors, and placements. They're all of people, and they all seem like that classical style of statue you'd see in a museum or in art books. Greco-Roman, perhaps. Warriors, lovers, priests, maidens, kings, queens... they're all represented here, a silent horde of grim-faced guardians and sentinels.

And one of them is *moving*.

My eyes widen, my jaw drops, and a scream rises like a balloon up from my lungs into my throat before it catches there.

Richard Charon treads barefoot across the grassy path away from his home, closing the distance between us with effortless ease. I still haven't found my voice— or my normal resting heartbeat—when he's suddenly upon me. Two bony arms rise up from his sides until he has his hands clasped on my shoulders, and I can feel his jagged fingernails dig in like claws behind my neck.

"Ethan Birch. What a marvelous surprise."

Of the three people I know that live here, Charon was the last one I expected to see.

"Hello, Richard."

I try to give him a casual smile, but his sudden and spectral materialization still has me thoroughly unnerved.

"What brings you all the way out here, Ethan?"

Vengeance.

"I was looking for Nolan, actually. Is he here?"

Charon carefully considers the question.

"He is not... unfortunately. Is it a matter of some great urgency?"

Like you wouldn't believe.

"It is. I assumed he's not at the office, since Isla told us to take the rest of the day off. Do you know where he is?"

"I do not... but I can help you find him. How about you tell me what this is concerning first?"

"I'd rather not, with all due respect. It's a private matter between me and Nolan."

Charon's eyes bore into mine like a drill.

"I see."

He holds me stationary in his grip for another moment or two, then releases me, turns, and drifts to a nearby bench.

"How about we sit down and talk, just you and I…"

"Richard, I'm sorry, but I really—"

"*Sit down.*"

He stands and waits for me at the bench. The sun dips behind an ominous, grey thunderhead high up above, tinting the yard around us and dispelling all the long shadows that seep out from the bases of these countless statues scattered around the lawn.

Engaging Charon in a battle of wills strikes me as a losing proposition. I can either do as he asks, I can refuse and just stand here, or I can return back the way I came and hope that the gate opens again for me when I get there. Clearly, acquiescing to the old man is my best option.

I walk in silence until I'm level with him beside the milk-colored marble bench. Once I get there, we sit down together side by side. For a long minute, neither one of us says anything. We both just look out over his sprawling estate, lost in our own private thoughts, and perhaps waiting for the other one to speak first.

Unbidden and uninvited, a mental photograph of Allie's decimated face and body appears at the forefront of my mind, and I have to swallow back the resulting emotion that it stirs up inside. Charon maybe notices something happening because he tilts his head ever so slightly in my direction, almost like he's keeping tabs on me from the furthest corner of his eye. Otherwise, though, his silence, his outward focus, and his perfect stillness are all unbroken.

It becomes obvious that his chess move was getting me to sit here next to him; now, it's my move.

"I don't think I can work for you anymore,

Richard."

He doesn't flinch.

"I am very sorry to hear that. May I ask why?"

How do I encapsulate everything I've realized since this morning and put it together in a cognitive statement? This is a conversation that should be happening with HR present and at the office, not alone with the company founder at his private villa home residence.

"I just—I've realized recently that the culture here isn't necessarily conducive for my work/life balance."

"You mean the unexpected trip to our cabin yesterday."

"That's a part of it, yes. But it's much more than that." I hesitate. "There's just a lot that's suddenly changed for me on a personal level. And without getting into all the specifics, almost all of it stems from this job."

"You mean your relationship with Portia… and how it affects your relationship with Allie."

I'm floored. I snap my neck around to stare at him in stunned disbelief, but he still has his attention locked on something—or on nothing—far, far away.

"What? How did—how do you know about that?"

Charon licks his thin lips before speaking.

"I told you that I try to make it my business to know as much as I can at all times about those I employ."

He then shifts his face far enough to meet my shocked expression head-on, and when he does, he's absurdly wearing a hint of a queer, twisted smile.

"Everyone knows about you and Portia, Ethan. You will forgive my saying so, but the two of you were not exactly… discreet."

My stomach ties up in knots. I guess it's no great

surprise that if Nolan and Isla both know about what happened, then of course Charon would know as well. But it still doesn't make this scenario any less embarrassing for me to experience in real time.

Charon's wisp of a smile flickers away as his expression calcifies.

"I believe you have misplaced your anger, though, Ethan... at being caught. While you have every reason to be incensed at the individual who sent those damning, pornographic images to your wife, you should know that individual no longer works at Olympus... and you should also know that individual was Bingham, not Nolan."

What? I don't believe it. Why would Bing do something like that? He doesn't have any reason to. Bing and I are friends.

This is absurd. How does Charon even know any of this anyway? It's not enough to just sit here and say he makes it his business to keep tabs on all of us; that's not a good enough answer.

The old man saves me the trouble of articulating any of these thoughts, though.

"I saw it with my own two eyes, Ethan. I wish I could say it was not so... but it was. I was the one who came across Bingham taking photos in the night. I am... ashamed to say that at first, I did not realize what he was doing. As soon as I did, I had him pack his bags, I called a car, and I sat with him until it came... explaining in no uncertain terms how he was to be excommunicated after such an egregious violation of privacy, integrity, and basic human decency.

"Tragically, however, it was not until after I saw that he was carried off... when I made to return your cell phone to your room where it properly belonged... that I noticed what he had done with those photos in sending them to your Allie. And all this... out of spite."

This isn't making any sense.

"Spite for what?"

The lines in Charon's weathered face grow deeper.

"Jealousy. Jealousy... would be my guess."

He pauses.

"You must understand, Ethan, that Bingham has long harbored an... *infatuation*... with Portia. To my knowledge, this infatuation has always been unrequited. I would also venture so far as to categorize it as an... *unhealthy* obsession.

"Now, I am no behavioral scientist... but when a young man already struggling with high occupational stress and a broken heart comes across the subject of his amorous fixation naked in the arms of another man... no less, a *married* man whom he considers a coworker, a role model, and a friend... well, perhaps then you can understand the warped motivation behind his actions... even if you cannot justify, excuse, or forgive the actions themselves."

I'm trying to comprehend all this information. Like a movie in my mind, I'm watching the events Charon describes take place from a vantage point outside my own, since I was unconscious at the time of their occurrence. But Bing, though? It just doesn't make sense.

After last night, I know better than anyone what it feels like to have done terrible things out of character while in a compromised state. Things you immediately regret and denounce with every fiber of your being, but things you still can't go back and change. Even though it was a different you who did them. Because all the terrible facts and circumstantial evidence says it was in fact you... no matter how much you wish with all your soul that it wasn't.

Still... Bing?

"I just—I can't believe Bing would do something like that."

Charon's bushy eyebrows narrow.

"Believe me: Bingham was not the man you thought he was. In truth, he was not the man I thought he was, either. But rest assured, Ethan, you need not worry about him... ever again."

It's so much to take in. If nothing else, I suppose it does explain his sudden disappearance this morning. I lean forward, drop my head into my hands, and sigh.

"*Man.* This changes everything. I came here to... well, I don't even know what I came here to do exactly."

Charon lays his hand on the back of my neck in a paternal gesture.

"I know what you came here for, Ethan."

"You do?"

"Of course. You came here for vengeance. You came here for Nolan."

I'm silent in my shame and confusion. Charon's grip gently tightens.

"Believe me. I understand. Nolan can be... tricky. I once made it quite clear to you that despite my great personal affection for the boy, I also had and have my reservations about his ability and judgment when it comes to certain matters. I sent you with him on the TrendBeat interview out of concern that he would do exactly as he did. Without exposing too much of his private life, suffice it to say that Isla and I took him in here as our houseguest to aid and support him in his battle against his own inner demons."

Charon shifts his weight completely so that for the first time since we sat down, both his face and his body are centered directly on me. His fingers are ice cold on my skin.

"We would be willing… actually, we would be honored… to do the same for you… should you now need a refuge… in your hour of need."

I readjust my own weight on the bench to break from his grasp.

"That's very generous of you, but I don't—I don't even know exactly what my home situation is. I had no idea about all this stuff. This changes everything."

Charon's look is almost piteous.

"Forgive me, Ethan… but what, exactly, does this new information change for you at home? Understandably, it alters your opinion on Bingham, on Nolan, and perhaps even on Portia. Hopefully, it does not alter your opinion… at least not unfavorably… on me, for what little role I played. But as far as Allie is concerned… how does anything change at all?"

"It changes everything!"

I spring up from the bench.

"She doesn't know about any of this! I didn't have a chance to tell her because I didn't know either—I saw the photos for the first time myself not long after she must have, and I didn't have any time to explain because I was already standing at my own front door, and then she was there. She doesn't know that I was drugged; she doesn't know about the *fucking brownies*, or that Bing had it out for me, or any of that. She wouldn't listen to me! But now if I tell her why Bing took those photos and why he sent them—"

"*Ethan.* Look at this situation from her perspective. Your wife sees photographic evidence of her husband sleeping with another woman. Unless you plan on selling her the idea that the images sent from your very own cell phone directly to her very own cell phone were somehow doctored or staged… why should her opinion change? Surely, she already put together that you did not *mean* to send her proof of your own infidelity. Why should it then matter to her that someone else did it for you?"

"But the drugs—"

Charon lifts his hand in the air to silence me.

"*Ethan.* In this country, no criminal is ever exonerated from his crime simply because he was inebriated or otherwise incapacitated when he committed it. I can tell you firsthand from three decades of experience that it is the same in marriage as it is in the criminal justice system."

"So, what are you saying? That I should just give up? My life is in *flames* right now, and you want me to just walk away and let it all burn down?!"

The old man folds his hands together in his lap and stares hard at me.

"Quite the contrary. I want you, first of all, to calm down… because nothing truly productive or lasting comes from putting rash, unfocused energy toward a solution. I want you to recognize that your wife is in shock right now… much the same as you are. I want you to trust an older, wiser man when he tells you that women, just like men, need time to process their emotions, both alone and with their loved ones. And, selfishly, I want you to reconsider leaving this organization."

Every muscle in my body trembles as emotion bubbles up into my chest.

"Did you do this? Did you do this to me?!"

Charon tilts his head.

"Did I do what?"

"Did you... *did you try to kill me last night?*"

My voice breaks. I've never been more desperate, furious, and downright terrified as I am right now in this very moment.

Charon doesn't speak; he stands instead. As he moves toward me, something starts to glow from behind his skull, and now I think I can see it again: that thin, terrible halo of flame from last night. I fall to the ground in a broken, quivering heap and lift up my hands like flimsy shields, closing my eyes and averting my face from it as I feel his awesome presence advance and then descend upon me all at once and all over again. In the quaking, crying darkness of hell, I wait for him to finish the job.

He doesn't, though. And when I finally open my eyes again and peek out at the world in front of me, not only am I still alive, but now he's here with me on the ground and in the grass. He is actually smiling; really, truly smiling, for once. And the halo is gone.

"Ethan. Believe me. I would never do anything to harm you."

My voice trickles out from my throat, little more than a whimper now.

"I—I saw you. At least, I *thought* I saw you... last night... at the cabin."

Charon's eyes glow faintly with interest.

"What did you see?"

I swallow.

"You... you had a gun... and there was a... a *fire*..."

He leans in closer so that I can feel the heat of his breath on my face.

"There was indeed a fire last night."

And then he smiles crookedly again.

"Our campfire, Ethan. No gun, though. Isla and I... we do not believe in them."

The air is getting warmer and somehow more suffocating around us.

"I—I did break the door, though. Didn't I? The crack? In the glass? Did... that happened. Didn't it?"

"Ethan. Your mind is playing tricks on you."

I want to believe him. What I saw last night—it just doesn't make sense. None of that makes sense. He has to be telling the truth. Why would he pull a gun on me? What motive would he have to hurt me—to hurt anyone? Even if I thought I saw the crack in the glass this morning, that doesn't mean anything. I either imagined it again, or maybe it really exists and I really put it there, but that still doesn't prove anything about a gun or... a halo of fire.

There's nothing there around his head right now. My mind must be playing tricks on me again. It's the drugs; the stupid brownies. I must still be feeling the aftereffects or something.

Charon licks his lips.

"Ethan... I know you feel hopeless right now; scared and confused... but I want you to know that you are not alone. I will not abandon you now in your hour of need. Let me be your refuge and your strength, an ever-present help in trouble, so that you shall not fear."

His black eyes flash as he leans in even closer.

"All you need to believe in is what you can see and feel and trust, here and now and always, in this moment and forever after. If you see me as only your employer, I am only your employer... but if you see me as your friend, I will be your friend... if you see me as a father, I can be a father... and if you see me as a savior, *I shall save you.*"

My vision shimmers.

"I—I don't know what to do..."

With infinite tenderness, he takes my hands in his.

"You do not have to know. You will not have to know. You must believe me when I say you do not need to know anything at all. Put your faith in me... put your faith in us... and what we have built here, and what we are still building. You cannot comprehend how lucky you are to be hand-picked for this... hand-selected for greatness... destined for immortality. You can have *everything*... without losing anything. But you cannot walk away from me now."

Something tickles my throat.

"Allie–"

"Allie... *and* Olympus. Work/life balance. Harmony. Union. Riches. Bliss. Peace. Ethan... you know where we are headed. I want you... I *need* you... to be the one who takes us there... all the way to the mountaintop."

I drink in my reflection from the black mirror balls of his eyes.

"What about Bing?"

"Gone forever."

"I mean... what about all the engineering work that still needs to get done?"

His lips crack into a thin, hungry smile.

"Can I share a secret with you, Ethan?"

I nod dumbly, utterly entranced. Charon removes his large cell phone from the breast pocket of his blazer, scrolls his fingers smoothly along the screen, and reverentially passes the device over to me like he's administering the Eucharist.

My breath catches. I don't believe it.

It's Olympus. Everything we've been working on is all here. All the design and engineering aspects, the functions, the apps-within-an-app, the user interfaces, the social networking, the membership circles, the support sections… it's all here already. It's all active and *alive*, right now, right here in the palm of my hand.

"I don't understand…"

Charon's feverish smile widens and spreads as someone or something lights the furnaces of his eyes, and bead-like orbs of fire begin to play and dance there.

"I have been fine-tuning everything myself for weeks now. I gave an extremely small circle of my personal confidants and advisors access to everything you have there in your hand for beta-testing, and then I selectively incorporated their feedback. What you are looking at is 1.0… what will release this Christmas. Barring any last-minute strokes of revelation or changes of heart… Olympus is finished."

He's not wrong. All of the components we've been working on are here; along with so much more. Every element and theory discussed at one point or another has been incorporated, but there are also things here that seem to be of Charon's own independent design and desire—things he never discussed with us, or at least not with me.

"Last night, while you were in the cabin by yourself.

You didn't actually figure anything out? Because you already had it all figured out? Because you already built it all by yourself?"

"Not without contributions from everyone on our team, of course. Please do not undersell or underestimate your part in this… or the parts of any of your colleagues, Ethan. The insights, ideas, and imagination you all brought to the table proved invaluable to me along the way."

I don't believe it.

"So… this whole thing, this whole job, this whole company. It's all fake."

Charon frowns.

"There is nothing *fake* about anything here."

"How can you say that? You have a hundred people in an office working on a project that you've already finished."

Charon takes a long, slow breath in through his monstrous nose.

"Ethan… if you can, try not to rush to judgment here. I want to help you see this through my eyes. Everything is real. We have assembled a team of the brightest, most innovative minds in the world… and we pay them… quite handsomely, I might add… for their contributions to the creative process. What difference does it make if I take those contributions that I pay for and utilize them in a manner that I see fit? Olympus is a collective… it makes no difference when, how, or, least of all, whom. All that matters is *what*… all that matters is what you hold there in your hand right now… all that matters is that you are a part of it."

I look down at Olympus in the palm of my hand. I'm sure it's just my imagination, but the phone suddenly feels heavier than it did when I first took it from Charon. Shakily, I extend the device back to him, and he takes it from me and tucks it gently back into his breast pocket like a baby bird in a nest.

"Why don't you just tell people the truth, then? Let them know the true nature of their work?"

Charon's eyes glint.

"It would not be the same. Desperation is the raw material of drastic change… and true innovation can never come easy. If I told every man and woman under my employ not to worry or fear failure, they would not *think*… and they would not *try*. Even in a deterministic universe, mankind needs to *believe* in free will and the power of choice… because the only alternative to progress is stagnation, and I will not let that sad fate befall them."

I'm really struggling with this, and perhaps Charon can see it in my face. He sticks his words into me one at a time with even greater emphasis and intensity.

"In legend, Prometheus steals fire for man and is sentenced by the gods to eternal punishment for this action. They strap him to a rock and send an eagle to rip out and eat his liver each day. Every day, the liver grows back… and every day, the eagle returns.

"In this same legend, however, those same gods later allow the hero Hercules to free Prometheus from his torment. Now, I ask you: do you think they simply forgave Prometheus… do you think they changed their minds… or do you think these events unfolded *exactly* as they planned them to?

"And if so, does it not then stand to reason that the gods actually *meant* for man to have fire all along? The end result is the same each way—man gets fire from the gods—but only one version becomes myth. Only one becomes *legend*. Only one has narrative... has drama... has real stakes and real consequences. There is nothing *fake* about it."

"Why are you telling me any of this? Why not just let me continue in blissful ignorance? Aren't you afraid I'll tell the others the truth?"

Gently, Charon takes my hands in his.

"Because I trust you, Ethan... and because I want you to have a seat at the table with us... up there with the gods in our story. Only a privileged few are fortunate enough to hitch their wagons to this particular star we call Olympus. Fewer still are entrusted with the knowledge that our star will never burn out or fade away... because I will not allow it to. Charles could not accept the great *divinity* of his position here with me... here with us. I told Bingham last night by the pool exactly what I am telling you now... *and it broke him.* But Nolan... and Portia... they both understand what I have given them. I know you will too."

I try hard to swallow. My throat has become very dry.

"They know about all this too? Nolan and Portia?"

Charon slowly tilts his chin downward.

"They know... and now you know as well. Think carefully, Ethan. What, *really*, has changed? Our work, our company, our goal... it all remains the same as it was before. The only thing that has changed is now you know, as they do, that *you* cannot fail. Consider this newfound revelation... a golden parachute, of sorts. You can try anything, think anything, do anything, be anything... without consequence. You can make things right with your wife, if that is what you truly wish...

because I will give you the time, the money, and the knowledge to make it so. But more importantly… I will give you everything you need to become the best version of yourself… to achieve your ideal state… *to achieve true transcendence.*

"All of this and more is possible… truthfully, it is more than possible… it is guaranteed… but only because of your position here. You directed development of Olympus… and now, Olympus is finished. But there is more great work… and there are more great undertakings to be done. The only difference is that now you are armed with the unique privilege and the divine knowledge that you cannot fail… you cannot be fired… you cannot lose… you cannot be killed. You are immortal… you are a god yourself. *But only if you stay.*"

My vision shimmers. It's all so much to take in…

And yet, it isn't. Charon is right about everything. Nothing has significantly changed. He did nothing wrong by completing Olympus on his own—it is his baby and his company, after all. My contributions, the work I've put in… it was all real. Maybe not all of it directly translated to the final product. Or maybe it did. I barely had a chance to really examine and explore that product; if it's anything like I know it is, I probably saw less than one percent of its total functionality.

Portia and Nolan both know the truth, too. They could handle it when Charon told them. Maybe I can handle it, too. Bing could not handle it. But he isn't here anymore… and that's a good thing. I thought Bing was my friend, but he went crazy, betrayed me, and tried to destroy my marriage out of jealousy and spite.

On my first day at Olympus, Portia rhetorically

asked what's not to like about this job—referencing the extravagant perks, the overall flexibility, the enormous paychecks. All of that still exists for me. The only difference is that I now have complete and utter job security. Provided I keep quiet about all that I've learned, and provided I refuse to let that knowledge 'break' me, I join the Charons' inner pantheon... and I become invincible. A god.

Maybe I can have it all. Allie, Portia, Olympus, fatherhood, fame, fortune. Why shouldn't I have it all? I'm sitting on a winning lottery ticket. Allie said it herself, and she was right. Millions of people would kill for this opportunity. I'd be a fool not to cash in.

And you know what? Portia was right, too. It *is* just sex. *Was*... is... whatever. It doesn't matter. What's fair is fair. Everything that happened was always only ever going to happen anyway. It's just the method of a deterministic universe working itself out. *Mysterious ways*, after all. Ultimately, if it's meant to be, it's meant to be.

My vision shimmers. It's all so perfectly obvious to me now, I can't help but laugh out loud. Why didn't I see it before? I have everything I could ever ask for and more. I'm right where I need to be. I always have been. And I always will be.

He is still waiting though, so I give him what he asks of me.

"I'll stay."

Charon squeezes my hands and bows his silvered head to me.

"Good. I knew you would make the right decision, Ethan."

There's a magic in the air around us. All my cares, my worries, my doubts, and my fears, they all melt and slide away from me down into the earth below.

"What do we do now?"

Charon produces something from his person and holds it up for me to see. It's the same ornate wooden box I've seen on Nolan and Bing. He opens the top, reaches inside, and then slips the container back into the deep folds of his clothing. When he unfurls his long fingers in my direction, there are two of them there in the palm of his hand.

"Provisions for the journey… for you are now called upon, my son."

My heart quickens.

"I don't know–"

"Trust me, Ethan. You are safe now, here with me and with the others in the kingdom of eternal life. Nolan, Isla, Portia… your Portia… they are all here already… and they are waiting for us. They are all just inside. Eat this and see the world as I do… as we all do.

"Viaticum is the nectar of the gods… the acolytes' ambrosia. Happy are those who are called to this supper… this communion under my roof. For you see now… that Olympus… Olympus is but a channel and a pathway… the means to an end… the final judgment test whereby only those who are truly worthy can be found, rescued, and then summoned here for congregation."

Charon's lids grow heavy, his nostrils flare, and his lips part as he slips the first one into his mouth and swallows. When he reaches forward with the second, I am ready for it. My mouth opens in time to receive the substance, light and airy and tasteless on the top of my tongue. He then guides my jaw upward with his fingers until it's over and done with.

"How long does it take?"

"It is already begun."

"What will I feel?"

"Everything."

"Should I be afraid?"

"Not anymore. Come."

Charon helps us both rise to our feet. He drapes a long arm over my shoulders as he ferries our bodies across the darkening lawn and slowly ever toward the giant wooden double doors of his domain. We walk in silence now as the rain starts falling down upon us like tears from heaven. When we've finally arrived, I turn to him.

"Richard… that day we first met… at the bar. Did you know who I was?"

Charon's mouth curls. His black eyes gleam in the radiance as he takes his time and devours this moment.

"I knew that you were special. I knew that all along."

He holds one of the doors open and gestures for me to go in first. It's pitch-black inside, but somewhere just up ahead, I can hear something. It sounds like a chorus of voices, chanting or praying or singing. It's the most beautiful thing I've ever heard. There's a light now too, faint and flickering in the distance, but quickly moving closer as I gaze upon it with tears in my eyes now.

The sound and light grow and grow until they finally unify and merge into a mass that reaches out and calls for me. I step inside to reach back, and when I do, Charon closes the door shut behind us. The mass surges up into a shrill rapture, and before long, I'm lost in it.

COMING SOON

HOPE'S LAST REFUGE

"Where hate cannot find you."

by

PATRICK MORGAN

Fall 2021

Acknowledgements

First and foremost, I want to thank you, my reader, for choosing this story and following the journey from beginning to end. Without you, none of this is possible, so please accept my most heartfelt gratitude for your time and interest.

Thank you to Christopher Bailey and all of your hard-working associates at Phase Publishing for continuing to foster my dream of being a successful author. I thank my lucky stars every single day to have been matched up with you all.

Thanks once again to Jenny Rudd and your team at Right Word Express for cleaning up my mistakes and believing in my stories. Not only do you make me a better writer, but you also teach me to be a better self-editor as well.

My thanks to Deborah and Kylie at Tugboat Design for creating such a gorgeous, eye-catching cover. You made the whole design process such a breeze, and I couldn't be happier with the final result. Can't wait for the next one!

A big thanks to Kayle Hill Publicity for helping me grow my readership as well as my public profile. Kayle, your ideas, plans, and picture-taking skills are only surpassed by your incomparable value to me as a treasured friend.

Speaking of friends, I'd be nowhere right now without mine. Thanks to each and every one of you for giving my life learning and laughter. There's not a day that goes by where I don't miss you all.

Thank you to my relatives and family members near and far for your unwavering encouragement and enthusiasm. More than anything though, thank you all for your boundless love.

Special thanks to Kasey Dailey and David Trisko for your unbelievably useful, unforgettably tense, and unquestionably hilarious three-way FaceTime feedback session. David, you are without a doubt the writer in my life I most admire and aspire to be like. I am forever in your debt. Kasey, no one compares to you when it comes to understanding storytelling, keeping me humble, and being my best friend. I release you from half of the debt you still owe me.

A massive thanks to my sister Megan and my brother-in-law Paul for letting me start this story on New Year's Eve while drinking champagne by myself and living in your guest room. Paul, thank you for sharing your beverage and tech knowledge with me alongside your feedback and for zeroing me in on the pills (and thus, the title). Lofus Ambrocius, thank you for unlocking this whole book for me on our road trip together and for selling me the rights to Snorkle-Orkle-Fitz.

Finally, thank you to my mother Sue and my father John for being my biggest believers, ambassadors, and role models from the moment you first brought me into this world. It can't be easy watching your child pursue one extremely difficult and competitive vocation in the arts only to pivot into another extremely difficult and competitive vocation in the arts. Your faith in me though is the fuel to my fire, and I'll never be able to put into words just how much I love and admire you both.

©2020 Patrick Morgan
Photo credit: Robert Atchinson

ABOUT
THE AUTHOR

Patrick Morgan is a writer, dog dad, and hammock enthusiast who currently resides in Austin. His previous novels, Realms and Apparent Horizon, were both released to critical acclaim.

Patrick's two great loves are the ocean and the New England Patriots, though he's also partial to Nacho Cheese Doritos dipped in cold Tostitos Salsa Con Queso (don't knock it till you've tried it).

You can contact him via his website at:

www.patrickmorganonline.com

CPSIA information can be obtained
at www.ICGtesting.com
Printed in the USA
BVHW050133140721
611841BV00012B/994